D1272733

FIC Nadel

Nadel, B.
After the mourning.

PRICE: $20.97 (afm/m)

WITHDRAWN
FROM THE
PETERBOROUGH PUBLIC LIBRARY

PETERBOROUGH PUBLIC LIBRARY   SEP -- 2006

After the Mourning

Also by Barbara Nadel

The Inspector Ikmen series:
Belshazzar's Daughter
A Chemical Prison
Arabesk
Deep Waters
Harem
Petrified
Deadly Web
Dance with Death

The Hancock series:
Last Rights

After the Mourning

Barbara Nadel

headline
review

PETERBOROUGH PUBLIC LIBRARY

Copyright © 2006 Barbara Nadel

The right of Barbara Nadel to be identified as the Author of
the Work has been asserted by her in accordance with the
Copyright, Designs and Patents Act 1988.

First published in 2006
by REVIEW

An imprint of HEADLINE BOOK PUBLISHING

1

Apart from any use permitted under UK copyright law, this publication
may only be reproduced, stored, or transmitted, in any form, or by any means,
with prior permission in writing of the publishers or, in the case of
reprographic production, in accordance with the terms of licences issued
by the Copyright Licensing Agency.

All characters in this publication are fictitious and any resemblance to real persons,
living or dead, is purely coincidental.

Cataloguing in Publication Data is available from the British Library

ISBN 0 7553 2137 5 (hardback)
ISBN 0 7553 3224 5 (trade paperback)

Typeset in Caslon by Avon DataSet Ltd,
Bidford-on-Avon, Warwickshire

Printed and bound in Great Britain by
Clays Ltd, St Ives plc

Headline's policy is to use papers that are natural, renewable and recyclable
products and made from wood grown in sustainable forests. The logging
and manufacturing processes are expected to conform to the environmental
regulations of the country of origin.

HEADLINE BOOK PUBLISHING
A division of Hodder Headline
338 Euston Road
London NW1 3BH

www.reviewbooks.co.uk
www.hodderheadline.com

To Grandma and Grandad P,
Grace, Evelyn, Ann and Thomas

Acknowledgements

Much of what follows in this novel springs from my own prior knowledge and experience. However, I would also like to acknowledge the debt I owe to the works of Dominic Reeve, the *Gypsy-English/English-Gypsy Concise Dictionary* by Atanas Slavor, and the Patrin Gypsy website (www.geocites.com/~patrin).

The Night of 31 October 1940, Eagle Pond, Epping Forest, Essex

I'd had a feeling it would end like this. Secrets do. The way of life this poor girl's people keep depends, to some extent, upon what is kept close and sacred between themselves. And, in a way, it is natural for most folk to have the odd secret or two. But this girl had been different. She had been consumed by what is hidden. I looked down at what her father had so recently uncovered on the ground and said, 'I can't touch her. I mustn't. This is something for the coppers.'

'But . . .'

'Someone's cut her throat!' I said as I, nevertheless, bent down to get a closer look at what remained of Lily Lee. As well as the gash across her throat there was blood around her naked private parts. Her once gay-looking dress, hitched up and ripped by whoever had done this to her, was covered with gore.

'If it's murder then we'll deal with it ourselves,' a man I recognised as a relative said. Not that many of the dark and dusty men around me weren't relatives of one sort or another to the dead girl. Gypsies travel with their own. They have loyalty to and affection for no others. However, the only reason I was grubbing about in the earth in Epping Forest in the middle of the night with a group of Gypsies was precisely because I wasn't one. Gypsy tradition dictates that dead bodies are both dirty and dangerous and cannot be handled in any way – except by what they call *gauje*, non-Gypsies. Because I am one of those, and an undertaker by trade, the Lee family, in the shape of Lily's little brother Charlie, had come to get me in the middle of the night to take care of the girl for them.

'Lily has been murdered and, and other things have been done to her too, I think,' I said, skirting around the subject of the girl's possible violation as best I could. Contrary to what a lot of people believe, Gypsies can be very strait-laced folk on occasion. 'The police need to know. I have to tell them. I can't do anything with Lily until they know. Whoever did this needs to be caught, and soon.'

None of the Gypsies, all of whom were men, spoke or moved. I admit, despite the circumstances, I found it restful. Ever since the bombing began back in September there's been hardly a moment of silence in my life. And I like silence. It's one of the reasons I do the work that I do. There had been a raid early on in the evening but that had been a long time before Charlie had appeared on my doorstep, insisting I get my new motor hearse out to drive over to 'our Lily'. I'd thought that Lily, like her sister before her, had just died. I hadn't imagined this – bloody murder on All Hallows Eve, the night when, barmy people say, the dead walk about. In my experience, the dead only shift when the living move them.

The sound of sobbing to my left caused me to turn in that direction. I could just make out the sharp profile of Lily's brother-in-law, Edward, crying his eyes out. As soon as he noticed me looking at him, he spoke. 'The police will find nothing,' he said. 'Nothing!'

I frowned. Was he telling me that the police wouldn't find anything because Lily had been murdered by someone in the clan? But that wasn't what Edward had meant. Lily's murder, he claimed, was a lot more complicated than that.

'It is the *muló* of Rosie,' he said, in his strange, foreign accent. 'It has always been. Everything Lily saw was the *muló*, come to take its revenge upon her.'

At the time I didn't know what a *muló* was, but I thought it had to be some kind of spirit or ghost of Edward's dead wife, Rosie. 'But why would Rosie want to hurt Lily? She was her sister,' I said. Although I don't hold with ghosts and suchlike, I am accustomed to having conversations of this sort with the many mourners who do.

'Because I did lie with Lily, that's why,' Edward said, as his chin descended on to his chest. 'While Rosie still breathed I lied with Lily. Now this is the end of it.'

He pointed to the blood-soaked corpse at our feet, then let out a tremendous howl, like a wolf.

Chapter One

Gypsies and tinkers have roamed the streets and forests in and around London for ever. Always set apart – feared sometimes, too – they ply their traditional trades, mainly for non-Gypsies: carving and selling pegs, weaving baskets, telling fortunes and knowing all there is to know about horses. It was this latter trade that first put me in touch with the Gypsies more than forty years ago when I was a nipper.

Hancocks have been in business as undertakers in the London Borough of West Ham since 1885. The company was started by my granddad, Francis – who I'm named for – then continued by my dad, Tom, until I took over when he passed away. Before the Great War, before those trenches in Flanders swallowed my soul, I can remember Dad taking me to see the Gypsies over on Beckton Marshes. A windswept and lightly populated part of the borough, Beckton Marshes is half wild and half industry. South of my home and business in Plaistow, Beckton is where the gasworks and its labourers' housing are. The wild part is where Gypsies, among others, ply their various trades, and other men take their horses for shoeing or for the exercise the big open spaces allow. I don't remember when I first went down there, but I do recall that Dad always took me and we always went to see a bloke called Nelson Smith. He shod the horses we've always used to pull at least one of our hearses and sometimes, when I was very small, he and Dad would exercise them too. Later on I did this myself together with Nelson's son, Horatio, the Gyppo who got me into this with poor Lily, Rosie and the rest of them up in the forest.

It all started on a Wednesday afternoon just over two weeks before Lily's bloody end. Although I was tired, like everyone is these days, I was having a stab at helping our office girl, Doris, with the books. Ever since the Luftwaffe started trying to bomb the East End docks to smithereens, Hancocks, in common with every other undertaking business east of Piccadilly, has been working flat out. And although I'm not really one for paperwork, I could see that Doris was getting into a bit of a pickle with it so I lent a hand. We spread out the big ledgers across my desk at the front of the shop, ready – as Doris is accustomed to doing – to put them away again should customers arrive.

Doris's brow was furrowed with concentration when she said, 'Wally Couch's son still owes for his old man's coffin, Mr H. Buried him almost a month ago.'

'I know,' I said, and offered her a Woodbine.

'Thank you, Mr H,' she said, as she took a fag from my packet and lit it. 'It ain't peanuts, the price of a coffin,' she added.

'Yes, but Reg Couch, well, he's—'

'Yes, yes, I know he's a *meshuggeneh*, Mr H. But you ain't a rich man. You can't just go giving out coffins to whoever and whatever—'

'Yes! Yes.' I held up a hand to stop her. Doris Rosen is a good sort. A nice Jewish girl from Spitalfields, who really cares about our business, and about me and my family too. But, like a lot of people, she doesn't and cannot understand the *meshuggeneh*, the madman, that is so big a part of Francis Hancock. The me who was little more than a boy when he joined the army to fight for King and empire in 1914 is not the same man who came back home with his soul cracked in two. I never cried myself to sleep before the Great War, I ate like a normal person, screamed only when I was shocked and ran for nothing but the bus. Now I run screaming from Hitler's nightly raids on our poor manor with things I can't even name gibbering and jabbering in my ever-wakeful head. Reg Couch was in the first lot too. But, unlike me, he has no business – no work at all, most of the time. He really is barmy, very much a *meshuggeneh*, which was why I had no intention of charging him what I knew he couldn't afford. Not that I could tell Doris that. 'I'll take care of Reg,' I said, as I lit a fag for myself. 'Don't you worry about him, Doris.'

The bell over the front door rang and we both looked up to see a dark, thin man with a big moustache holding on to his cap in the doorway. He seemed embarrassed but I knew from experience that this was just the awkwardness that so many Gypsies experience when they move in *gaujo* society.

'Horatio,' I said. I walked forward to offer him a chair. 'I hope you being here doesn't mean a loss of some sort . . .'

'Rosie Lee has finally gone,' Horatio replied, as if I should have known both who she was and some of the circumstances surrounding her passing.

Doris put the ledgers on the floor while I said, 'I'm very sorry for your loss, Horatio.'

'Died sudden, Mr Hancock,' the Gypsy said, without any obvious emotion, 'so nothing was done proper. It's why we need you. We'll pay.'

I heard Doris mutter words to the effect of 'You'd better!'

under her breath, which I hoped Horatio hadn't caught. People can have strong opinions about Gypsies, especially when it comes to money.

I tried to lead Horatio to a chair but he wouldn't accept it. 'If you'll do it, Mr Hancock, we'll have to go now,' he said. 'And you'll need to bring a woman.'

I sat down and said, 'Now, look, Horatio, what's all this about? Was this Rosie a relative of yours?'

'Yes.'

'So . . .'

'She died before we could wash and dress her, Mr Hancock,' he said. 'Now she's gone, it's too late. No Romany can touch her. One of your kind, a *gaujo*, must do it. But because you're a man you'll need a woman *gaujo* with you too. It's our way. Them who've passed can be dangerous and need respect. And Rosie's mum is foreign and they're much more careful about tradition than us English men.'

'I see.' Most real English people consider the Gypsies foreign, wherever they were born, so Horatio's way of speaking about the bereaved mother might have been seen as a little strange. But I'm used to him and the way he speaks, so I accepted that this woman, though yet a Gypsy, might come from somewhere I did not understand. 'So where—'

'They have their *'atchin 'tan* up by Eagle Pond,' he said. 'The Lees been stopping there in winter many long years.'

'Christ Almighty, that's in the forest!' I said. 'Miles away! Couldn't you have got a firm from Walthamstow or Leyton out to do it?'

'But we want you, Mr Hancock,' Horatio said calmly. 'Me and my family've known you and yours for a long time. The washing and the dressing has to be done by a *gaujo* we can trust.

Then you must bring her here until the funeral.'

It was, of course, a compliment, even if getting up to Eagle Pond, which is on the edge of Epping Forest between Leyton and Wanstead, is no mean feat. Five miles if it's an inch, and with wrecked buildings, unexploded bombs and the possibility of daylight raids always on the cards, going so far out of my manor – away from London and into Essex – wasn't something I really wanted to do. But on the other hand Horatio had shod and exercised my horses for years. He'd never overcharged me and he'd always done a good job. On top of that, now that we had the motor hearse, it wasn't as difficult to get about as it had been with just the horse-drawn carriage.

'Well, seeing as it's you, Horatio,' I said. 'But as for a woman to help me, both my sisters are out at the moment.' Not that either my older sister Nancy or Agnes, the younger one, are accustomed to helping out regularly with the washing and dressing of our bodies. Our apprentice boy Arthur generally does that with me.

'What about her?' Horatio said, pointing straight at Doris.

'Ah, well . . .'

'Don't matter that she's a Jew,' he said airily. '*Gauje* is *gauje*. Romanies don't pay no mind to religion.'

Epping Forest, and that area of empty country just south of it called Wanstead Flats, has always been somewhere for Gypsies, travelling shows and the like to pitch their camps. Dad used to take us kids and our mum over that way years ago – sometimes we'd even go along with Nelson Smith, Horatio and his brother George Gordon. Our dad enjoyed the horse-riding stunts some of the Gypsies used to do, while Mum liked to buy baskets and be among women who looked as she did and still does. My mother – the Duchess, my sisters and I call her, on account of her very proper way of going on – comes originally from Calcutta in India. Dad was a soldier out there for many years until he came home with his very dark wife and little baby girl to help old Francis with the business. That Mum, despite being a 'wog', was a good Catholic like the rest of the Hancock family helped, but my grandmother never accepted her. Granny H, as we all called my dad's mum, only ever took to fair-skinned, blue-eyed Agnes. Mum, Nancy and I were never really in the running for Granny H's affections. Not that Agnes, or Aggie as she's called at home, and I ever suffered much in any other event. But people other than Granny H could be unkind about the Duchess and Nancy. Their darkness has always stood them apart, except among the Gypsies. Up in the forest the Duchess could pass between the travelling folk without comment. 'Of course, the Gypsies came from India long, long ago,' my mother would say, as she smiled at the unsmiling women around her. 'Their tribe is quite different from the rest of us, but India is where their journey began.' I told Doris about this as I drove her and Horatio up through Leytonstone. Moving away, as we were, from the Germans' prime target, the docks, both Doris and I became almost painfully aware of how much lighter the bombing had been in these areas. Most of those Victorian 'villas', as they're called in Leyton and Forest Gate, were just as they always had been. They were and remain very smart. Down our way, the poor end, we were getting a lot more than our fair share.

'Your mum ain't no Gyppo,' a scandalised Doris responded, as I parked the Lancia on the side of the Snaresbrook Road in front of Eagle Pond. 'She's a lady.'

I smiled. In spite of her agreement to come along and help

me with this deceased Gypsy woman, Doris remained highly suspicious of those we'd come to assist. According to Doris and, she said, her husband Alfie too, Gypsies were 'tea-leaves' and 'bandits'. 'If it wasn't for you, Mr H, and that Gyppo being your mate,' she said, as she tipped her head towards Horatio, 'you wouldn't see me here for dust.'

In spite of being a rural-looking, wooded clearing on the edge of our tightly crowded London, 'here' was a poorer place even than we'd just come from. Not all Gypsies have those colourful covered wagons for which they are rightly famous. Some, like this group, use carts to move from place to place. They live in tents and in an English October that's a bleak prospect. As we followed Horatio into their camp, those familiar suspicious dark eyes bored into me yet again. However, unlike my encounters with Gypsies in the past, this time was not characterised by any movement or offers of entertainment. They all, men and women, sat around their smoky wood fires crying and, in some cases, raking their fingers down their long, grief-stricken faces until they bled. On the outskirts of the group other people, obviously not Gypsies, watched the scene, baffled.

'Christ!' Doris said, as she moved in front of a woman whose face was wet with blood and tears and whose tattered clothes reeked of smoke, damp and leaf mould.

'Romanies can't do nothing until the body is buried,' Horatio explained, as he headed towards a particularly small and mean black canvas tent. 'No eating, washing, drink just tea and wine and smoke baccy.'

'So you all do nothing?' I asked, anxious, I must confess, to learn how they could manage like this.

'Yes.'

'But how do you—'

'We pay the *gauje* to do most of it,' Horatio said. 'And those not of the family, we boil the kettles for the drinks, make the arrangements, get baccy.'

'We? But you said you're family to this girl, Horatio.'

'I'm family in as much as all Romanies is family,' he replied. 'I can do things. I can get you . . .' he pulled the front flap of the tiny, filthy tent to one side revealing the blood-soaked body of a girl and a familiar clergyman '. . . and the vicar. Important – man in touch with God should be first to see the dead one. It can calm the *muló*, the spirit, what can be wild with anger.'

On seeing the state of the corpse, Doris turned aside. The clergyman smiled. 'Hello Frank.'

'Reverend.'

He came out of the tent, straightened, and we shook hands warmly. Ernie Sutton, Anglican priest of St Andrews, Plaistow, had been an early playmate of mine. Many was the time we'd swung together on ropes around lamp-posts as nippers. As the tent flap flopped down after him, Ernie took me to one side and said softly, 'Rosie Lee, the deceased, died of cancer. At my insistence that chap Horatio got a doctor up here, a fellow called Wright from Leyton. But it's all quite straightforward.' He sighed. 'The girl died naturally . . . if, of course, you can call death natural at her age.'

'How old is she?' I asked.

Ernie shrugged. 'Sixteen, twenty at the most. And before you say anything else, Frank, she was married, in common with most Gypsy girls, and that is her husband over there.'

I looked towards the pond where a tall young man stood sobbing into the wind. At his feet stood a small, perplexed blond child.

'It doesn't help that half of Canning Town happens to be camping out here at the moment,' Ernie said. 'Gawping away. You'd've thought they'd seen enough misery, wouldn't you?'

Canning Town is one of those manors that abut directly on to the Royal Docks – the Victoria, the Albert and the George. With Silvertown, Custom House and North Woolwich, Canning Town supplies most of the manpower for the docks as well as for Beckton gasworks, the Tate & Lyle sugar factory and lots of other industries beside the Thames. It's been blasted to bits ever since the raids started in September. The bombed-out can be billeted elsewhere, but to go through all the official processes takes time and a lot of families have ended up in tents out in the forest. In that way, so they say, they can have some control over what happens to them and their nippers. If they let the authorities take care of them, more often than not the poor sods are given billets in the same area they came from, which means they'll suffer raids every night again and have to go down into tiny damp air-raid shelters. Just thinking about it makes me sweat. If I was bombed out I might very well come out to the forest or the Flats. The police can say what they like about how gangsters and other unsavoury types do their business alongside the decent folk among the trees these days – but in the forest a person is out in the open.

'Anyway, Frank, are you and Mrs Rosen . . .' Ernie smiled briefly at Doris '. . . going to make a start?'

'Er . . .'

'I can bury her on Thursday, if that's all right with you,' he continued. 'The Almighty and Jerry willing, I can do two o'clock in the afternoon.'

I was about to say I'd check my appointments when I got back to the shop but Doris, who knows everything about Hancocks, said that I could do that date and time, so we agreed it with Ernie, and with Horatio when he came over to see what we were about. Rosie's family, he said, would be content with that.

Once Ernie had gone and Horatio had finished boiling a pan of water for us, Doris and I set to work on Rosie Lee. Someone, probably her husband, had put another set of clothes, which had obviously been the deceased's Sunday best, beside the body in the tent.

'Poor little thing,' Doris said, as she walked gingerly around the body, settling eventually at its head. 'All that blood!'

'Mr Sutton said she died of cancer.' I gazed at the young, if strained, face of the corpse before us – still not visibly at peace: great clots of blood lay like pieces of liver between her thighs. I've seen such poor women before. When cancer gets into a woman's womb it's a terrible, painful, bloody death. 'Come on, let's get her washed as soon as we can.'

Doris, who had never washed, dressed or even touched a dead body before, stuck out a hand for a cloth and said, 'I'll wipe her face.'

I let her do what she felt able to while I concentrated on the rest. After all, the Gypsies couldn't see us and I couldn't in all conscience put Doris through a full-scale washing of a corpse this bad. Cancer rots from the inside out, so little Rosie was far from wholesome. In a way, I suppose, I was deceiving the bereaved who, I knew, expected Doris to do most of the work, but I didn't feel bad about it, given the circumstances. In this job you have to treat every corpse and every bereaved family differently – give them what they want, and do what's best at the same time, if you can. If you can't, you just have to do whatever's possible.

After Doris and I had done as much as we could with the water we had, I went outside with the bowl to get some more from Horatio. He was squatting by one of the fires in the middle of the camp, watching the water pot suspended above it with rapt concentration. As I moved towards him I saw that a few of the non-Gypsy gawpers Ernie had pointed out had started to move beyond the edges of the travellers' camp. The Gypsies seemed not to notice but I did, so I went over.

'What do you want?' I asked a particularly large old bloke with anchors tattooed on his forearms.

He frowned. 'What you doin' here?' he said. 'Ain't you that undertaker from up Plaistow?'

People sometimes say the East End is like a collection of villages. There's truth in that, especially if you're bonkers and Anglo-Indian as I am. Even those who've never used our business know about Hancocks. I'm the village idiot.

'Yes,' I said. 'I'm here to remove a body from the camp. I think these people want to be left alone to grieve.'

'There's coppers about,' the man said, ignoring me and moving ever more forwards. 'Military, asking questions, going through things.'

In my experience, Military Police, rather than ordinary coppers, could mean only one thing. 'They must be hunting down deserters,' I said, my blood freezing. Back in my war, the Great War, deserters had been shot. I have done it myself. I have stood in a line with other soldiers and shot at boys who only did what the rest of us wanted to do. I can still see myself doing it sometimes, at night, in the dark. It's not only the bombs I run from when the raids get going. My brain is much more dangerous than any Luftwaffe pilot.

'I don't trust no coppers, military or whatever,' he said, as he

15

thrust one meaty hand into his jacket pocket and brought out a pipe. 'I don't want to answer no questions off of no one. I'll wait here until they've gone.'

'I've just told you these people are—'

'I won't make no bother for the Gyppos,' he said, as he lowered himself to the ground beside Horatio. 'I ain't got nothing against them.'

The Gypsy looked at me and nodded, then refilled my bucket from his pot. Not speaking to coppers of whatever kidney is something that East-Enders and Gypsies have in common. Although unspoken, it had been agreed that the man and whoever was with him could stay. It was the start of an association between the Gypsies and the bombed-out that was to have a big impact on all of us in the weeks to come.

When I went back into the tent, Doris said, 'So, what happens between now and the funeral, Mr H?'

'Once we've got Rosie cleaned up I'm going to put her in that nightgown over there,' I said, pointing to a threadbare white garment that lay on the ground. 'We'll transport her in that.'

'We not putting her in her best things, then?'

I lowered my voice. 'I can't clean her up properly here, Doris. If we put her in a nightdress now, we can take her Sunday best with us and I can put her in it back at the shop.'

'Yes, but won't they—'

'I'll bring the shell in here in a moment and we'll put Rosie and the clothes inside,' I said.

'Well, Mr H, if you think that's kosher . . .'

A few minutes later I left the camp with Horatio and went back to the hearse. We took the shell, a flimsy makeshift coffin we use until the right 'box' has been made, into the camp and through the flap of Rosie and her husband's tent. As we passed, carrying the emblem of mortality, all of the Gypsies wailed loudly and the tearing of clothes and faces increased. This group, I noticed, were a mainly short and very dark bunch. There were a few blonds among them – there generally are in a big group – but not many. Few of these had ever bred with the *gaujo*.

Getting Rosie into the shell wasn't difficult even if I only had Doris instead of my usual assistants, Walter and Arthur. The poor girl had been so eaten by the cancer there was nothing much left of her. Whether Doris would be able to carry one end of the shell and help me back to the hearse remained to be seen, though. Now that Rosie was inside it, I realised that not even Horatio could help me. However, his new-found *gaujo* friend with the tattoos was glad to lend a hand and we moved back towards the vehicle with a small woman in tow, her face a mess of scratches.

When we drew level with the car, Horatio nodded at her and said, 'She's Rosie's mother. The dead can't be alone before they return to the earth. She must sit with her. In your shop.'

'What? For three days?' I said.

'Yes. She'll not trouble you for food. Just a little tea sometimes and a cigarette,' Horatio replied. 'She's foreign but she speaks some English. She can't leave her daughter now. Not until the funeral.'

How I would wash Rosie properly and put her clothes on, I didn't know. The little Gypsy woman climbed into the car with a determined expression on her heavy-featured face.

Doris turned to me and said, 'So, what now, then, Mr H?'

Chapter Two

Rosie's mother's name was something queer and foreign but she said we were to call her Betty. She reckoned she was about the same age as my younger sister Aggie. I, at forty-seven, am the middle in age of my parents' three children. Aggie is thirty-six and the mother of two nippers, currently evacuated to Essex. Her husband, a right fly-by-night in everyone's opinion, went off with another woman a long time ago. By contrast, Betty Lee still had her husband who, she said, earned money from the activities of a dancing bear. The whole group were show-people – some of them, like Betty, and Rosie's husband, Edward, had come originally from Rumania, or so Betty said. There were fortune-tellers, dancers, magicians and basket weavers. All eight of Betty's remaining children were involved in one way or another.

'My eldest girl, Lily, she has the Head,' Betty said to the Duchess one morning, when the latter brought her some tea.

'The head?' my mother enquired.

It was two days since I'd brought Rosie and her mother back to the shop with me. Since Betty wouldn't leave her daughter even when a raid was on, I'd had to tell her I wasn't finished with Rosie. But she understood and she let Aggie and me wash and dress her daughter, and even watched when the Duchess gently brushed out the girl's long black hair. Betty had deemed the result 'beautiful'. She gazed at the corpse from across our little storage room.

'It's a great marvel,' Betty said, her dull eyes seeming to give the lie to such an extravagant statement. 'It talks, opens its eyes. When Rosie is in the earth you must come and see this great attraction.'

And then the wailing, which the Duchess had grown accustomed to, began again so she and I left Betty alone.

'Betty reminds me of the mourners I used to see at Hindu funerals,' my mother said, as we climbed the stairs up to our family's flat. 'Christians are so restrained by comparison.'

She wasn't and isn't wrong there – although 'restraint' isn't a word I'd have used about any of the funerals I organised, with the exception of paupers', until this last year. By that I don't mean that there was a lot of emotion before this war began. That's not the English way. But there was always a show. There were horses draped in black crêpe pulling the hearse, and mutes carrying huge ostrich-feather wands. Everyone attending was in full mourning and the memorial to the deceased was the biggest the family could afford. Not that many families could afford much, but they'd scrimp and pawn and beg for a funeral. This is a poor borough where generations of men and women have worked themselves to death. For years a slap-up funeral has been the one way that broken-backed dockers and women used up in childbirth can have their brief moment of glory. Now, thanks to Mr Hitler and his mates, that's changed. With most of the women out at work as well as the men, there's money for all these things but no time. You have to bury the dead quickly in case of a raid. There are no mutes, few horses and even fewer flowers. There seem to be a lot more tears, though. But when you've seen your old dad or your sister or your best friend blown to pieces in front of you it changes things – and people. I know.

When the Duchess, who has very bad arthritis, and I finally made it to the top of the stairs, we went into the kitchen and had our tea with my older sister Nancy. Nancy, or Nan as we call her, is a spinster. Bitter, because she feels the darkness of her skin has put the kibosh on anyone being interested in her for marriage, she spends most of her time looking after the Duchess and saying the rosary.

'How's that . . .' Nan couldn't think what to call Betty '. . . Gyppo?'

'Tired,' the Duchess replied, as she sat down and picked up her cup. 'Keeping vigil is wearisome.'

'I don't know why,' Nan said, as she watched me roll, then light a fag. 'Ain't like she's praying or nothing, is it? Them type don't have no religion.'

'Ernie Sutton's burying the daughter up at the East London,' I put in, by way of information to my sister.

'Oh.'

Of course, being buried an Anglican wasn't and couldn't be as 'good' as if the ceremony had been Catholic but it gave Nan pause, which was no bad thing. At that moment Aggie came bustling in, all perfume and blonde hair rolled up into a great big sausage at the back of her head.

'Can I have one of your fags, please, Frank?' she said, as she lifted my tobacco tin off the table in front of me.

'Well . . .'

'Ta.' She laughed. Although her hair is dyed, Aggie has bright blue eyes and baby-fair skin. She works with a gang of other 'girls' down at Tate & Lyle's sugar factory in Silvertown.

Although I knew she was about the same age as Betty Lee, Aggie and the Gypsy couldn't have been more different. For a start Aggie looked ten years younger. Nan, watching her sister roll a cigarette, sniffed ostentatiously. Aggie, who has always taken the view that it is better to attack than be attacked, said to her, 'I like smoking. Mind your own beeswax.'

'Agnes . . .'

'Well, she's always looking,' Aggie said to the Duchess, with a shrug. 'Everything I do she looks at! When I smoke, when I get myself ready to go out for a drink . . .'

'You haven't been to Mass.'

'No, I haven't,' Aggie said to Nan. 'I don't believe in it. And, anyway, Frank don't go either. My church is called the Green Gate,' she continued, naming a local pub I knew she went to. 'Like it or lump it.'

She poured herself a cup of tea and sat down next to me to drink it. A rare silence descended on the Hancock table, only broken by the Duchess, who said, 'Agnes, you have probably been to more music halls and fairs in recent times than the rest of us.' Nan snorted but we all, even Aggie, ignored her. 'Have you ever heard of an attraction called the Head?'

Aggie frowned. 'The Head? No. What—'

'Betty says it's a great marvel. Her eldest daughter has it. She has invited me to go and see it one day.'

'The Head . . .'

'Yes. I imagine it is a head on its own, as if separated from its body . . .'

'Oh, it's the Egyptian Head you mean,' Aggie said. 'I saw it at a magic show on the pier at Brighton before the war. My old man took me.' She looked down quickly at the floor, then up again almost immediately, smiling.

'So?'

'It's a head of a girl, if I remember rightly, in a box on a table. Opens its eyes and speaks.' Aggie shuddered at the memory. 'Creepy.'

I've always been interested in how tricks and illusions are done. My earliest experiences of magicians took place in Epping Forest where I watched turns performed by Gypsies and travellers. When I got older I watched magicians at the music halls and the odd end-of-the-pier show or on beanos out to Southend or Brighton. I've seen girls sawn in half, men and animals seemingly disappear and even a very good levitation act. But I'd never, at that point, seen a disembodied head. I admit I was intrigued. I've always thought that I should be able to work out how such tricks are done, but I've always lacked either the time or, since the Great War, the will to do so. After all, when you've already gone mad, as we all did in the end out on the Somme, who are you to decide what's real and what isn't?

'You know Betty won't come down the Anderson,' Nan said to me, in that sudden, sharp way of hers.

'Eh?'

'The raid, last night,' She gave an exasperated sigh. 'She wouldn't come down the shelter with us. Just sat there with her daughter, wailing.'

'It's their way,' I responded simply.

And I knew anyway. As soon as the sirens went I made myself go and check to see what Betty Lee might want to do. The Duchess and the girls were already down the Anderson shelter in the backyard and I invited the Gypsy to join them. But she declined. 'I cannot leave Rosie,' she said, so I made ready to go outside as I usually do. I can't be anywhere enclosed during a raid. I have to be out, running as a rule. Running from

22

bombs and fire and my own memories of being enclosed, in a trench, in the last lot, unable to escape the terror of being buried alive. Because blokes did get buried alive back then. I've seen men and their horses sink and choke to death in the mud of northern France and Belgium. Just disappeared they did, into shell-holes the size of churches.

'Well, when you get a chance, ask Betty what my fortune might be, won't you, Frank?' Aggie said, as she put her empty cup back on the table and stood up. 'Find out if she can see a new pair of stockings anywhere on the horizon. I'm off to work now.'

I watched her go with a smile on my face. A lot of people, Nan included, think that Aggie is flash and cheap, but she's a bright girl and, what's more important, she has great heart. With her old man long gone off with another woman, her two kids in Essex and a job in the sugar factory next door to the Nazis' main target, the docks, she'd have every right to be a bit grim. But Aggie takes what Mr Churchill says very seriously and she keeps her chin well up. 'That Hitler can think again if he reckons he's going to stop me going down the pub,' she said, when the Duchess once suggested that perhaps going out in the evening wasn't always a good idea.

Later on that day, in the early afternoon, Ernie Sutton came to visit Betty Lee to talk to her about her daughter's funeral. They were not together for long, and at the end of it he told me, 'She just wants that girl in the ground now. I don't think she understands or cares too much how we do that.'

But, then, as Horatio had told me from the outset, Gypsies, or Romanies as he likes to call his people, don't have too much to do with religion. It makes what happened shortly afterwards all the more barmy and just downright strange.

*

I don't always go to wakes. I'm not always invited. But this time I was and I went. What had happened in the church had been what I'm used to in a funeral. However, behaviour at the graveside had been wild and this wake, I felt, in a Gypsy camp away from religion, was going to be even more different still. I wasn't wrong. As we entered the encampment I saw a young boy set light to a large pile of women's clothes on the outskirts of the area.

'All the things of the dead must be destroyed,' Horatio explained, when he saw me looking puzzled at the scene. 'If you don't then *marimè* will hang about.'

I frowned. My apprentice lad Arthur, who'd also decided to come to the wake, said, 'What's that?'

'*Marimè* is bad things,' Horatio said. 'From the grave. Even speaking the name of the dead is bad.' And then he went off to greet his brother, George Gordon, who was standing in the midst of a gaggle of black-clad old crones.

In reply to the confusion on Arthur's young red face I said, 'He probably means bad spirits.'

'What? Like mediums and that?'

I didn't know. But Arthur was puzzled and obviously bothered, so I said, 'Yes, just like mediums and that.'

Some of the food and drink for the wake had been prepared for the Gypsies by the family of the large bloke with the anchor tattoos on his arms I'd met on the day that Rosie died. He was called, I discovered, Sidney Clarke or 'Nobby', which he preferred. For such a rough-looking sort he seemed to have a good heart. 'My missus and a couple of the other women from our manor done part of the spread,' he said, as he stood with me gazing down at the food laid out on sheets on the ground. 'Gyppos or not, they lost their girl and that ain't good.'

Later he told me about the brother and father he'd lost when his parents' house in Silvertown took a direct hit. No wonder he and his wife couldn't bring themselves to go back to the docklands. It's natural to want to be away from so much death. Maybe, I thought, the Gypsies had it about right when they wiped out the names and things of the dead.

Travelling people generally sit on the ground when they eat, especially when it's a big do involving the whole lot of them. In fact, even non-Gypsies like Nobby sat once the beer came out, so I, too, got down on the grass that was, as grass is in October, none too dry. As funeral spreads tend to be now, it wasn't elaborate but there was Spam, pickled onions, bread cut into sandwiches with potted meat, and some sort of cake that I didn't touch. Ever since the rationing business began things like cake have contained some strange ingredients. I hear Nan talking about grating up carrots and parsnips and shoving in lentils, so I tend to give cakes a wide berth. There was some meat I was told was hedgehog. This is real Gypsy food from the countryside. I didn't trouble myself with that either. But the weather wasn't bad for the time of year, so I supped my beer and looked around at the Gypsies' small village of tents and carts and at their big, contented horses. The scene recalled many happier times for me, and I was wondering idly where Mr Lee's dancing bear and other attractions, the Head included, might be when my eye was caught by the deceased's beautiful sister. Lily Lee was small, curvy, and, dressed from head to foot in black, looked exotic and mysterious. Not that those features alone single out a Gypsy girl. Lily Lee, though, had something else besides, a sort of delicate dreaminess to her eyes. It was something that made her beautiful rather than just pretty. She sat at the far end of the spread with her parents, her brothers, and sisters, and Rosie's loudly weeping husband.

There wasn't, or didn't seem to be, any organisation, so people just tucked in as and when. Arthur and I sat with other *gauje*, like Nobby Clarke, and talk was, as ever, of the war.

'Them military coppers been all over this forest like a rash,' Nobby told me, as he sank his third glass of stout. 'They've got a whole list of men they want to get their hands on – spivs and gangsters a lot of 'em, but also deserters, poor sods, and a couple of foreigners too,' he said, with a knowing tap of his nose.

Foreign spies – those creatures we have to avoid careless talk for. Nobby, I felt, had a quite different attitude to foreign spies than he did to deserters. It was one with which I was in accord. Spies are dangerous and need to be stopped but frightened boys should be left in the forest until this horror is over and done with. That's what I believe.

We all tucked in and then, after a while, George Gordon rose and went to what had been Rosie's tent. Alone, he took out plates, cups, pictures and jewellery, which he proceeded to smash in front of everyone. I imagined it was all part of the process Horatio had told me about – getting rid of the deceased's goods for fear of bad spirits. Rosie's father sat like an oak while this went on. Her mother and husband screamed. Again, just as it had been at the graveside when many of the mourners had thrown coins down on to the coffin while tearing at their chests and faces, it was raw and distressing. Rosie's brothers joined in too, beating the ground with fists still wrapped around cigarettes, saying words only some of which I could understand.

'They're a lively lot, aren't they?' I heard Nobby's missus say to Arthur. Not that I caught what Arthur might have replied because it was at this point that Lily screamed and sprang to her feet. Trembling with what looked like fear, she pointed a dirty finger at a tree.

'She's here!' she said. '*Oh, dordi!*'

'Lily!' Rosie's widowed husband shouted. 'Lily!'

For what seemed like an age there was nothing but silence. No one around me ate, drank or moved. Some people were later to say that they stopped eating mid-chew, so alarming did the girl appear to all concerned.

I alone, I think, moved to look up at her. Lily's face wore such an expression of terror that it was almost painful to see. 'She's here!' I heard her say again, then something else in another language. Many of the Gypsy women hid their faces in their scarves, muttering until rendered mute by the strangeness of the situation. All other voices besides Lily's became silent.

'Our Lady,' Lily said, her voice trembling as it formed the words, 'is here!'

Now no one so much as breathed, or so it seemed.

Much to Nan and the Duchess's disgust, the Church has not featured in my life to any great extent. Most of my old mates who were killed out in the trenches died deaths I still see in my mind, in red and black blood-drenched detail. Only one of my mates survived along with me and he's left with half a face. Whether that's any better than having only half a mind like me, I don't know. But one thing I am sure about is that God didn't help me get through any of it. That said, I know religion: I had it drummed into me at a very early age. I know who 'Our Lady' is.

Rosie's husband was up on his feet now. 'No,' I heard him murmur. 'No.' He started to run towards Lily. I watched him and was probably almost as shocked as he was when he was brought up short by the actions of a red-headed woman, who had now thrown her arms around the Gypsy girl's neck. This woman was *gaujo*, one of us. Later I found out she was a neighbour of Nobby Clarke and his missus.

'A vision of the Virgin!' she screamed at all of us present. 'This girl has had a vision of the Blessed Virgin Mary! Well, for Gawd's sake, act humble, you lot!'

Still no one spoke or moved.

Lily turned her head towards the woman and began, 'No—'

'Just like at Lourdes,' the woman continued. 'The Virgin—'

'No!' Lily turned back to the tree. 'No, it's Our Lady, ours, she's come—'

'To save us from Hitler!' I heard someone else, another *gaujo*, say.

Yet again Rosie's husband made to move towards Lily but this time a glance from the girl prevented him. He put his head down and just stood, his eyes, almost alone among that party, averted from the scene unfolding in front of us. People began moving forward, slowly at first.

'What's all this, Mr H?' Arthur said, as suddenly the whole camp erupted into a great nightmare of Gypsies wailing, women rushing towards Lily trying to see what she was still so obviously seeing and *gaujo* men swearing as their beer glasses spilled over the ground, toppling under the weight of the feet of the faithful.

If I hadn't been in company with so many others I could have thought that what was happening was just a part of my own madness. I sometimes hear, and even see, things left over from the Great War – a death rattle, a disembodied leg, a man's scream of agony. But this wasn't like that. This madness was real.

'It's a sign, is what it is,' a rough woman said. 'A bleedin' wotsit, you know, a miracle.'

'The war'll end now she's come. You'll see,' someone else said. I heard the distinctive sound of hymns being sung by several old women.

I looked at Lily Lee's face over the heads of the many 'faithful' that had rushed towards her and thought, *I don't know what this is.*

It wasn't real, for me it just couldn't be, but it wasn't not real either. Lily was seeing something. I felt that if I could only get close enough I would glimpse a reflection of it in her eyes. I could see, or rather I sensed, that her people, the Gypsies, were feeling somewhat the same. There was no joy among their number, only confusion. Like me, or so I thought, they only pay lip service to religion. The poor buggers couldn't understand what was going on. They'd buried Rosie as an Anglican yet here was her sister coming out with all this 'Our Lady' Catholic stuff. Ernie Sutton, though not a Catholic, would have known what to do or at least what to say, but he'd had to go back to the East London cemetery to bury a couple of little 'uns from Upton Park. It was diphtheria, not bombs, as took them, so Ernie said.

'Well, this is a bit of a bleedin' turn-up,' Nobby Clarke said to me, as he watched his wife go over to Lily and gently touch her hair. 'Barmy, if you ask me, mate. But, then, that's women for you, ain't it?'

'Yes . . .'

I looked across into the trees and saw that the raised voices around the camp were beginning to attract attention. Men in uniform moved towards us with rapid, military steps.

Chapter Three

I know a lot about desperation in wartime. In the first lot it mainly afflicted us soldiers. My own belief is that the human brain just isn't capable of taking in the level of horror you find on a battlefield so it sort of switches itself over to a different channel, like changing the programme on the wireless, as we used to do before this war began. For some, that different programme is disappearing into a dream world but for others, like me, it's running, or rather trying to run, as far away from that horror as it can. Some take refuge in their religion. I've fought beside blokes who could see the Virgin Mary or an angel right in front of their faces. Not even my mates were immune. Almost the last thing an old Jewish pal of mine said to me was that he'd seen a rabbi moving among the dead in the mud, all robed up and floating three feet off the ground. My pal, like the people who were now flocking to Epping Forest to see Lily Lee and her 'miracle', was convinced that what he had seen meant something good. He died the next morning and the Great War dragged on for another two years.

A lot had happened since Rosie's funeral the previous Thursday. For a start-off, or so it was said, the Military Police had been obliged to cut down on their other duties in favour of crowd control. The forest around Eagle Pond was, apparently,

31

packed out, not just with the inevitable crop of newspaper reporters but with thousands of Londoners and lots of other people from all over. Every one of them wanted the same thing: some sign from the Virgin Mary that the end of the bombing was at hand. No one wants to live with the fear we have – no one. It was a busy day for me the following Monday when I heard our family priest, Father Burton, enter the shop.

'Hello, Father,' I heard Doris reply, to the priest's customary dour greeting. 'Mr Hancock's just about to go out. He's laying to rest poor old Mrs Ewers – don't know whether you knew her but—'

'It's not really Mr Hancock I've come to see,' I heard Father Burton say. 'It's Mrs Hancock and Miss Nancy.'

'Oh, well, that's nice,' Doris said. 'The ladies like to have company, 'specially, yours, I know, Father.'

'Just want to make sure that none of my parishioners is getting hoodwinked by this nonsense up in Epping Forest.'

'Oh, the Gypsy with the—'

'The Gypsy no one has been able to wrest from her filthy tent since her so-called vision last week,' the priest said stiffly. 'As if a savage like that would be granted the privilege of miracles! She's not been to see a priest or a divine of any sort since this all began. It's most irregular. How can the Bishop make a judgement about such a thing without talking to the person involved? Now, or so I hear, the Gypsy camp is awash with the ignorant and gullible, touching the tree the girl was staring at and, no doubt, being roundly fleeced by the Gypsies for doing so!'

'I'll go and tell Mrs Hancock you're here, Father,' Doris said, as she pushed her way through the black curtains at the back of the shop and into the place where we sometimes keep our deceased. Most people, of course, keep their dear departed at home with them until the day of the funeral. But sometimes, as in Rosie Lee's case and with bombing victims too mangled for their families to bear, that isn't always possible. So I have, not a nice posh Chapel of Rest like some more prosperous firms, but something as close as I can afford to it. I was just reaching over to retrieve the lid of May Ewers's coffin when Doris went past me towards the stairs. Knowing how I feel about priests and suchlike, she mouthed at me, 'Miserable old git,' and I smiled.

The tiny shrunken woman in the coffin had been, it was said, a music-hall hall singer in the years before drink took up her every waking moment. I'd known her a bit and she was a loud, coarse and funny old girl. She'd had no family, which was why she was on her own with me in our room. Just before I put the lid over her dried-up old mug I leaned in to the coffin and said, 'Tell you what, May, I'll go up to the forest after work and see what's going on for both of us, shall I? If Father Burton doesn't like it, it must be quite a carry-on.'

I was intrigued, I admit. Work and family commitments had meant that I hadn't been able to get far beyond the shop for some days. But now I had some time I resolved to go and find out what was going on. I thought I might also collect some twigs for the fire while I was at it.

I called out into the yard for Arthur to bring me a handful of nails.

You see some sights, these days, but nothing had prepared me for what met my eyes around Eagle Pond. There were thousands of them, men – some in uniform and some in civvies – women, children, mostly sitting when I arrived, in that way they do when they're sheltering down the Underground.

Waiting. The nippers were playing with their few little toys, occasionally whining, the women knitting, drinking tea, the blokes leaning up against the trees, smoking. It's true that on the Underground fights do sometimes break out between people, women mainly, over choice little bits of platform, but when a raid is on it can be quiet like this.

It was late afternoon when I arrived and I came into the forest in the same way I'd done on my first visit to the Gypsy camp with Horatio. This time, however, my path was quickly blocked by a rough couple of lads I'd seen briefly at Rosie's wake. Dressed in cut-down trousers and faded flat caps, neither of them could have been older than fifteen.

'Who are you?' the taller and younger of the two asked me, as he sucked nervously on his short clay pipe.

I removed my hat and was about to answer him when a man I recognised as Rosie and Lily's father approached. 'It's the undertaker,' he said to the boys, and then, to me, he added, 'We made full payment for my girl.'

'Yes, Mr Lee,' I said, 'of course you did.'

'Then why have you come? You're not a believer in miracles.'

He was maybe my age, maybe younger, it was difficult to tell. When a face is as brown and lined as Mr Lee's, it could be almost any age you care to mention. All I could see with any degree of certainty was the contempt that crossed the deep-set eyes, which were almost hidden by his battered felt hat, as he used the word 'miracle'. But, then, he was a Gypsy and, Lily notwithstanding, I had expected no more nor less.

'I wanted to see what was happening for myself, Mr Lee,' I said. 'I've heard so much since I was here last week.'

'The women do no wrong reading palms and cards for the *gauje*,' Lee said, as he gazed across at several women sitting

34

over by 'Lily's' tree reading the palms of a group of blonde-haired girls. 'My wife, she even reads for the soldiers.'

'The Military Policemen?'

He shrugged. 'The soldiers keep the people back from my daughter.'

'I expect some people would like to touch her,' I said, remembering what had happened when the 'miracle' had first occurred. Vague memories of stories about Lourdes and how the local folk had wanted to touch Bernadette came into my mind.

'Lily keeps to her tent,' Mr Lee replied. 'She has the Head for company. Come and have some tea with me, undertaker.'

I suppose that even those who are completely convinced about the existence of the 'unseen' can't believe in everything. But I was still shocked that Mr Lee should dismiss Lily's 'miracle' while making out the famous Head to be as real as the grass on the ground. But then, as I drew nearer to his tent and I saw the beast that was tethered in front of it, I felt that maybe it had been the showman talking when Mr Lee had spoken about the Head.

'This here is Bruno,' the Gypsy said, as he rubbed the bear's head with a large, rough hand. 'He likes to dance.'

Down on all fours, as he was now, Bruno didn't look that big. Brown in colour, he was a bedraggled chap and where the chain that tethered him to the ground met the collar at his neck there was a bald patch, which, though not inflamed, did not look comfortable. As he stared up at me I had the feeling that the bear didn't trust me, but why should he? I'm human and humans make him dance, most probably when he'd rather be doing something else. Beyond stunt-riding acts, I'm not a great one for animal turns.

'Bruno comes from the forests where my wife was born.' Mr

PETERBOROUGH PUBLIC LIBRARY

Lee invited me to sit down with him outside his tent and watch the kettle come to the boil over his fire. We sat in silence, which is something Gypsies do very well, in my opinion. Only later when the tea was made were we joined by others, all men, including Rosie's husband, Edward. Not one of the other men addressed or even appeared to notice the tall, thin *gaujo* with the top hat sitting next to Mr Lee. But they put questions to me, in their own Romany language, through him. They could all, including Edward, speak English, but seemed to choose not to. I thought at the time there might be something in the Gypsies' traditions about certain individuals not speaking directly to *gauje* after funerals. And maybe there is, but I know no more about that peculiar conversation now than I did then.

'He asks, why do you think so many people come to see what only my daughter can see?' Mr Lee said, as he twitched his head in the direction of a ragged, elderly man on his left.

'Well, I suppose it's because what Lily sees, or says she sees, is the Virgin Mary, Jesus's mother,' I replied. That was what the papers were reporting and what I had heard with my own ears. 'What does Lily herself say about it?'

Mr Lee shrugged and would, I believe, have remained silent if Lily's brother-in-law had not been about to speak. Mr Lee cut Edward off mid-breath. 'Lily talks to the Head.'

I knew that since the first 'vision' Lily hadn't been out of her tent. That was why there were so many people in the forest: they were waiting for the next dramatic development. The Duchess, who – sadly from Father Burton's point of view – was very interested in what was happening up in the forest, had told me that at Lourdes Bernadette's Lady had made several appearances scattered over a few weeks. Those visions and the later ones in Portugal towards the end of the

Great War involved people being cured of illnesses and prophecies being made. And, of course, those were the real reasons why so many people had dragged themselves up to the forest. I was looking out now at not just a sea of Catholics but of Protestants, Jews and probably a few Hindus too. People in wartime need answers, and if those answers are miraculous, well . . .

'The Head, Mr Lee,' I said, 'what—'

'My daughter makes her living from the Head,' Mr Lee cut in sharply. 'If you've sixpence you can see it.'

I did, so I put my hand into my waistcoat pocket to retrieve the coin but was stopped before I could think of handing it over. 'Not now,' Mr Lee said, with a frown. 'As I said, my daughter is talking to it, alone.'

Then he, and I, looked across at Lily's tent and the group around the fire became silent as the daylight slowly faded into night. Even when the sirens went, none of them moved. I, of course, sprang to my feet as if I'd been shot from a gun. Even though I was out in the open, which is far preferable to being inside the shelter or the shop, I wasn't yet on the move and I needed to be. I lifted my hat to take leave of my hosts but, as I always do at these times, I could only stutter my apologies. 'I, er, I, m-m-must . . .'

'Yes, you must run from death,' Mr Lee said, with what appeared to me an unusual amount of understanding.

'Th-thank you . . .'

'We must all run and hide from death,' he continued, and then he said, 'but you don't have to worry about that tonight, undertaker. Tonight you will come to no harm. The bombs will miss you.'

I ran from Mr Lee's fire and the company of the silent

Gypsies and headed towards the path that snakes around the edge of the pond. The way Mr Lee had spoken about death led me to think that his own view of it was possibly as something human beings could outwit. Death played games that we could win, if we were careful. I wondered whether it was the Gypsies' knowledge of this game that gave them their so-called predictive powers. After all, if you know how an enemy thinks you're half-way towards defeating him, or so I've heard.

The first explosions came as I was trotting past what must have been the last duck left on Eagle Pond. Poor scrawny object, it didn't know whether to run from the vast yellow and orange lights in the sky or from me when I drew level with it. Had I been in my right mind at that time I would have had the bird, wrung its neck and taken it home for Sunday dinner. But by that time I had gone far beyond 1940 and the poor old docks getting a pasting yet again, well away from the duck and how nice he might go with a couple of spuds and some runner beans. The blood from the trenches was dripping into my brain, the screams of those drowning in mud throbbing in my ears. I ran and ran until I couldn't breathe another breath and then I sat down in the middle of the Snaresbrook Lane and I cried. *Christ Almighty*, I remember thinking when dawn finally came, *if Lily is waiting for some sort of message from her Lady it had better be a good one*. Atheist I might be but I needed a miracle just as much as the rest of the poor sods laid out on their little bits of blanket in the forest – waiting. Mr Lee had been right, though: I'd not come to any harm that night. I started to make my way home through the mist-covered woodland. I had completely forgotten to collect any twigs.

*

'You've got to stop buggering off like this, Frank!' Aggie said, as she pulled me in through the shattered front door of the shop. 'Look at this mess! The Duchess is beside herself!'

'Ag—'

'We're three women on our own,' my sister continued. 'I know you have your problems, Frank, but we can't cope. Bomb come down over Balaam Street and we caught the blast. Look at it!'

It wasn't only the shop: all the windows at the front of the flat had blown in and the blackout curtains hung in ribbons, fluttering into the street. Balaam Street is a fair way from us, coming off the opposite side of the Barking Road, so the bomb that hit down there must have been big. I shoved what was left of the shop door shut with my foot and stared down at my desk, which was now covered with a thick layer of broken glass.

The Duchess, who stood between the black curtains at the back of the shop, said, 'You'll have to get Walter and Arthur to board everything up when they get in.' Mainly she was exhausted and smelt strongly of friar's balsam, which she'd been sniffing for some days now in an attempt to ward off a cough.

'Yes, I know.'

Of course, a lot of businesses had been boarded up since early September. Compared to some we had been lucky. But I still didn't like it. Boarded-up businesses had plucky slogans like 'Still here!' painted over where their windows had once been; boarded-up businesses worked in darkness.

'Francis . . .' My mother began to cough again.

'Why don't you go back upstairs, Duchess?' I said hardly able to look her in the face. 'Make a cup of tea.'

'I would if the kitchen were not covered with glass,' she

39

replied, in a tone that was harsh for her. 'The blast has shot the glass from the parlour right through to the kitchen sink.'

I glanced up at her, aware that I had tears in my eyes. 'Mum, you're not well. I'm sorry . . .'

'Francis, I have a cold, I am not about to die,' the Duchess replied.

'Yes, but I should've been here.'

'Blimey, Mr H, what's all this?'

I turned to see Walter Bridges, our occasional pall-bearer, push open what was left of the shop door and crunch his way across the glass-strewn floor towards me. He looked around doubtfully, took off his hat and said, 'You're going to need this boarded up, you know.'

'Yes, Walter,' I said, as I turned away from the strong smell of beer on the old fellow's breath. Walter isn't as young or as sober as he might be, but with all the young men in the forces who can choose their workers? 'A job for you and young Arthur, I think.'

'Well, if you have any boards, Mr H, I—'

'This is an undertaker's business, Walter,' I said. 'The one thing we have plenty of is wood.'

'What? Coffins?'

'No!' I've never been able to work out whether Walter is lazy or stupid or both. 'The off-cuts is what I mean. Bloody hell, Walter, the carpenter'd skin me if I boarded my windows up with his coffins.'

Our carpenter is the younger brother of a bloke who was in the first lot with me. When the Great War started there were four lads in that family. Only our carpenter, who was too young to go into the forces, survived. Now he makes coffins for us and for some of the other firms round here. He's a good lad, and rather than throwing away the off-cuts or taking them for himself, he lets us have them. And if the Duchess hadn't been so careful with the fire we would have burnt the lot. While Walter went out the back – to fetch a load of planks and nails, I hoped – I looked across at my mother.

'Thrift is a sacred word,' she said, as she smiled at me. 'Did you bring any twigs back from the forest with you, son?'

I was about to own up to having become, once again, a mad, frightened fool when the door opened on a small group of men wearing the uniform of the Corps of Military Police. The man at their head – who wore sergeant's stripes – saluted and took off his helmet. 'Mr Hancock?' he said, in a voice I've always associated rather more with commissioned officers.

'Yes,' I said. 'Can I help you, Sergeant?'

'Maybe,' he said. 'Can I have a word?' He was, I imagined, about twenty-eight, well-built and very blond. Aggie, who is partial to that type of fellow, was smiling like a person with tetanus.

'Well, as you can see, Sergeant—'

'Williams,' he interrupted. 'Corps of Military Police.'

'Sergeant Williams,' I said, 'we've taken a bit of damage here so if you want a chat it might be better if we go out the back to my store-room.'

'That should be all right.'

I was about to ask Aggie to organise some tea for the sergeant and his blokes when Walter came bustling in with a bundle of planks in his arms. 'You know you've got a stiff out there, don't you, Mr H?' he said. 'Some fat geezer.'

Mr Alexander McCulloch had dedicated his life to the butchering trade, which meant that he had had little time for relationships, much less marriage. He'd also been a mean, unpleasant old sod, which was why I'd ended up with him rather than his one surviving relative, his brother. 'Keep him down at your place until the funeral, will you, Mr Hancock?' Albert McCulloch had pleaded. 'There'll be an extra ten bob in it for you.'

I smiled at Sergeant Williams. 'I'll just go and sort it out round there.'

Calling Aggie to help with the refreshments, I went outside to tidy Alexander McCulloch away into the backyard. As I left I heard the sound of Walter hammering misshapen planks across what had once been our windows. Soon Hancocks would be trading in darkness.

Sergeant Williams took the delicate little cup and saucer, one of the Duchess's best, from Aggie with a smile.

'Two sugars?' she breathed.

'Thank you,' he said, then waited patiently for my sister to leave. She took her time until she flashed a glance inadvertently at me and saw my expression. She didn't notice that he wasn't showing the slightest interest in her. He was probably a good ten years, maybe even more, her junior.

I offered the sergeant a fag, which he declined, then said, 'So what's all this about, then, Sergeant?'

'I understand, Mr Hancock, that you were at the wake for the Gypsy girl in Epping Forest when all of these "miracles" began.'

'Yes, I was,' I said, and proceeded to tell Sergeant Williams what my involvement had been.

'I wasn't there myself, the day these visions began,' he said, 'but as you must have noticed the Corps have been up there in the forest for some time.'

'Yes.'

'There's all sorts up there. Spivs and gangsters on the run from the law, dodgy types concealing dodgy goods among the trees. But we're not really in the forest because of them. We're military and as such we're concerned with national security and military matters. Deserters hide in the forest.' I had to make myself continue to smile at him. 'We're looking for four at the present time.'

'Are you?'

There must have been an edge or a tone in my voice that he didn't like because he said, 'Is that a problem?'

I studied the sawdust-covered floor of the store-room and said, 'No.'

He paused before he spoke again. 'Good.' And then, after another pause, during which I lifted my eyes to his, he said, 'We're also searching for a couple of foreigners, people we're obliged to intern for the national good.' He put his hand into the top pocket of his battledress and pulled out several photographs. I knew at least part of what was coming next. Doris's father-in-law, a German Jew, had been interned for six months at the beginning of the war. It had nearly killed the poor old bugger.

'This is Heinrich Feldman,' he said, as he handed me a photograph of an elderly Jewish man. 'And that is his wife, Eva.'

She was quite a bit younger than him but I'd known that anyway. Heinrich was a clock-mender and had done a very nice job for me once on my dad's old pocket watch.

'They used to live in this area. Had a shop in Upton Park, so I believe,' the sergeant continued. 'They were born in Germany so the law must be applied. Do you know these people, Mr Hancock?'

'No.'

'There's talk, you see, in some quarters, among those who may call themselves socialists, that because some of these people are Jews they shouldn't be subject to internment. But they are Germans, Mr Hancock, and we believe they are hiding in Epping Forest.'

'Well, I wish you luck in finding them,' I said, as I handed the photographs back to the sergeant.

'As you can imagine, what with all that miracle chaos, we haven't been able to move around quite as easily as we normally do,' he said. 'And, of course, the Gypsies aren't exactly helpful. A strange, dark people.' He stared pointedly at me as he spoke.

'Yes.'

'And talking of Gypsies, here's another reason my chaps and I are in the forest.' He handed me a small, indistinct photograph of a dark, rather fierce-looking young man.

'His name is Martin Stojka,' the sergeant said. 'We've received intelligence that he's in the forest. He's required to be interned.'

'He's a German?'

'A German Gypsy,' he replied. 'Have you seen either the Feldmans or this man in or around the Gypsy encampment at Eagle Pond, Mr Hancock?'

'No.' Of course, I, like most people in West Ham, knew the Feldmans and wouldn't have told the authorities where they were even if I'd known. But I didn't, any more than I knew about this Stojka fellow.

'We've searched the Gypsy encampment, with a view to finding Stojka, but we've come up with nothing.'

'Then maybe he's moved on or was never there,' I said.

'Or maybe the Gypsies are still hiding him somewhere,' the sergeant replied, as he sipped his tea slowly. 'The Eagle Pond group are the only Gypsies in the forest at the moment. They look after their own, that lot.'

'Don't we all?'

He looked up at me sharply, wondering, I could see in his face, what someone like me might be. Was I a very pale black or just a dark white man? It's a look I've seen many, many times.

'Well, the fact is, Mr Hancock,' he said at length, 'you've been up to the camp a few times and it's said you know these Gypsies.'

'Well . . .'

'His Majesty and his armed forces would therefore be very grateful, Mr Hancock, if you could keep your eyes and ears open for any unusual people, the Feldmans and especially Martin Stojka in your future dealings up in Epping Forest.' He leaned in close to my face and said, 'They trust you. You buried one of them, didn't you?'

'Yes,' I said.

'You know the horsemen from Beckton, Horatio and George Gordon Smith?'

'Yes.' He knew a lot about me, this Military Policeman. I frowned. 'Why do you want this Martin Stojka again, Sergeant?'

'Because he's a German,' the sergeant said levelly. 'He's also, it's said, vicious and dangerous. Anyway, all Germans have to be detained, you know that.'

'Yes, but—'

'Just keep your eyes peeled, Mr Hancock,' he said, as he put his cup down on one of the coffin stands, then rose to his feet. 'My lads and I are always about. If you see or hear anything you should pass it on immediately. And don't try to do anything yourself, don't be a hero. Whatever sub-group these people might belong to, whatever stories may be going around about what Hitler is doing to them, they are first and foremost Germans and the enemy. If attacked, they might kill you.'

I thought about telling him the story of Doris's father-in-law Herschel Rosen, but thought better of it. That poor old Herschel had suffered in that awful camp they'd sent him to wasn't going to impress or soften this bloke. He was, or rather I thought he was at the time, one of those who goes beyond patriotism into something that is an enemy of any sort of understanding. But I said I'd do as he asked and bade him goodbye cheerfully enough.

Aggie, who was almost breathless with excitement, watched him and his men go with a sigh on her now painted lips. 'What a dish!' She turned to me. 'Oh, Frank, are you going to be seeing him again?'

'Not if I can help it,' I said, and at the time, I meant it.

'Oh, you mean git!' Aggie cried.

I walked out into the yard, passing Walter on his way to the front of the shop with more wood. Arthur, who had only just arrived, was looking into Alexander McCulloch's coffin with a frown.

'He out getting a suntan, Mr H?' he said.

'Something like that,' I replied, and then I asked Arthur for a fag, which he gave me without further ado. We stood beside the not-so-dear departed, smoking in silence. Even the back of our building, which had not been touched by the blast, was filthy and studded with shards of glass.

46

Chapter Four

Later that afternoon, once I'd screwed the lid down on Alexander McCulloch's coffin and my lads and I had boarded up most of the windows, I went into the kitchen to get a cup of tea. I knew that my sisters were out and I had thought that the Duchess was asleep but then I saw her thin, black-clad figure standing motionless at the kitchen window and I said, 'Penny for 'em?'

She turned and smiled. She's seventy years old, my mother, and still beautiful. 'My thoughts? Well, Francis, I was thinking that someone ought to go down to Canning Town for some sweets.'

I went over to the kitchen range and lit the gas underneath the kettle. 'Sweets? You'll be lucky. What do you want sweets for?'

'I'd like some Victory Vs to soothe this cough,' she said. 'I would also like some sweets for a journey I intend to make.'

Like me, the Duchess is tall and thin, so I never have to look down at her. 'Where are you planning on going, Duchess?'

'Well, that poor woman who lost her daughter, Betty Lee, she invited me to see her other daughter's attraction, the Head. You remember, Francis.'

I did, although I couldn't really see my mother putting herself out so much as to go all the way to Epping Forest just to see some side-show.

'Nancy and I have decided to go tomorrow afternoon and I thought it might be nice for us to have some barley sugar or something like that for the journey.'

I'd had my suspicions, of course, but now I was certain. If the Duchess was going up to Epping Forest with Nancy, she wanted to see the 'miracle'. She wouldn't go directly against Father Burton's orders, of course, she'd use the mysterious Head as a cover story and be perfectly calm about telling the priest so, when eventually she had to.

'So, if you have time, Francis, I would be obliged if you could go to Murkoff's for me,' she said. 'Their sweets are so much better than anyone else's.'

'Duchess,' I said, 'the chances of my finding some sweets even at Murkoff's—'

'Well, if you don't find them there, then maybe you won't mind trying elsewhere in Rathbone market,' the Duchess said, as she turned pointedly away from me. 'You could even see your friend who lives there, Miss Jacobs, couldn't you? I'm sure she'd be glad of the company.'

Ever since my mother had met my 'friend' Hannah Jacobs, some weeks before this, I'd wondered how much she'd worked out. Aggie, I knew, was fully aware of what Hannah was and what she meant to me. But the Duchess? Well, I knew she knew that Hannah was Jewish, and I suspected she had knowledge of some amount of 'involvement' on my part. I could be pretty sure, however, that she didn't know that Hannah was a prostitute. If she had I do believe that Rathbone Market and even Murkoff's would have been very much out of bounds.

That she waved me off when I left, with a smile, was also a strong clue.

'I'll come with you and Nan tomorrow,' I said. 'It's like a madhouse up round that pond and I've no work on in the afternoon.'

The Duchess coughed, then smiled again.

'Eva Feldman's parents disappeared, so they say,' Hannah said, as she pulled her dress over her slip, then lit a fag. 'She got together with old Heinrich, who already had a brother over here, in Bethnal Green. That was three years ago.' She looked down at the floor sadly. 'Jews can't leave Germany now.'

'Hannah, love, I would never tell the Military Police or anyone else where the Feldmans might be, even if I knew,' I said. We both dress very quickly after one of our 'afternoons' so I was sitting on the bed by this time with my shirt and everything else done up to my neck.

'I know.' Hannah isn't a pretty woman, she's seen far too much of life for that, but in spite of her age – forty-seven like me – and the fact that she dyes her lovely brown hair yellow, she's beautiful. Many years before I met her, Hannah left her very religious family, disowned by them, to marry a Gentile boy. But that didn't work out so she had to make her living any way she could. At first she was literally on the streets, but now she lives with a couple of other 'old girls', who work in the house of an elderly abortionist called Dot Harris. I am one of Hannah's few regulars. I am also, I like to think, something more on occasion too.

'Anyway, I got the feeling that the person the sergeant really wanted was the Gypsy, Stojka,' I said. 'He made him sound dangerous.'

'Like the Feldmans?' Hannah shook her head. 'You know, the Commies say that the Nazis have been killing the Gypsies for years. This Stojka has probably run here for his life.'

'But, as the sergeant said, they're all German,' I said, unconvinced even as I uttered the words. The Communists, or Commies as many call them, are strong in this part of London. Committed to the betterment of the working classes, a lot of Commies are Jews and they are, in my experience, very well informed. Hannah knows a few, and if they were saying that the Nazis were killing Gypsies I was inclined to believe them. After all, even if Joe Stalin chooses to ally himself with Hitler that doesn't mean every Commie on the planet thinks likewise. Doris's husband Alfie, for one, thinks that the Soviet leader is simply playing for time.

'Well, if you don't go up to the forest again for a bit, you won't have to get involved in none of it, will you?' Hannah said.

'I've said I'll take my mother and sister up there tomorrow afternoon,' I replied. And then I added, 'To see this Gypsy girl having her "vision" hopefully.'

'Virgin Mary supposed to be, isn't it?' Hannah said.

'That's certainly what people want it to be and, to be fair, the girl Lily did call whatever it was "Our Lady". But putting aside for a moment the fact that I can't believe in such things, there's something not right about it all.'

'What do you mean?'

I picked up a fag I'd rolled earlier and stuck it into my mouth. 'Well,' I said, 'when some old girl from Canning Town started jumping around about it being the Virgin Mary, Lily said, "No."'

'What changed her mind?'

'I don't know whether anything did.' If my memory served

me right, Lily had just stopped saying it wasn't the Virgin Mary. She had also, I remembered, stopped her brother-in-law saying something too.

'Maybe it's a swindle,' Hannah said, after a pause. 'You know how dodgy Gypsies can be.'

'I thought you felt sorry for them,' I said, as I lit my fag.

'I don't think they should be hurt,' Hannah said, 'but I'm connected to the real world too. Gyppos are dodgy, H. Talking of which, they have paid you for that girl's funeral, haven't they?'

Exactly like Doris. 'Yes,' I said impatiently – and this time I was telling the truth.

'Good.' Hannah smiled. 'So, you're off to Eagle Pond tomorrow, then, are you?'

'Yes.'

She sat down in the small hard chair beside the range and sighed. 'Well, maybe I'll take a trip out there meself. Get a bit of country air. Maybe our paths will cross. I should at least see this thing for meself.'

'Not likely to be much to see,' I said. 'Lily hasn't had any visions since the first one.'

'A lot of people are living in hope that she does,' Hannah said. 'I should see what there is to it.'

'Yes, you could come with us . . .'

'No.' Nan wouldn't be any too pleased, but the Duchess, in blissful ignorance of Hannah's calling, would be charmed. After all, I am forty-seven and I've never been married, which means that my mother is willing to consider most women for me now. The religion, of course, is a stumbling-block, but that isn't nearly as big a problem as Hannah's low feelings about herself. I've proposed several times and she's always refused me. She reckons she isn't good enough to marry a decent man like myself. What, she wonders, would she say to my mates and my neighbours if they ask her what she did before we met? She's also afraid, and with good reason, that one or other of them might recognise her. And that is a problem even I must accept. 'No, I'll pop along in the afternoon and if we meet we meet.'

'OK.'

'Anyway, I might, if I'm lucky, see that military copper your Aggie was so sweet on,' Hannah said mischievously. I'd told her about that and we'd laughed together just before we'd had our little bit of passion. 'He sounded lovely.'

'Mmm.' I hung my head in the way I am inclined to do when I'm upset, even though I knew Hannah was only pulling my leg. Looking the way I do, I sometimes find big, fair, younger blokes intimidating. They can so easily look down their noses at a 'wog' like me – and I can't retaliate. I have nothing to look down my nose at them for.

Hannah smiled. 'Oh, don't get down in the dumps, H,' she said. 'I'd rather have you than some bloke who spends his time out hunting for innocent people to bang up in some filthy camp. And, anyway, the military don't do nothing for me. I've been with soldiers, you know.'

I tried to smile at her but I couldn't. Even the mention of other men in her life upsets me and she knows it. Hannah realised she'd gone too far and came over to kiss me. Then, without another word, she made me a cup of tea, which I drank in silence. It isn't easy loving a woman in her line of business.

Lily Lee, it was said the next morning, had left her tent in the middle of a raid at just after midnight. Dressed in red she stood in front of 'her' tree and began to talk. Some said she sobbed a little, too. She was seen first, before it all went mad, by a small boy called Eric. He said the Gypsy girl was saying how sorry she was to thin air, asking it to forgive her if it could.

Of course, Eric's mum, once she discovered that her boy was missing, got up and went to find him. What she, a worn-out mother of twelve from Silvertown, saw was Lily Lee communing with the Virgin Mary in front of her six-year-old son. Eric, his mother later told the *Evening News*, was 'holding his hands up like he was praying'. That woman woke everyone else, screaming, 'She's come back! The Virgin Mary ain't given up on us!'

Mayhem followed, apparently, the still mourning Gypsies screaming, over-tired kids running all over the place, causing mischief, and East-Enders not being at all like the people who went to see Bernadette at Lourdes. Nobby Clarke told me about it the next day: 'All they wanted to know, kept on asking, was about the war. You had geezers shouting, "Tell us when the fucking war's gonna end!" and "Ask God to send us some fags!" Went raving mad, some of them.'

What was missing from all the accounts of that second 'vision' was anything about Lily herself. She didn't, or so it seemed, speak to 'Our Lady' after Eric had inadvertently blown the whistle on her. But, then, until Sergeant Williams and his lads arrived to intervene, she was a bit too busy beating off women who wanted scraps of her clothing. In the *Daily Sketch* the following morning, the reporter, who hadn't been anywhere near the event, described it as 'Outrageous. Those people who lost control of themselves should be ashamed.' He went on to talk about how unBritish it all was and how maybe Mr Churchill would like to put a stop to it personally. But Mr Churchill, as we all know, is cleverer than most and that article got no reaction from Downing Street. After all, whatever else she might be doing, the Virgin of the Pond, as Lily's experiences were coming to be known, was giving people hope. Because as well as the madness that attended the girl's visions there was also contentment. I saw it for myself when I took the Duchess and Nan to the pond the following afternoon.

Chapter Five

'Oh, I think that the fact that they're singing, and hymns too, is quite delightful,' the Duchess said, as Betty Lee led her and me towards Lily's tent.

Betty surveyed the massed hordes in the forest with a rather more jaundiced eye. 'Makes you *dinilo* all day and all night long.'

'But everyone looks so happy,' the Duchess continued. And she wasn't wrong. Everyone we met had a smile on his or her face. Nan said it was the grace of the Virgin entering their souls. Although how she could say that and then refuse to meet the presumed channel through which Our Lady communicated – Lily Lee – I still don't know. The Head and all the 'mumbo-jumbo', as Nan called it, aside, I would have thought she'd be curious at the very least. But she wasn't, so the Duchess and I left her sitting with another spinster she knows from church, Miss O'Dowd, and took Betty up on her offer to see Lily's Head.

Until this point I'd never actually spoken to Lily Lee. But as I entered the shabby, patched tent, I removed my hat and said, 'Good afternoon,' to the stunningly beautiful young woman sitting on the floor in front of me. With more curly black hair than you usually see on three average women, Lily Lee was also far more rounded than most Gypsy girls, who are generally skinny. But, like the first time I'd seen her, it was Lily's eyes that held me. Large and dreamy. Very good eyes indeed for a visionary.

'The undertaker,' Lily responded matter-of-factly.

'And his mother,' Betty said to her daughter, before slipping out into the open air.

'Sit down,' the girl ordered, and indicated that the Duchess and I should lower ourselves on to a damp, filthy blanket on the floor.

'Miss, my mother has a cold—'

'The Head won't come if you don't sit down,' Lily said, which, to me, had to mean that the illusion was somehow based on what angle a person viewed it from.

'Oh, well,' the Duchess said, with a smile, 'if we must sit, we must sit. Help me down, would you, please, Francis dear?' She took off her small black pillbox hat and reached up towards me.

I picked her up, then lowered her down at my feet. She's light as a feather, poor old girl. Not that Lily watched with anything that appeared to be compassion. Although lovely, her face also had a hard cast at times, like her voice, which could be as sweet as it was throaty. Once I'd settled the Duchess I sat down beside her and waited for something to happen. There wasn't much in that tatty old tent – just a pile of rags that probably constituted Lily's bed, a bowl for washing, animal bones and fur hanging from the ceiling and a little table surrounded on three sides by a black fabric screen.

Lily, who was still wearing the long red dress she'd been seen in the night before, shuffled over to one side of the table, just behind the black screen, lit a small clay pipe and said, 'The Head is very ancient and knows all things. It speaks many languages, one of which is English. You mustn't come near or the Head will disappear, although you can ask it questions. The Head is a man of our people who was a great magician. His name is Django.'

And then she called him. '*Django! Django, av!*'

There was a light that I can only assume came from a tear in the top of the tent, which illuminated the surface of the table. Beyond Lily's pipe, there was no smoke, nothing to distract a person's attention and no sound whatsoever. So how the head of a dark, moustachioed man appeared out of thin air on that table top I couldn't then imagine. Slowly, slowly, as if coming skin by skin into being the Head materialised and blinked its black-rimmed eyes. During this process I glanced away for the merest second so the thought about how it might have been done took my breath away.

'Django.' Finally I saw Lily smile. She said something else to the Head then in their language and he replied, I think, '*Va.*'

Lily, who was obviously accustomed to chivving along dumbstruck *gauje* from this to the next attraction, said, 'Ask something of Django. He knows everything.'

I looked at the Duchess, who was, I could see, without a thought in her head, then cleared my throat and said, 'Well, good afternoon, Django. It's very nice to meet you.'

'It is most pleasant to make your acquaintance too,' the Head responded, in a rather high, sing-song voice with an accent I couldn't pin down for the life of me. The moustache, I could now see, was not real but painted on to his face.

'So, er, how old are you, Django?' I said, feeling a bit of a fool to be talking to what had to be an illusion in that darkened, dirty tent.

'I am nearly two thousand years old,' the Head responded proudly. 'I have seen the Romans rise, fall and disappear completely.'

'Oh, that's very interesting.'

'I have seen Julius Caesar walking by the Nile river with Queen Cleopatra.'

'Egypt.'

'Yes,' the Head replied. 'Our people stayed in that country for a while.'

The Duchess, though religious, is not a stupid person and I could feel her shaking with some sort of emotion. The Head was aware of it too. 'You, lady,' it said, 'I think that you want to ask Django some question.'

The Duchess coughed, looked at me and then at Lily before she addressed herself to the Head. 'Well,' she said, 'I wanted to know, Django, whether you ever went in your long travels to the land of Palestine.'

'You are a Christian woman, lady?'

'Oh, yes.'

The Head smiled. It was not a pleasant sight. Quite apart from the situation, which was eerie, Django seemed ugly, leering and had very blackened teeth, which, again, I felt at the time had been done to him with makeup. 'I saw your Christ enter Jerusalem on a donkey and I saw Him die upon a cross,' the Head said, with what appeared to be great seriousness.

'Did you? Did you really?'

'Yes.' The makeup around his eyes creased and melted as he suddenly, unnervingly, smiled again. The look of it and what he, this actor, and presumably Lily Lee were doing made me sick. The Duchess is a sincerely religious woman and what they were feeding her here wasn't nice.

58

'You know, lady, it was the Gypsies that made the nails that crucified your Christ. No one else would do it. So it is said. So people say.'

'Django,' Lily Lee's face was troubled now and she'd put her pipe quickly to one side, 'the lady don't need to know—'

'Everybody thinks there was three nails, to smash the hands and the feet together, but there was four.'

Lily Lee grabbed a battered cardboard box, then said something, in whispers, which sounded very hard, to the Head. He said something back and then, with genuine regret on his face, he said to me, 'I am sorry, sir, for upsetting the lady. But I can see she wants to know everything about Christ. She is a seeker for the truth and a person of clean spirit.'

'Yes, well, that's as may be. But that sort of detail is not nice,' I said, at the exact moment Lily Lee covered the Head with the cardboard box. For probably no more than a couple of seconds I heard it pleading and babbling in its box, and then it went silent.

'The Head is gone,' the girl said, before removing the box from the table to demonstrate this to us.

'Probably for the best,' I said, then couldn't help adding, 'Can't have parlour tricks upsetting people's beliefs, can we?'

Lily dropped her eyes to the ground.

'Well, that was very interesting, my dear,' the Duchess said to the girl, as I helped her to her feet. 'Who do I pay? Is it you or—'

'You buried my sister,' Lily said to me. 'You can both go free.'

'Oh, how generous,' the Duchess said, as she made her way out through the tent flap and into the open air. 'And very interesting too. Francis, I will just stand outside for a little while . . .'

59

'All right, Duchess,' I said, as I glanced – fiercely, I imagined – at the Gypsy girl still leaning on the Head's table.

'It's not a parlour trick,' Lily Lee said to me, once my mother had gone. 'The Head is real.'

'Oh, in the same way that your "visions" are real?' I said.

'You were there the first time. You saw me see—'

'I saw you see something, yes,' I said. 'But I don't think it was the Virgin Mary and neither do you, do you, Miss Lee?'

'I—'

'I'm not saying that what you're doing here is a bad thing,' I continued. 'Your visions have made a lot of people happy, given them hope. But I know you don't believe it. I heard you deny it was the Virgin with my own ears. And this Head thing, well—'

'Sssh, the Head will hear you!'

She had real fear in her eyes, but I told her I wasn't fooled because I believed sincerely that I wasn't. Smoke and mirrors was what I thought – smugly, I confess – as I left the tent Lily Lee shared with the Head. How was I to know there was any more to it than that?

'Tell your mother to make a tea from coltsfoot for her cough,' the Gypsy called, once I was in the open air. ''Tis very powerful for a bad chest.'

Nan was having a nice conversation with Miss O'Dowd, who is quite her equal in the spinsterhood stakes, when the Duchess and I found her again. I think it's the bottle-bottom glasses on top of the tiny, disapproving eyes that disturb me most.

'Have a good time with your Gypsies' magic, did you?' Miss O'Dowd said sourly, as we approached.

The Duchess smiled. 'Very interesting,' she said. 'You know

that Lily even offered a cure for my cough? Coltsfoot, apparently.'

'Father Bowers, who is a friend of Father Burton, says that all types of magic and country ways come straight from the devil,' Miss O'Dowd said, in that limp, almost apologetic way she has.

'Oh, well, must be damned, then,' I couldn't resist responding.

'Not you, surely,' a sharp, familiar voice said behind me.

I turned and raised my hat. 'Miss Hannah Jacobs.'

'In the flesh.' She was wearing an old if still stylish costume in cherry red. The skirt was short, as most women's tend to be now, and it showed off her legs really well. Made up to the nines, as she always is when she goes out, Hannah had piled her hair up at the back of her head in a big French pleat, and topped it off with the fan-shaped hat I like so much. She looked a treat.

I heard Nan and the O'Dowd woman sniff disapprovingly in unison, but I ignored them and instead I reacquainted Hannah with the Duchess.

'It's very nice to see you, Miss Jacobs,' the Duchess said, as she took Hannah's hand and shook it between her own twisted, bony fingers. 'You, like myself, must be curious about what is happening here in the forest.'

'Yes. It's amazing.'

Apart from Nan and Miss O'Dowd, we all chatted companionably until the Duchess suggested that perhaps Hannah and I might like to walk around while she sat with 'the girls'. 'You know that Lily's father has a dancing bear,' she said to me, as I bent down to bid her goodbye. 'There's plenty of card-reading and perhaps Miss Jacobs would like to see the Head.'

'Yes, Duchess. We'll see. Don't get too cold out here, will you?'

'Francis, please don't fuss,' she said as she waved us on our way.

I noticed that Hannah had frowned at my mention of the Head but I rolled my eyes to the sky and indicated that we should set off quickly while we could.

Once we were out of sight of my family I took one of Hannah's hands.

'Had your pocket picked yet, have you?' she said.

I smiled. 'No.'

'How much they fleece you for a butcher's at the dancing bear?'

'Nothing,' I said. 'I haven't seen him – this time. But I have spoken to Lily Lee.'

'The Gyppo gifted with visions.'

'If you want to put it like that, yes.'

'She's a fake,' Hannah said. 'And?'

I put my hand into my pocket and took out my fags. 'I want to say yes,' I said, 'but not because of the visions. She just did a dreadful parlour trick for the Duchess and myself, a head on a table . . .'

'Oh, the Egyptian Head. I know the bloke who does that,' Hannah said dismissively.

'Do you?'

'David Green, calls himself the Wazir of the Pharaohs. His family lived next door to my auntie Esther in the Montefiore Buildings on Canon Street Road. Me and David was quite close as kids. Slimy thing when he grew up, mind. Been doing the halls with his magic act for years.'

Magicians are close about the secrets of their trade so I knew that if I asked, and even though I was a mate of Hannah's, this Green bloke wouldn't tell me how the Head trick worked. But I felt I'd like to see another version of it so that I had something to compare with what Lily was doing.

'Do you know where David Green is playing at the moment?' I asked.

'No, but I can find out,' Hannah said. 'He ain't no oil painting, though, David Green. You have been warned. Short, fat, bald and sweaty.' She pulled a face. 'Weird, he is, not in a nice way.'

She seemed disturbed, but then she said, 'Not like you.'

It wasn't easy getting away from the hordes in the clearing around the pond – there were even people camped among the trees. But after stepping over whole families of knitting women, not to mention numberless dirty-faced kids, we eventually came to a spot where we could be relatively private. I put my arms around Hannah and kissed her.

'You know I charge extra for doing it out of doors, don't you?' she said, once I'd disengaged myself. 'You get leaves and twigs in your clothes and up your wotsit.'

I laughed. I hadn't paid Hannah in the accepted sense for years. I take her out, get her some coal, slip her the odd coupon when I can, and I've paid her rent on a couple of occasions when she couldn't. But I never pay to sleep with her. I give her what I can and I'd do that whether she slept with me or not. I love her.

'Oh, I don't want to do anything, love,' I said, as I cleared some grass for us to sit on under an oak tree. 'Just being alone with you is nice.'

Hannah brushed away a few stray leaves before she sat down, pouting her red lips with distaste. She's a proper city girl and not too fond of the countryside. But once we'd sat down and lit our fags, Hannah settled, and even sighed contentedly when I moved her head on to my shoulder. I was about to close my eyes for a few minutes when something caught my attention further and deeper into the forest. It started as a flash of red. It might have been anything – a bird, a discarded blanket blowing through the trees – but it was a person, wearing something red, and as it and the other less distinct body beside it moved closer, I saw that the red thing was Lily Lee's dress.

'Leave me be!' I heard her say, followed by the low, if indistinct, rumble of a man's voice is reply.

'That's the girl who has the visions,' I murmured to Hannah.

Hannah looked in the direction of the voices, then turned back to me. 'Who's she with?'

I shook my head. 'I don't know.'

Closer to us now, I heard Lily again: 'I'm saying nothing because there's nothing to say! I can't help you, leave me be!'

'Lily!' The voice was loud but it wasn't unpleasant.

'No!'

'Lily, no one's going to get hurt. I promise!'

'No!'

She ran straight past Hannah and me, but she didn't see us. Her dress was pulled down at the neck and I looked at Hannah, who returned my gaze knowingly. 'Someone up to something she shouldn't,' she said.

But I wasn't sure. What Lily had said to the man struck me as more of a refusal to give aid rather than lack of desire for sexual relations. Not that the man appeared to follow her. Maybe he knew that Hannah and I were in the area. Or maybe he didn't want to get involved in the great mass of people we could now see swarming towards and around the young woman in red – hundreds of them, trying to touch her, asking her, 'Has Our Lady told you when it's all going to end?' or 'Ask Our Lady about our Derek, please – will you, Lily, darling?'

'Christ, H, this is barmy,' Hannah said.

'Yes,' I agreed. But inside I recognised that I felt different. Apart from the blokes I knew who claimed to have seen things in the first lot, I, like millions of old soldiers, know the story of the Angel of Mons. Quite what was seen by the British troops in the skies above that battlefield in 1914 no one can know. Some said it was an angel, some a whole company of the things; others had seen St George and there were even blokes who claimed it was all down to King Arthur and his Knights of the Round Table. But somehow the Hun were held back during that battle and thousands of our lads were spared. Whether it's true or not hardly matters. The Angel of Mons gave people hope and, if you discount the enemy soldiers involved, it or they hadn't hurt anyone. Lily's Lady, Our Lady of the Pond or whatever people might choose to call her, seemed to me to be in the same category – or, rather, she was for the time being. A chill wind was sweeping into Epping Forest that wasn't entirely due to winter coming on. Its origin, I felt, was in the uncertainty I'd experienced when I'd watched Lily having her first vision – the sense that I didn't know what I was witnessing.

We left the forest at just before five. The light was beginning to go, and the Duchess and Nan were anxious not to be caught far away from home if or when the bombers came over. Neither of them had ever been inside a public shelter and they didn't plan to do so now.

'You can't breathe in some of them places for the smell of, you know, the toilet,' Miss O'Dowd said, to my scandalised sister, as we all made our way back to my car. 'And there's women down there no better than they should be, allowing men all sorts!'

Hannah and I, following the Duchess and the other two women, gripped each other, laughing silently. What Miss O'Dowd would have done had she known about Hannah I didn't dare think about and as for my sister . . .

'Oh, blimey, it's a hearse!' I heard Miss O'Dowd say, as we all turned into the Snaresbrook Road and she beheld the Lancia.

'Well, you know our Frank's an undertaker, Dolly,' Nan said, in my defence.

'I can't get in no hearse! I thought you said your brother had a car!'

'He does. It is a car,' Nan said.

Miss O'Dowd crossed her arms across her chest and shook her curly red head in disapproval. 'Oh, no, Nan,' she said. 'I can't get in there. Hearses are for the dear departed. I'll get the bus.'

'It is getting dark, my dear,' the Duchess said, as she tapped Miss O'Dowd's arm. 'I don't think we should leave you here alone.'

'I'll be all right, Mrs Hancock,' Miss O'Dowd replied, with only a tiny shudder at my mother's foreign touch. 'I've got me rosary and a St Christopher for journeys, and with Our Lady so close by, I can't come to no harm, I don't think.'

'Not bothered that the visions might be part of that Gypsy magic the priests say come straight from the devil?' I couldn't resist asking.

Not that Dolly O'Dowd gave me an answer: she just stuck her nose in the air, told Nan she'd see her at Mass on Sunday, then headed off up towards the Eagle pub.

The Duchess shrugged, then turned to Hannah. 'Well, you,

I hope, will accept a lift, Miss Jacobs. It is so cold and damp now. If I recall correctly, you live in Canning Town, don't you?'

Hannah accepted my mother's offer so I drove back through Forest Gate, Leyton, through Stratford and back into the rubble and filth that is now the Royal Docklands. One other thing I noticed from that drive was that people get thinner the closer you come to the river. Further south from Canning Town, right on the Thames, had to be home to people who were all but transparent, I thought.

Chapter Six

Stella Hancock is my dad's older brother Percy's girl. In her early fifties, like our Nan, Stella is a spinster who, until that terrible night for her in late October 1940, lived with Uncle Percy in New City Road, Plaistow. There's a lot of women Stella's age without husbands or children. Victims, you could say, of the Great War, although not all of them see themselves in that light. My cousin Stella is one who does, her single misery displaying itself as a propensity to 'nerves'. It didn't take a great stretch of the imagination to picture what the ARP found when they dug out the stair cupboard Stella had been hiding in when the house next door took a direct hit.

'I've never seen nothing like it,' the warden, a local tailor in his other life, said. 'Stood up with her hands braced agin the ceiling of the cupboard, hair on end, pinny in shreds, her gob wide open like a bleedin' cod.'

'There's no sign of anyone else, I suppose?' I asked, as Doris came into the shop with tea for the warden, Johnny Webb.

'You mean your Uncle Percy?' The warden shook his head sadly. 'No, sorry, Mr H. Just your Stella, I'm afraid. Barmy as a coot too, which is why she's down the cop shop.'

I waited for Doris to go before I asked, 'But why didn't they bring her here? The police know our family.'

'Coppers only managed to stop her screaming half an hour ago.' Johnny moved his head close to mine. 'Look, Mr H,' he said, 'it's up to you. I'm just here to tell you because I think you should have the choice – you're family. The coppers want to take your Stella up to Claybury. And we all know what that means.' He sipped his tea noisily and appreciatively.

I breathed in deeply, then shuddered. Claybury is a grim Victorian asylum just to the north of Walthamstow. It's where they take East-Enders when their minds break under the weight of the work and the poverty that follows almost everyone here from the cradle to the grave. With its ice-cold baths and the numerous other punishments available to the staff when patients fail to 'behave', Claybury is a place of nightmares for a madman like me. I know I could be put inside its walls within a heartbeat. Just one outburst in front of the wrong person would be enough. I felt myself sweat.

'I'd better get over there, then,' I said, as I took my jacket off the back of my chair and stood up. 'Thanks for letting me know, Johnny.' I shook his hand.

'Oh, you're welcome, Mr H,' Johnny Webb replied, as he finished his drink and stood up too. 'I'm so sorry I had to bring you such bad news. We'll carry on looking for your uncle Percy, but . . .' He shrugged.

'I know.'

'Well, I'd best be going and let you get on,' he said. 'Let me know how it goes with your Stella, won't you, Mr H?'

'I will.'

I patted him on the back as he left my dingy, boarded-up premises. A lot of people criticise the ARP and sometimes with good cause but, like any group of people, you have good, bad and on occasion villains too. Like most people, I've heard stories about wardens looting bombed-out houses. But that's not Johnny Webb. Like me, he just wants to get on with his job and his life and make enough money to feed his family. Unlike me, he still has one window left in his shop.

'You've got them two sisters up Green Street, Bella and Alice Goring, at twelve,' Doris said, as she came back into the shop carrying the business diary.

Green Street, even using the horse-drawn hearse, is only a few minutes from the shop so if Arthur and Walter got busy preparing the vehicle and I got my skates on, I could get over to the police station to see how Stella was before the Goring sisters' funeral. After all, if she was really bad I'd have to let them take her to Claybury. If she wasn't I'd speak to the Duchess and the girls about her billeting in with us. They'd welcome her, I knew. Even if she was barmy they'd take her. I just wasn't sure whether *I* could take her if she was screaming or crying all the time.

I put my hat on and said to Doris, 'I've got to go out for a bit. I'll be back at eleven.'

Doris frowned. 'Yes . . .'

'Tell Arthur and Walter I want the hearse and the horses spick and span by the time I get back,' I said. 'Make sure the lads are well supplied with tea, won't you, Doris? It's cold out there today.'

I know some of the blokes up at Plaistow police station. One of the constables, Fred Bryant, has held a torch for our Doris for some time. He knows she's married but he pops in to 'say hello' from time to time. He's more than a bit of an idiot. Not that I had come to see Fred this time. I went straight to his guv'nor, Sergeant Hill, who took me to a small room at the back of the building, which was quiet, he said.

'We've one of the nurses from Samson Street Hospital with her,' Sergeant Hill said, as he opened the door on Stella, who was staring straight ahead of her like a person in a waking dream. 'She's calmed down a bit now, but you'll just have to see what you think, Mr Hancock.'

In her younger days, Stella had been blonde like our Aggie. Now her hair was a sort of soft grey, which wasn't unattractive, even if the straight cut she had on it was far from flattering. But thin and largely disregarded, by everyone but her own, Stella was, like Nan, pretty worn down and haggard now. First I smiled at the little young nurse beside her, then took one of my cousin's hands and said, 'Hello, Stel, you've been in the wars a bit, haven't you, love?'

She looked through rather than at me, so I went on, 'Stella, it's Frank. You know, your cousin Frank Hancock, Uncle Tom's son.'

Still she didn't speak. Her only reaction was the production of a thin trickle of water from her left eye. I squeezed her hand and said, 'If you want you can come home with me, love, Auntie Mary, Nan and Aggie'll be so pleased to see you.'

Stella made a squeaking sound in her throat, like a bird.

'Stella?'

The little nurse shook her head sadly and mouthed, 'Shocked.'

As if I didn't know, but she was only a kid and she was doing her best.

'I tell you what, Stel,' I said, after a pause, 'I need a couple of gas mantles for the flat, so what say I go next door to

Bedwells, get them, and then come back for another chat in a couple of ticks?'

Still Stella failed to respond. But I got up and made my way out of the room with a promise to 'see you in a mo' on my lips. Bedwells, the general store next to the police station, was not, of course, my destination. Although I could see that Stella was going to be bad, probably for some considerable time, I didn't want to give her over to Claybury without some more information, so I made my way back to the front desk and Sergeant Hill. When I got there, however, I found that he wasn't alone. Three Military Policemen, all strangers to me, were with him.

'Oh, well,' I heard him say, 'if that's the law then that's that, I suppose. I've always found him, and her, to be very respectable people.'

'That's the whole point about being a spy,' a spotty young private said. 'You'd never know.'

'Private . . .'

'They're enemy foreigners,' the young man responded curtly. 'Who knows what they're really doing here?'

'Still,' Sergeant Hill said dubiously, 'Heinrich Feldman . . .' Then, seeing me, he cleared his throat and said, 'Ah, Mr Hancock . . .'

I, of course, knew a little about the search for Heinrich and Eva Feldman from my recent conversation with the 'dishy' Sergeant Williams. I'd denied all knowledge of the Feldmans to him. These MPs, who might or might not have been Williams's boys, looked at me with ill-disguised disdain. But youngsters are not that keen on people in my profession.

'Sergeant Hill,' I said, 'could I perhaps have a bit of a chat about Stella?'

'Yes, of course,' he said, and after first taking leave of the MPs he ushered me through into the back office where we talked together about our Stella.

'I see 'em all the time,' he said, as he sat down behind a big desk covered with candle stubs and lit his pipe. 'Bomb 'appy, they wander about talking rubbish many of 'em. But your Stella, well, she's always been a nervous woman, hasn't she, Mr Hancock?'

'Yes.'

'So Claybury . . .'

'I do know about places like that, Sergeant,' I said. 'Not to point the finger, you understand, but I don't always think that asylums are necessarily the best places for people with bad nerves.'

'No.' He looked up sharply at me, Hancock, the barmy bomb-happy old soldier always on the run from Hitler's Luftwaffe. He'd seen me out and about when a raid was on and both he and I knew it. 'No,' he repeated, 'not everything is as it seems, is it, Mr Hancock?'

He'd been in the first lot too, so I imagined that was what he had to be talking about. But then there was the Feldman couple, that nice old clock-repairer and his wife – the young MP had mentioned the word 'spy'. 'People can be surprising,' he said. 'Yes.'

Suddenly I'd made up my mind. 'I'm going to take Stella back to our place, Sergeant,' I said. I couldn't think about Claybury. 'Give her a chance. See how we all get on.'

He was uncertain, I could see, but he nodded.

'I know she's always been a bit barmy, but she isn't generally loud or a problem,' I said. 'And even when people do have troubles they generally keep to their character, don't they?' He didn't reply or respond in any way. 'Sergeant Hill, have the Military Police caught up with Heinrich and Eva Feldman?'

'You know I can't say anything about that. Careless talk and—'

'A Sergeant Williams came to see me the other day,' I said. 'He's looking for deserters and others up in Epping Forest . . .'

'Yes, I know.' Then he frowned. 'Why did he come to see you?'

I told him about my first visit to the Gypsy camp and my experience of the original 'miracle'. 'Sergeant Williams mentioned the Feldmans to me,' I said. 'He said I should keep an eye open for them if I visited the forest again.'

Sergeant Hill smiled. 'I bet you didn't, though, did you? I bet you didn't even say you knew them.'

I smiled too. Both the sergeant and I are East-Enders: I didn't have to explain anything to him. 'Williams was also keen to find a Gypsy, another German,' I said.

'Yes,' Sergeant Hill sucked thoughtfully on his pipe before he said, 'Everything's about spies at the moment. The Feldmans, this Gypsy. I don't believe all of it, myself. It's not Williams in charge up in the forest, it's an officer, Mansard, a captain. It's a bit of a mess up there in the forest if you ask me, what with the Gypsies, this "vision" business and the MPs going about their work. Captain Mansard wants that Gypsy particularly. We have to find him soon.'

'Do you know why?'

'Even if I did I couldn't tell you, Mr Hancock, discreet as I know you are. I mean, blimey, if Heinrich Feldman or any other Jew for that matter can be a Nazi spy, who can an honest patriotic copper trust, eh? You tell me.'

As I stood up to go I said, 'I don't believe the Feldmans are spies, do you?'

'People throw words around without thinking much of the time, especially the military.'

'So you don't think they're spies, then?' I said.

Sergeant Hill looked at me steadily, then said, 'You want to take your Stella off now, then?'

'Yes, I'll take her,' I said, with a sigh. 'Don't want her babbling nonsense where someone might hear and get the wrong idea, do we? I mean, if Jews can be spies, why not nutcases?'

Sergeant Hill, I knew, was aware of my views about internment. When our Doris's father-in-law had been interned for six months, she had told Constable Fred Bryant all about it and about my useless efforts to stop it. Fred blabs so the whole station had to have known Doris's and my business. But Sergeant Hill just shrugged his shoulders helplessly and let me leave without further comment. For my part I was saddened that the Feldmans had, or so it would seem, been caught and I knew that Hannah would be upset too. Eva Feldman, particularly, had suffered so much already under the Nazis. What, I wondered, as I made my way back to Stella, was the state of play with the Gypsy Martin Stojka?

Having Stella at home in our cramped flat wasn't easy for the next few days. I was very busy and didn't have to bear the brunt of it – that was done by the Duchess and my sisters. Poor Nan even had to share what few clothes she had with Stella, our cousin having lost the lot. Not that Stella seemed to care much, of course. To look at her face was like staring into an empty bucket. Towards the end of that week I came home one evening to find the Reverend Ernie Sutton in our parlour with the still silent Stella.

'I met Ernie outside the Abbey Arms,' Aggie said, grabbing hold of me just before I went into our dark and now very quiet parlour. 'Nan and Mum keep going on about how our Stella's a soul in torment, so I got her a priest.'

'Wrong religion,' I said, but smiled at my sister. 'Well done anyway, Ag. Ernie's a nice bloke.'

'I just want somebody to get her to talk,' Aggie said, as she walked towards the kitchen. 'Gives me the heebie-jeebies, her just sitting there like two penn'orth of Gawd 'elp us. I've put your shirts in the copper. Christ knows if we'll ever get them dry but—'

'Thanks, Ag,' I replied, as I went into the parlour.

We had finally managed to tell Stella that Uncle Percy had died the previous day. When the Duchess began to explain, however, Stella put her hands over her ears and screamed. I felt that the sooner I could arrange a funeral for Percy the better, although even I couldn't do it with absolutely nothing – not yet. Any bit of flesh would have done or even a piece of clothing at a pinch, but so far the Auxiliary Fire boys had come up with nothing. Uncle Percy had vaporised and an 'empty coffin' do was, I knew, on the cards.

When I went into the parlour I found a calm, if still silent, Stella seemingly hanging on Ernie's every word.

'Your auntie Mary has said that you can stay here for as long as you like,' I heard him say, in that gentle, low-toned way he has. 'Your dear dad is with God, Stella, but you have your Auntie Mary and Nancy, Agnes and Frank. You've people, which is more than many folk have got.'

Her eyes were wide and unseeing like a lunatic's. I must

admit that even when Ernie eventually got Stella to acknowledge his existence, I had a moment or two of wishing I'd never taken her in. It's something I wasn't proud of then and I'm not now.

When Stella had had enough she got up and went to be on her own in Nan's room. As we watched her leave, Ernie said, 'She's a long way to go, Frank. The shock has taken her very badly. I wish I could do more. I could come back . . .'

I said I thought that might be a good idea, as long as Ernie didn't mind providing comfort to someone outside his own flock. Just the idea of it made him smile. 'We all do our bit wherever we're needed, these days,' he said. 'I mean, look at you and me and those Gypsies.' And then, suddenly, he frowned. 'You were there when the girl had her vision, weren't you, Frank?'

We hadn't spoken since Rosie Lee's funeral – there's little time for anything apart from work, these days – so I now took the opportunity to unburden my soul, in part, to the Reverend Ernie Sutton. When I'd finished my story he said, 'You know, I've had a conversation with Philip Burton about this and we're both worried.'

'Father Burton's very anti-mystical,' I said. 'Always has been.'

'And probably with good reason,' Ernie said, as he offered me a Passing Cloud. 'People get hysterical around such things. They build up expectations about what might be about to happen.'

'Oh, I know it can't be real,' I said, as I took one of his fags and lit it. 'But there are a lot of happy people up there in the forest at the moment.'

The gas in the pipes hissed as it made its way sluggishly

towards the single mantle that we lit in our now completely boarded-up parlour.

'What do you mean it can't be real?' Ernie asked. 'Just because you're an atheist?'

'No.' I told him of how Lily had originally denied that her vision was of the Blessed Virgin. I told him about how her brother-in-law had behaved and about how the look of the girl had puzzled and, in a way, frightened me too.

'Well, it isn't typical of this type of thing,' Ernie said, when I had finished. 'As Philip pointed out, the Virgin usually – at Lourdes and that place in Portugal, Fatima – speaks to the recipient. She asks the person to come back again or bring others. Sometimes there are prophesies and instructions. But with Lily Lee there was nothing.'

'Because it isn't the Virgin Mary,' I said. 'Lily's seeing something, talking to something . . .'

'But nothing divine?'

'I don't think so. I don't know,' I said. 'But something isn't right.'

'All those people up there are expecting a miracle,' Ernie said. 'If it's a hoax they're going to be angry and disappointed.'

I puffed at my fag for a few moments. 'I don't think it's a hoax exactly, Ernie.'

'Then what is it?'

'As I said, Lily is seeing something. But it's difficult. On the one hand I feel she's genuine but on the other I know she performs parlour tricks.' I told him about the Head. 'But anyway,' I said, 'there's so many people up there now that if the coppers or anyone did try to go in and break it up to prove it was a fraud they wouldn't have much luck.'

Ernie sighed. 'But where is it going to end, Frank?'

'I don't know, mate,' I said. 'There's so much going on in the forest, what with the MPs all over the shop searching for deserters and gangsters and foreigners . . .'

'The Feldmans.' Ernie shook his head. 'I heard. A bad business. Poor Heinrich and Eva.' He paused. 'Frank,' he said, 'Father Burton, myself or someone in the Church needs to speak to this Lily Lee before all this goes too far. You've been up there a few times – you had Betty Lee here . . .'

'Yes, we did. It was a strange time, I can tell you!'

'I don't doubt it,' Ernie said. 'But I expect you got some sort of idea about what they're like from having her here, didn't you?'

'A bit, I suppose, not enough to make me an expert but if you want me to go up to the forest with you I'll do that,' I said. 'I can't add anything to what I've already told you except that . . .' I recalled the last frantic time I had seen Lily Lee, out of her tent and obviously afraid.

'What?' Ernie prompted. 'Except what, Frank?'

'Except there's a man wants something from her,' I said. 'I don't know who he is or what he wants. All I know is that she's not letting him have whatever it is.'

And that was all I did know. As far as I could tell, Lily Lee lived – discounting the Head – alone and without obvious involvement with a boyfriend. Still grieving for her sister, she appeared to be quite distant from the rest of her family and, in fact, from the whole group. There was some awe among the Gypsies regarding her relationship with the Head that, considering it was a parlour trick, had to have been put on for my benefit. I began to wonder who the Head might be, whether I had seen him about the camp and if, in fact, it had been the Head with whom Lily had argued when I was in the forest with Hannah. If it was, Lily was more controlled by than controlling her parlour trick. The thought made me feel quite cold.

'We should go and see the Gypsies soon,' Ernie said, as he was leaving later on. 'I'll speak to Philip Burton and then I'll get back to you, Frank.'

Chapter Seven

The following day was so hard it almost killed me. Like most people now, I'm getting used to hiking across piles of rubble. When every night and some days bring wave after wave of German bombers what can you expect? Even working in a shop without any daylight and only intermittent gaslight is something you can get used to. The workload isn't, because in my line of business a lot of work means a lot of death.

We started in the morning with one old boy from Upton Park and a box full of God-knows-what that was supposed to be an ARP warden from five minutes down the road. I'd known him a bit so after that one, which was held up at the East London, I felt I had to put my head around the door of the wake. The warden's wife, a plump, toothless woman in her thirties, seemed to want to cry on my shoulder rather more than she should so getting away wasn't easy. I hadn't slept the previous night so I was tired even then. The old fellow from Upton Park had been very big, and with only Arthur and Walter fit to bear – often we have Doris's husband Alfie, or members of the deceased's family – I'd had to turn to and help.

By the time we got to New Barn Street to pick up the body of an old girl who had died a natural death, I was even more tired and quite sore about the shoulders. Arthur, who had just learned to drive the motor hearse, was in a mood because everyone that day had requested the horses and the last thing I needed on top of all that was the Luftwaffe. Walter was about to put Charlotte Twigg's coffin lid on when the sirens went.

'Jesus, not again!'

I shot him a stern look. Charlotte's daughter, Esmé Dixon, was in the room and didn't look amused.

'Better get down your Anderson, Mrs Dixon,' I said, as I ushered both her and Walter out of the small family parlour.

'But what about Mum?' the woman asked, as she staggered shakily into her long, dark hallway.

It wasn't the first time that had happened so I was ready for at least one of the relatives to want to take the dear departed down to the shelter with the rest of the family. The first time I'd had to restrain one grieving son until he came to his senses.

'I'd be obliged if you could find some room in your Anderson for my two lads,' I said, as I pushed Walter and Arthur out towards the scullery before me.

'But Mum . . .'

'Your mum's dead, love,' I said, as gently as time and events allowed. 'My lads are alive.'

She looked at me with fury, then told one of her sons to take Arthur and Walter down to the shelter. I thanked her, then made my way back to the hearse.

'What about you?' she called after me.

'My place is with the horses,' I replied, which, of course, was in part the gospel truth. Our geldings Rama and Sita have nice quiet natures, especially Sita, but when the bombs start coming down the poor things get very scared. 'It's all right, boys,' I said, as I unshackled the horses from the hearse. 'Come on.' I took their bridles and walked them forward out of the way of the empty carriage behind. 'Come on, my good boys.'

My horses trust me, but those first explosions, which were taking place down at Silvertown, made them bare their teeth and roll their eyes. 'Sssh.' I held their bridles tightly, pulling their flanks in towards my body. Even though we weren't touching I could feel their sides trembling with terror. Inside my head the things that remain from the trenches started to scream and rave as the bombs descended over the East End, and all I could see in front of my eyes was blood. Rolling down my face, pouring into a gutter that was not a gutter any more but a trench full of the bloated dead faces of all my old mates from 1914. With the horses in tow I couldn't run, however much I might have wanted to, so the three of us shuffled around in the middle of New Barn Street, moving in strange uneven circles. We must have resembled some hellish animal turn at the circus.

I suppose that, from beginning to end, the raid only lasted an hour. But holding on to the horses while I temporarily lost my mind had taken its toll. When finally, and only with help from Walter, I managed to get the boys tethered to the hearse again, my shoulders ached something rotten. As I bent down to pick up the few little bunches of flowers that had been on the hearse before the raid, Arthur came over and said, 'Mr H, you'd better come inside the house. Something terrible's happened.'

The late Charlotte Twigg's parlour was now almost unrecognisable. Just over an hour before, the oak sideboard had been set with the bottles of beer and ginger wine all ready for the wake. Now it had been smashed in half by a hissing gas pipe, which hung from the back wall like an angry snake. The hard chairs that had been lined up around the wall were splintered to matchwood. Worst of all, however, Esmé Dixon and her daughter Ruby were screaming their heads off because Charlotte Twigg had been blown clean out of her coffin and up against the window, which had let in light from the yard. With her head out of the now empty casement and her legs dangling over the remnants of the sideboard, Charlotte Twigg looked like a broken rag-doll.

'Gawd help us!' Esme Dixon screamed. 'Bloody Jerries! Look what they've done to Mum!'

Charlotte's coffin had ceased to exist so I knew I'd have to go back to the shop and see if we had another suitable for her. 'Get these ladies out of here while I try to sort this out,' I said to Arthur. The boy nodded, then began gently to lead the women out into the glass- and metal-strewn yard.

Just before the Heavy Rescue boys arrived to deal with the gas and the general devastation along New Barn Street, I walked over to where Charlotte Twigg hung and grasped one of her cold, smashed hands. I said nothing out loud, but in my head I promised her that it'd be all right in the end, that I'd get her to where I knew she needed to be. The dead have to be protected on their last journey – the living can so often put the kibosh on it with their violence and selfishness. This is what I do. It is almost entirely why I exist.

As I walked back out into the street, I heard one of the ARP wardens talking to a copper. 'Virgin Mary up Epping still ain't put a stop to the Luftwaffe, then,' he said, laughing.

'Oh, that'll all die a death soon, you mark my words,' the copper replied, also with a chuckle in his voice.

But one bombing raid wasn't going to change what was going on up in the forest – the promise of Lily's vision was too powerful for that. Hannah, who had been, unbeknownst to me, up in the forest when the raid was on with her friend Bella, was to tell me about it later that evening. When, drawn and exhausted, I got home after my day from hell, she was waiting for me in the shop.

'Them military coppers took that Gypsy camp apart today,' Hannah said, once Doris had given us tea and gone off home. 'People were going bonkers.'

'Well, the Gypsies . . .'

'And the rest of them too,' Hannah said. 'Women screaming as how it was sacrilegious and suchlike. Some blokes even tried to fight the coppers – there's so much feeling for this "miracle" thing up there. But they done it anyway. The officer in charge, he just bowled in and had all the Gypsies' tents down in a couple of minutes.'

'Even Lily's?' I asked.

'So people said. I never got close enough to see for myself,' Hannah replied. 'But those as did said that the girl just stood there and let this officer knock her tent down with his stick.'

I thought about the table with the Head and asked, 'What was in Lily's tent? Do you know?'

'Well, that was queer,' Hannah said, as she sipped her tea, and then lit a Woodbine. 'After what you said about that Head, I thought people would be able to see at least something of it. But, no. Apart from a few rags, the tent was empty so I heard. People were amazed by the girl's poverty. Some of them mad old Irish bags you get round here were going on about how that proved Lily had to be a saint. You Christians don't half set a lot of store by having nothing!'

I smiled.

'Mind you, what I did see, afterwards, was that Military

Police officer and he was none too pleased,' Hannah continued. 'I heard him talk about the Gypsy you told me about, that German, to one of his men. He said that catching him was all that mattered and that if he found out any of the Gypsies or anyone else had been lying to him they'd be for the high jump.' Hannah pulled a face. 'I didn't like him, H, that officer. Some bloke told Bella it was him what found the Feldmans.'

Sergeant Hill up at Plaistow had told me about Captain Mansard and his need to find the Gypsy Stojka. It occurred to me, not for the first time, that perhaps Stojka was more than a rather leery Gyppo who just happened to be a German too. There had to be reasons for basically attacking the Gypsy camp in opposition to all the 'faithful' up in the forest, who now considered Lily and her people to be almost at one with God Almighty. I wondered, too, whether this action by the MPs was just one of many. After all, I had never found out who Lily had been talking to when she'd run away crying from someone when I'd been up at Eagle Pond. Maybe Mansard, Williams or another of their blokes had pressed her on the subject of Stojka. Although why they would think she might know something I couldn't imagine. Lily and her folks were – except Betty and Edward, who were Rumanians – English Gypsies, as far as I knew. They certainly weren't German. There was no reason, Gypsy blood aside, why they should know this Stojka chap at all.

'So how was it up at the camp when you left?' I asked Hannah. 'Are the MPs still up there?'

'Yes,' she said. 'Last me and Bella saw, they were watching the Gyppos put their tents back up again. It was quiet, but not a good atmosphere. I got the feeling the coppers won't move now.'

'They're between the Gypsies and the people?'

'Yes.'

I shook my head in despair. 'Well, that's all very good until Lily starts having her visions again,' I said. 'If the MPs try to keep them back from "their" Virgin there'll be hell to pay. There's some right hard nuts up there, and what with the MPs having rifles . . .' I sighed. 'As Ernie Sutton said to me only yesterday, someone, he thinks a clergyman, needs to talk to the Gypsies and find out what's really going on – if that's possible, of course.'

'Gyppos are close.'

'Yes, I know, but if the MPs are putting pressure on them they might welcome some help. They might need it. I think I'll speak to Ernie.'

There was a great deal of doubt in Hannah's eyes, but I picked up the telephone receiver to see whether I had a line or not and when I found I had, I called the Reverend Ernie Sutton without further ado. In spite of my tiredness, just one hour later I found myself driving Ernie and Hannah slowly through the dusky blacked-out streets, over to Eagle Pond and the unusually subdued Gypsy camp.

'We don't know anything about this man you speak of,' Mr Lee said, in answer to my question about Martin Stojka. 'These soldiers here,' he pointed to the group of MPs on the perimeter of the camp, 'they just come and tear our tents down.'

'Because they're looking for Martin Stojka, yes,' I replied. 'He's a German Gypsy. Didn't Captain Mansard ask you about him?'

'No.' Mr Lee turned his face away from me as he spoke. 'No one said nothing, just smashed up the camp.'

I noticed that Lily's tent, unlike the others, was still flattened out on the damp ground. 'Where's Lily?'

The Gypsy shrugged.

'And the Head?'

'Alive.' Then, turning to Ernie, he said, 'Would you like a beer, Reverend? We can have no fire because of the German aeroplanes, but if you want to come into my tent you will be welcome. The season grows cold at night now.'

Ernie smiled. 'Yes, thank you.' As we followed Mr Lee towards his tent, he said, 'Maybe he'll talk when he's not being watched.'

'Maybe,' I agreed, as I glanced at the many Military Police who surrounded the camp. Only with great reluctance had they allowed Ernie and me in to see the Gypsies. Ernie's position as a vicar had secured it for us in the end. But they hadn't allowed Hannah to enter and she was, I knew, waiting with the 'faithful', anxious to get back to her home and 'work'.

Mr Lee placed a bottle of Mackeson in Ernie's hands and led us into his tent, which, like his daughter's, was damp and covered with strange pieces of animal bone and feather. Before we had a chance to sit down he said, 'As you are men who work with life and death, I can tell you things.'

Ernie and I positioned ourselves on a long pile of rags.

'Yes, I know the military men are looking for a Romany from Germany,' Mr Lee said, as he rolled and lit a short, dark fag. 'But they don't tell me.'

'Then how do you know?' I asked.

'From my daughter Lily.'

Did the girl, I wonder, now have the gift of mind-reading as well as being a visionary? 'How did Lily know?'

'The young sergeant, Williams, told her. He is in love with

my daughter. He bothers her sometimes,' Mr Lee said, in that matter-of-fact way a lot of Gypsies in this country seem to have. So maybe it had been Williams I had heard talking to Lily the first time I'd been up to the Pond with Hannah. Perhaps their encounter had been of a romantic nature.

'So why do the MPs think that you or Lily or anyone in your group would know about the fugitive Martin Stojka?'

'Because he and us are all Romanies,' Mr Lee replied. '*Gauje* believe we all know one another. They also think we have powerful magic, that we can do impossible things.'

'Well, to be fair, having a head with no body that can talk is pretty magical,' I said. 'And now this "miracle"—'

'I don't know nothing about that,' the Gypsy cut in quickly. 'What Lily sees is given only to her. I don't know why.'

'Between ourselves do you think that her vision is of the Virgin Mary?' Ernie asked. 'Honestly?'

Mr Lee shrugged. 'There's just horses, bears and the road in my life,' he said. 'If people choose to believe something, that is their business. If my daughter has religion, that is something that she alone knows. You'll need to speak to her.'

'You haven't?' Ernie asked, disbelief in his voice.

'Ever since Rosie died she has talked almost only to the Head,' the Gypsy replied.

'I heard her talking to a man in the forest a few days back,' I said. 'If that was Williams . . .'

'My daughter, whatever is happening to her, won't go with no *gaujo*,' Mr Lee responded gravely. 'You talk about religion, but religion is nothing. The *romanipe*, our way of life, our beliefs and our people, that is everything.'

'So you've warned Sergeant Williams off?'

'Lily has,' he said. 'She doesn't want him. He and the others came just before my other daughter died, looking for bad people in the forest. Lily told him then she wouldn't look at no *gaujo*. She tells him now. When he goes he will forget her.'

'And if he doesn't?' I asked. 'Lily is quite the famous girl at the moment, Mr Lee.'

'It will pass,' he replied, with what I felt was a lot of confidence. 'Lily is Romany. She will move on and be forgotten.'

Both Ernie and I felt that what he was saying, in a roundabout way, was that he didn't believe in Lily's visions. Not that he had in any way colluded with his daughter to trick people. That his wife and some of the other Gypsy women were selling fortunes and other goods to the hordes of religious *gauje* in their midst was neither here nor there. Gypsies, like most travelling folk, take advantage of opportunities as and when they come along, whatever those opportunities might be.

'You know that if Lily continues to see things and the Military Policemen try to keep the people from her there could be a riot?' Ernie told the Gypsy as he sucked hard at his bottle of beer.

'Why would they try, the policemen, to do that?' Mr Lee asked.

'Because they have it in their heads that you know where this German Stojka is,' I said. 'They may try to withhold Lily to put pressure on you to give this man up. You're the only group of Gypsies in the forest . . .'

'I tell you, we don't know such a man from Germany. He, Williams, he's punishing my daughter for not going with him,' Mr Lee said gravely. '*Gaujo* men always think bad things about our women.'

'Be that as it may,' I replied. 'But if Lily starts seeing whatever it is she sees and the MPs stop people going to her, there'll be trouble. People might get hurt. The reverend and I are here to see what we can do to stop that.'

'Well, you'd better speak to Williams and his boss, then,' Mr Lee replied. 'It is all out of my hands.'

Ernie Sutton shook his head. 'But, Mr Lee,' he said, 'senior churchmen will come up here to see your daughter. They have to reach some sort of, well, decision about what . . .'

'They can come and they can see,' Mr Lee replied. 'Ain't stoppin' 'em.'

'Mr Lee, they'll come to see whether they think Lily's visions are genuine. If they think they're not, then . . .'

'They entitled to theirs opinion,' Mr Lee said, in a philosophical manner. 'Mind, who can say what is or is not in the world unseen do have to be a better man than me.'

I for one didn't know about that. Father Burton at least, if he deigned to come at all, was not inclined to an open mind.

'And Lily,' I said, 'she's the one, after all . . .'

'Oh, Lily is far away in the forest now,' Mr Lee said. 'What the soldiers done, it upset her.'

'On her own? But it's getting dark,' I said.

Mr Lee relit his roll-up. 'She's got the Head with her. She'll come to no harm.'

Hannah hadn't seen Lily Lee any more than anyone else had. But like the good listener I knew her to be, she'd kept her ear to the ground among the confused crowd of people who were being held back from the Gypsy camp by the straight-faced MPs.

'She just disappeared,' Hannah told me, as soon as Ernie and I caught up with her in what was becoming a very dark night indeed.

'So no one saw her go?'

'A lot of people saw the MPs knock her tent down,' Hannah said. 'But Lily weren't in it. I don't think this lot,' she nodded at the huge crowd of people beyond the Gypsy camp, 'would be as calm as they are if she had been. They all believe bleedin' mad stuff here – begging your pardon, Reverend,' she said to Ernie. 'Apparently, according to some, the Virgin Mary's due to battle the Luftwaffe in the skies above the forest tonight. I didn't hear whether Jesus and God were also involved but . . .' She changed the subject. 'The officer in charge here, Mansard he's called, I think I've seen him before, H.'

'Have you?' I wondered whether he was one of her customers, and my blood began to pound with anger. But I didn't want to start a conversation about that with Ernie at my side. After all, he didn't know, as far as I could tell, what Hannah did for a living and I was keen to keep it that way.

However, before I could say anything else, Hannah continued, 'Yeah. I don't know where but I've a feeling it might have been up home.'

'Up home' for Hannah is not Canning Town, where she lives now, but Spitalfields, where so many Jews have their homes and businesses.

'Military types go all over the place,' Ernie said, 'especially these days.'

'Yes.'

What sounded like many hundreds of gasps made us all glance up. There was nothing, as far as I could tell, to see.

'Oh, there she is, Gawd bless her!' a fat, tired-looking woman standing just in front of one of the motionless MPs said.

'Where's who?' Hannah asked, as she peered into the darkness to where the woman was now pointing. 'Lily?'

'The Blessed Lily,' the fat woman corrected. 'Gawd love her.'

Ernie and I squinted into the darkness until I saw the lone, bedraggled figure of a young girl drag itself slowly towards us. People cheered, some sang – the MPs gazed upon the crowd with menace and fear, and at a barked order from somewhere they made their weapons ready to fire.

I turned to Ernie and said, 'This is madness.'

'Lily! Lily!' the people chanted.

'Here she comes!'

'What the Virgin say to you, love?' one old man asked, as the girl, her face and clothes covered with mud, made her way past the MPs and attempted to get to her people. 'The war over, is it?'

She ignored him. As she pushed forward as quickly as she could, all I heard her say was, 'Leave me alone! Leave me alone!'

When she drew level with me, however, I remembered what Mr Lee had said to Ernie and me about Lily when we were in his tent and I said, 'Where's the Head, Lily? Is he . . .'

'He's with me,' she replied, and frowned. 'He's always with me. You just can't see him.'

What she said and the way she stared at me made me feel cold. When the bombs are raining down and I'm out running away from the blood and the nightmares in my mind, I know I can't always tell what's real and what isn't. Sometimes things appear that could be true of what is going on now and what went on in Flanders twenty-two years ago. But occasionally my 'visions' are not easy to interpret, even for me, and with the Gypsies' seeming ambivalence to the Head and its reality, this was one of those moments. What on earth could Lily mean by saying that the Head was with her? Even I could see that she was alone. But before I could ask her to tell me more she had gone towards her mother and father, who had come out to wait for her in the wake of the commotion. Hannah, Ernie and I watched with the many thousands around us as Lily embraced her parents, then followed them into their tent. As she did so, Bruno the bear gave a contented growl from his place behind their canvas home.

'Oh, well,' a bright young girl, with a cup of steaming beef tea in her hands, said, as the crowd began to break up, 'I suppose that's all the miracles we're going to get tonight. More tomorrow.'

The MPs on the perimeter of the camp seemed to relax, but not enough to want to talk to either Ernie or me. If senior churchmen wanted to verify Lily's miracles then they, like any other citizens, could do so. The young privates we attempted to speak to made it clear that they'd deal with that eventuality as and when.

On the way back to the car I did look towards the bit of forest Lily had come from earlier, and I thought I saw a figure that could have been a military type sheltering there. Was it Sergeant Williams? Neither Hannah nor Ernie had seen whoever it was but later I remembered that I hadn't seen Williams in or around the camp prior to that 'appearance'. Had he, Lily and even the Head been out in the forest doing or saying things that they didn't want others to hear? Was I going barmy even thinking that the Head was with them (or anyone else for that matter)?

Neither Hannah nor Ernie spoke to me about any of the things we had seen and done in the forest on our way home to the East End. All three of us were anxious to get back before the sirens went, as we all knew full well they would. Hannah and Ernie wanted to be near their own shelters when that happened and me, well, I just didn't want to have to take responsibility for anyone other than myself. I didn't want to have to make my girl and my mate safe before I took off, running away from the sounds and sights that torture me. When the bombs fall I have to be above the ground in a place I know I can look in the eye whatever might be about to kill me or make me go off my nut. It's important for us old refugees from the mud of Flanders that we die above the ground.

As she got out of the car Hannah, said, as if remembering something, 'Oh, H, tomorrow night you're taking me out.'

I frowned. Of course, I always like taking Hannah out but I was alarmed as this arrangement had slipped my mind.

'To the Hackney Empire,' Hannah said, 'to see my old mate David Green.'

'David Green?'

'Blimey,' she said. 'Brain like a sieve, you've got! The magician bloke with the Egyptian Head turn.'

'Oh, yes.'

Now I remembered. The Egyptian Head. I'd wanted to know how like or unlike it was to Lily Lee's attraction. Now I was going to find out.

Chapter Eight

I'm not, in general, a great one for music-hall turns. If you get a girl or a fellow with a really good voice and a rousing set of songs, that's nice. But a lot of the other acts can leave me cold. A case in point was the 'Comedy Partnership of Bertie Rouse and his "Cheeky" Niece Harriet'. The joke in this case was that the 'girl' was actually a forty-five-year-old bloke in a blond wig and a dress, which might have been funny if either of them had known any jokes. But the Rouses, just like the three poor old buggers who did a bad turn of the Wilson, Keppel and Betty type, were useless and I realised early on that I should've been drunk before I set foot in the place. Outside the concert parties to entertain the troops there's little new blood on the halls, these days. There's little new blood out of a uniform.

Hannah and I had caught a bus up to Mare Street, Hackney, which is where the old Empire is, just after I shut up the shop at six. It had already been dark so our journey was gloomy – on account of the blackout – and very, very cold. October was turning into November, which, in my book, is winter.

'All Hallows Eve tomorrow,' I said to Hannah, as I buried one of my arms in the deep pile of her astrakhan jacket.

Hannah said, 'What's that mean?'

'All aboard!' the bus conductor yelled, to anyone who might still want to get on to a bus where, on account of the blackout light we have to put up with, everyone looked deceased.

'All Hallows Eve is when the dead are supposed to come back to haunt the living,' I said. 'There's all manner of customs and frightening stories about it.'

'Sounds horrible,' Hannah said, then lit a fag and changed the subject. 'Here,' she said, 'I wonder if they've got one of them ventriloquists on the bill tonight. I like them.'

But Hannah was to be disappointed – if not as much as I was. She did find some of the entertainment funny and she did tell me off for being what she described as 'so bloody miserable'. But by the time the interval came, bringing with it a shower of fag ash all over my trousers from the bloke sitting next to me, I wanted to see this David Green bloke do his stuff and go. Luckily for me, I didn't have to wait long.

'There you are,' Hannah said, as a short, fat balding man walked on to the stage. 'The Wazir of the Pharaohs as promised.'

It didn't take me long, in common with most of the audience, to realise that the Wazir was as drunk as a lord. What should have been card tricks, easy for a skilled sober man, became acts of pathetic comedy in the Wazir's trembling hands. People laughed, of course they did, and if the Wazir himself had not seemed so surprised and hurt, I would've thought that perhaps his act was meant to be funny.

'Blimey, he's gone down the pan,' Hannah said, as she shook her head over the antics of her old friend David.

'He's drunk,' I said.

'I know. Never used to be, in spite of everything,' she said.

'Wonder why he's so sloshed now.'

Some embarrassing nonsense with silk scarves followed, after which the Wazir, whose only concession to anything Oriental was an exotic scarf flung about his shoulders, said, 'And now for the high point of my act – the amazing, astounding and magical Egyptian Head!'

One of the stagehands moved into the wings a screen I'd noticed earlier at the back of the stage. Behind it was a booth in which there stood an apparently empty table. The Wazir, who stood to one side of what was almost exactly the same arrangement as the one I'd seen in Lily's tent, waved his magic wand dramatically in the air. Smoke appeared, as if it was coming out of the stage, covering the table and part of the booth.

Some wag in the audience shouted, 'Them Egyptian fags ain't 'arf strong, ain't they?'

I laughed for the first time that evening. But all the time, as I watched the smoke clear around the Egyptian Head's table, I was thinking. Anything could have been happening under all that smoke. Something obviously was. But with Lily's Head the illusion had just appeared. No smoke, except that from the girl's pipe and, except for the few moments I'd looked away from it to the Gypsy, the Head had just come into being before my eyes. And although Django, with his sinister made-up face, had been unnerving, he hadn't been funny like this one.

'Behold, the great Abu Abdul!' the Wazir said, in a voice I imagined he thought sounded grand. 'The famous, the impossible Egyptian Head of old Cairo!'

Like everyone else I beheld. God alone knows how old he was, but his face was sunken at each side, which suggested that the Egyptian Head didn't have a tooth in his bonce. The fez on top of it all was several sizes too big, which didn't help to make the illusion any more regal. Old the Head was, but mysterious and special he was not.

'Oooh,' moaned the Head, and then again, 'Oooh!'

I looked at Hannah, who looked back at me primly. This magician was an old friend of hers, after all.

'Great Abu Abdul, you sound as if in pain,' the Wazir said, in what, to his credit, was only just starting to be a Cockney accent. 'Can we help you, O seer and magician of the mysterious desert sphinx?'

As in Lily's tent, I could see right under the table to the curtains at the back of the booth. This Head, like the other, floated on a table top. Whether it was concealed under the table or hidden somewhere else, there had to be a body somewhere.

'O mighty Wazir, it was the terrible Pharaoh Tutikamin what done for me!' the Egyptian Head said, in an accent that owed more to Canning Town than Cairo.

Hannah nudged me. 'What's David doing with that old geezer? He had some pretty girl when I saw him years ago.'

'The Wazir of the Pharaohs has obviously hit hard times,' I said.

'He ain't just hit 'em,' Hannah replied. 'He's gone right under.'

Fortunately we didn't have to put up with too much more of the Egyptian Head act. After the Wazir had finished and before the next act, 'Freddie the Dancing Dalmatian', could come on, Hannah and I agreed to go backstage.

In spite of his performance, I still wanted to meet the Wazir David Green. I wanted to ask him why he'd never passed in front of the Egyptian Head at any time. Lily Lee hadn't either.

*

'Hannah Jacobs, as I live and piss!' The little fat man now wearing a rusty Homburg over his shiny pate took my girl into his arms and squeezed her. She didn't seem entirely comfortable with it.

'Blimey, it has to be twenty years!' He pulled away from Hannah the better to study her. 'Still gorgeous, girl.'

'David . . .'

'Come in! Come in and have a drink,' the magician said, as he waved us into his tiny, dust-grimed dressing room. Looking now at me he said, 'Husband?'

'Friend,' Hannah said, before I could.

David Green, the Wazir, smiled. 'You still . . .'

'Mama and Papa don't speak to me and I still make my living in that way with . . .' Her voice petered out.

But the magician shrugged, indicating, I imagined, that he knew what Hannah did. He went over to the battered chest and mirror that passed for his artist's dressing-table and poured some gin into a cracked half-pint glass. He handed this to Hannah, then turned questioningly to me.

'No, thanks,' I said.

'Suit yourself,' he said. He offered Hannah his dressing-table chair. 'Sit! Sit, Hannah! God, it's good to see you!' He poured himself a truly enormous drink and laughed. 'Old sinners like us, thrown out of our nests, we should stay together.'

But his face, which became suddenly very red, told another story: that he regretted what had just been said.

'Yes,' a grave-faced Hannah replied. 'Davy—'

'Christ, no one's called me "Davy" since before the Flood!' He laughed again, maniacally as drunks do. He was, it seemed, as much a refugee from the Jewish heartlands as Hannah. I wondered whether the drink had been his offence or whether he drank to dull the memory of whatever had happened many years before.

'So, you caught the act,' he said.

'Yeah.' Hannah took her fags out and lit one. 'Egyptian Head was a woman last time I saw it.'

The magician sighed. 'She left me.'

'To go back to the Pyramids?'

He shot her an unforgiving look.

'Back to Barking, then, was it?' Hannah said, and then, with a quick glance up at me, got down to the business of why we had come. It seemed that she didn't want to linger here. 'Listen, Davy, my friend Frank here, he wants to ask you something about your act.'

David Green pulled himself up to his full height of, at most, five foot three, and said, 'A magician never reveals his secrets.'

'Mr Green,' I said, 'I don't want to know how you perform your Egyptian Head illusion—'

'Well, that's fucking good, then, isn't it!' he said spitefully, and threw a quarter of a pint of gin down his neck. ''Cause I ain't telling ya!'

'Davy!'

'What?' His belligerence was as quick as it was shocking. 'So, the turn stinks. I've still got my pride, you know! I thought, Hannah, that you'd come to see *me*!'

He fancied her, or so it seemed.

'Davy, you and me were never . . . You were a mate. You *were*.'

'Yes, well, if I'd been more than that maybe a lot of trouble would have been avoided.'

'Oh, don't you blame me for what you done!'

'Little Hannah Jacobs, so prim and nice and don't-touch-me,

what became a whore for the *goyim*!' As if he knew he'd gone too far, David Green stopped and his flabby face drained of all colour. 'Hannah . . .'

Her face was like a thunderstorm. 'Oh, that's rich coming from a bloke who likes to fiddle about with little girls! Thought that might have slipped me mind, did you?'

'Sssh!' He took another swig from his glass, then put one shaky finger to his lips. 'No one knows . . .'

Hannah looked at me. 'Davy here stuck his hands in the rabbi's daughter's knickers. Blames me for it, so I now learn.' She glanced at him and said, 'He was twenty-eight and she was seven.'

'No, no, no, no!'

I'd never seen Hannah like this before: nasty. I felt quite sorry for the poor bloke – or, rather, I would have done if he hadn't been a pervert.

'Just because I left our manor before you don't mean I don't keep in touch with people,' Hannah said. 'I know everything about what you done, Davy Green. Why'd'ya think I only come to see your show once in twenty years, an old mate like me? And we was good mates, but after what you done . . . Now, my mate Frank wants to ask you a few questions and I would suggest that you answer him – and polite, like, too.'

There was a moment when I thought he might hit me but then, maybe because deep down he knew he was too drunk and flabby to do me any harm, he slumped, sat down on his dressing-table and said, 'So, Frank, what can I do for you?'

It wasn't a comfortable situation and I could see he resented me, but I asked what I had to anyway.

'I want to know,' I said, 'whether it's possible in the illusion for the magician to stand in front of the booth and therefore in front of the Head?'

I'd given this some thought and I had an idea that mirrors had to be involved – not that I knew how at that moment.

'I won't say why but no,' he said, 'that ain't possible.'

'Are there mirrors under the table?' I asked.

'Reflecting the audience? Don't be daft!'

'No, reflecting something else,' I said. And then a solution came to me. The body of the Head had to be somewhere. 'If the mirrors come to a point in front of the table they'll reflect the curtains of the booth that surrounds the act, won't they?' I became, I admit, quite excited by my idea. 'It'd give the illusion from the front as if the Head was floating on top of the table. But the body would have to be behind the mirrors, wouldn't it?'

David Green did not reply.

But it would explain why Lily had kept to one side of not only Django but the booth. If mirrors were in use she would have had to, as the Wazir had had to. The 'Head', if this solution was correct, had to appear through a hole in the table top. It made sense if, in spite of everything, I still had a creeping feeling that Lily's 'Head' was somehow 'real'. Partly it had to be because she was a Gypsy, with all the mysterious associations those people attract. I knew it was stupid, but then, in his next breath, David Green threw the question wide open again.

'Course, I did see it done once with the magician walking in front of the act,' he said. 'When I was in the Kate, I was posted to Egypt, Alexandria. Shit-hole it was but there was this bloke, Arab, done this turn like it was something real. Don't know how.'

'What do you mean "real"?' I asked.

'His Head, this Arab bloke's, it was truly just a head,' David Green replied. 'I walked all round it, right close up.'

'And you couldn't see any trickery?' I asked.

'No,' the magician replied. 'Not a bit of it. Give me the right willies, I can tell you.'

''Ere, Davy, want to go for a pint, do ya?' The voice was old and it came from a familiar head, which had just poked itself around the door of David Green's dressing room.

'All right, Stan,' David Green replied, and Abu Abdul's head disappeared as quickly as it had materialised.

'Stan, see,' David Green explained, after the old man had left, 'needs his body. If he didn't he wouldn't look half as funny as he does when he's smashed out of his head on light and bitter.'

I had seen no one in the Gypsy camp so far who could have been Lily's Head, yet he had to be there somewhere. Whatever David Green's Arab had done in Alexandria had to have been an illusion in itself. A head couldn't live without a body – could it?

We left the Empire at just before nine and as we walked out into the cold night air we peered up nervously into the blackness of the sky. No Jerries as yet but I, like millions of others, knew they would come.

'I'll take you home,' I said to Hannah, as I moved her in what I hoped was a southerly direction. It's not always easy to know in the blackout.

'Yes, but if there's a raid you can run off like you do,' Hannah said, as she squeezed my arm affectionately. 'I'll find a shelter. I'm a big girl now.'

I smiled. Although she doesn't understand, no one who wasn't in the first lot can, Hannah accepts how I am in raids and doesn't try to stop me doing what I have to do.

'Your old mate Davy turned out to be a bit of a character,' I said, after we'd lit the fags we knew we shouldn't in the depths of the blackout.

'He's a dirty bastard,' Hannah replied simply.

'And you really, really don't like him, do you?'

'He fiddled with a young kiddie.'

'So why did we go and see him, Hannah?' I said. 'If you dislike him?'

She sighed first, then smiled up at me. 'Because you wanted to find out about the Head and Davy's the only person I know who does that sort of thing.'

'I would have lived if you hadn't, love,' I said. 'I'd do anything rather than hurt you, even indirectly.'

'And that's why I took you,' Hannah said. 'Because you'd do anything for me.'

'Oh, Hannah.' I went to kiss her but she turned away as she sometimes does when I show her what she feels is too much affection. Even without her 'work' on the streets dividing us, we can never be together on account of our respective religions. So we both know that what we have is hopeless. It just hurts Hannah a little bit more than me, I think, when I show her my feelings.

Experience told me to change the subject. 'So, David Green,' I said, 'did he go to prison or . . .'

'No.'

'No?'

'Just as we take care of our own, we also punish them,' Hannah said. 'David Green won't be going back to his old home in the Montefiore Buildings or anywhere else off the Highway till the day he dies. Not after what he done and what was done to him.'

'I thought you said he put his hand in the little girl's knickers?'

'Oh, he done a lot more than that, H, believe me,' Hannah said. 'He ruined that child for ever.'

It was cold, but after those words I felt even colder. What David Green had done was inhuman. I could only imagine how those who had found out about it had punished him.

'How do you know all about it?' I asked Hannah. 'Whatever was done to Green was done outside the law, and I imagine people wanted to keep it quiet. And you . . .'

'Even dead as I am to my mum and dad, I got to know about my little cousin and what David Green done to her.'

I stared down at her, and she said, 'Yes, my uncle Nathan is a rabbi and, yes, some men in my family did break David Green's nose and his ribs for his pains. Got off lightly, I'd say. I don't think he's ever had real relations with an adult woman. Maybe if I had given in to his sweaty wandering hands when we was both children . . .'

'You can't think like that,' I said, reeling inside from yet another new piece of information about Hannah. It's always the same with my girl. 'There's no excuse for rape, Hannah,' I said. 'There's enough ways that men can deal with their urges . . .'

'Using women like me, yes,' Hannah said.

'Hannah . . .'

'Put them fags out!' a loud voice yelled, from somewhere in front of us. 'There's a fuckin' war on!'

We threw our fags down and walked on in silence. Such overpowering darkness as you get in the blackout is quite suitable for some trains of thought. I've always known that East-Enders look after their own – Jews may do it one way and Gentiles another but basically it all comes out the same. Everyone has their own customs and traditions, including the Gypsies in the forest. But punishment is universal and people treat certain crimes very seriously indeed. David Green, I now felt, had got off lightly, as Hannah had said, and, as a consequence, was a very lucky man. In some quarters, maybe away from men of religion like Hannah's uncle, he might have been killed.

The sirens started up then, as they always do, with a hellish rising wail.

Chapter Nine

People often say after something terrible has happened that they had bad feelings beforehand or a premonition about it. Most of the time, of course, that's a load of rot. But the next day I did feel strange – or, rather, what passes for strange with me. We all worked hard. Two families in Boundary Road had gone down with diphtheria some time before. Now the first deaths had occurred – two little sisters in one family and a girl of sixteen in the other. Five nippers were still fighting for their lives in the isolation hospital, and both sets of parents looked like ghosts. When I went round to the first house, the Wattses', to measure up and offer my condolences, the mother said to me, 'I don't see no sense to it, Mr Hancock. I don't see God or Jesus or none of it in nothing.'

Her eyes were grey, dry and dead, as if she herself had already gone beyond the normal state of living flesh. I had a cup of tea with her and she gave me a pilchard sandwich, just the one, that she had made especially for me. For the very poor, producing even a tiny piece of food is a source of pride so I had to eat it, even though I can't stand tinned fish. Then she said, as I was leaving, 'That girl up in Epping Forest supposed to have seen Mary – you seen that?'

I nodded.

'More like the devil she's seeing,' Mrs Watts said, before she closed the door behind me. 'It'll end in tears, you mark my words.'

People say such things all the time and usually they mean nothing. But I got back to the shop and the feeling of doom increased when I found that my wand had been smashed to matchwood in the previous night's raid. An undertaker's wand, which to most laypeople is just a silver-tipped stick, is important to those in my line of work. Traditionally it was used as a weapon to keep ne'er-do-wells and grave robbers away from corpses. But there is an older interpretation: that the wand might be a magical implement designed to give spiritual as well as physical protection to the dear departed. I don't believe that, but I inherited the wand from my father, who in turn had got it from his.

'I remember Granddad saying he bought that from an old bloke who'd actually used it on Resurrection Men,' Nan said, as she bent down to help me pick pieces of the shattered wand off the floor. 'Beat them up he did as they tried to steal a corpse from its coffin for the doctors up the London Hospital.'

So-called Resurrection Men were rogues and toughs, who stole bodies for doctors to practise their anatomy skills on. Resurrection was rife in the nineteenth century, especially in the East End where there was a deluge of interesting deaths and diseases. The London Hospital at Whitechapel was always, unofficially, in the market for such corpses. Dad had told me that story about the wand and its history too. It fitted in well with my own beliefs about myself and my work. Only the dead can be innocent, in my opinion. The living kill, maim and torture their fellow creatures, and their inventiveness in this regard seems limitless. Not even the innocent dead are safe – I was in the trenches, and I know. But I have always done what I can to protect those I personally serve, and the wand had been a very important part of that.

'What am I going to hold when I walk in front of a coffin?' I asked Nan, as she folded bits of wood and silver into her full-length apron. 'Dad would be shocked rigid. I'm going to look like anyone else.'

My sister Nan doesn't smile or show affection very often, but this time she made an exception and put her hand on my shoulder. 'Dad's dead,' she said softly, 'so he don't care. And as for you looking like anyone else, that just ain't possible.' She turned away then and later, when we talked again, it was of other things.

But the point had been made: who is like me around here? Some people say that I look like this or that Jewish actor, this or that Spanish or Italian boxer. But I don't. I'm a tall version of the little Indian men who come selling carpets door-to-door, I'm like the Gypsies, Mr Lee, Horatio and his brother George Gordon. Jews are good at entertaining people, while Italians and Spaniards have a reputation for being romantic. I am none of those things. I'm an undertaker and now I was an undertaker without a wand. It made me want to cry.

I went out into the yard, where Arthur and Walter were cleaning the hearses.

'Bad luck that is, Mr H,' Walter said, with a sharp intake of breath when I told him about the shattered wand. 'Very bad.'

'Load of cobblers, more like,' young Arthur countered.

'Oi!' The older man raised his hand to the youngster. 'Bleedin'—'

'Yes, Arthur, I don't think you should talk to Walter like that,' I said, as I pushed the older man's hand down once again. 'But

I do hope you're right and not him.' I smiled. 'What we need now is a spot of good luck, don't we?'

But we, or rather I, didn't get it. Later on that night, All Hallows Eve when the fearful dead walk abroad, Lily's young brother Charlie came to take me to the forest where his sister's body lay covered with blood. It was only after I'd seen Lily Lee in death that my story became for ever connected to that of the Epping Forest Gypsies.

I left the travellers with the body while I went off to find one of the Military Policemen. I was a bit surprised that they weren't already clustered around Lily – they had seemed to be just about everywhere the previous day. But when I saw a large group of them staring downwards only a few hundred yards from where the Gypsy girl was lying, I learned the truth. If, however, they hadn't told me that the body on the ground was that of Sergeant Williams, I would never have known. What lay there was little more than meat.

'Made a terrible mess of himself,' Captain Mansard said, with extreme distaste as he gazed down at the body, whose face had been shot clean off.

'You think he killed himself?' I asked. I was shocked: Sergeant Williams had seemed far too steady to do anything like that.

Mansard was a tall man, almost as large as me, but he still looked down his long, straight nose at a man in a top hat in the middle of a very dark night. 'The .38 Smith and Wesson still in his hand may provide a clue,' he responded harshly, as he waved the dull beam from his torch up and down Williams's body. 'Who the hell are you?'

I told him. I also told him that I hadn't noticed the revolver in Williams's right hand mainly because I was too busy looking at the Bowie knife in his left.

Mansard bent down to the knife, then called one of his men, a Private Jones, to come over.

'You say this Lily girl is dead,' Mansard said, as he watched Jones examine the knife in the hands of the corpse.

'Yes,' I said. 'From what I can see her throat was cut. I imagine whoever killed her used a knife.'

'We mustn't draw what could be incorrect conclusions, Mr Hancock,' Mansard said. 'There will have to be a proper investigation into these events.'

'So the civilian police . . .'

'One of my men is already on his way to the police station,' Mansard said. 'We can't investigate Williams's death ourselves. I expect the local constabulary will call in Scotland Yard. The death of a Military Policeman is not a thing to be taken lightly.' He then asked to be taken to see Lily's body. On the way, I explained to him what the Gypsies – or, rather, Lily's brother-in-law, Edward, believed about her death: that it had been brought about by the angry spirit of her sister, Rosie. I also pointed out to him the significance of the date: All Hallows Eve.

'Superstitious rot,' Mansard said, as we pushed our way through heavy rain-soaked tree branches and cruel bushes already devoid of their foliage. 'But given the girl's new-found fame we will have to tread carefully. What the crowds of gawpers will do without their direct line to the Virgin Mary, I don't know. Christ, what a mess!'

'I done it. I killed her,' Edward said, as soon as he saw Mansard. 'I lied with Lily so Rosie's *muló* killed her on the night when all spirits take their revenge.' He wept bitterly and very loudly.

'Don't be so bloody stupid,' the captain muttered, as he pushed roughly past the weeping Gypsy and made his way to the body. 'The dead can't get up and walk about, whatever the date may be, you stupid Aborigine!'

This annoyed me considerably, but I followed him anyway and, once he was hunkered down beside the corpse, I lowered my voice and said, 'I think that someone might have interfered with her. You know, sexually . . .' There was a lot of blood over her crudely exposed private parts. I remembered what I'd said to Hannah about her old mate David Green and how there was never any excuse for rape. There isn't.

Mansard turned to me. Even by the thin light from his torch I could see that he was extremely pale. 'We'll wait and see what the civilian police say about that,' he said. 'It would be foolish to connect this – outrage with the death of my sergeant.'

'Captain, the girl and Williams – he was attracted to her . . .'

'Don't tittle-tattle to me, Mr Hancock,' Mansard hissed. 'George Williams was a decent fellow. I won't have gossip. Do you understand?'

I wanted to say something about the knife I'd seen in Williams's dead hand, but I didn't. He knew I'd seen it, and I imagined it wouldn't occur to him to interfere with evidence. I was, in fact, proved wrong in this regard, but not in the way I had imagined.

I couldn't take charge of Lily's body until after the doctor the coppers had called had seen her. If he decided she'd been murdered I'd have to wait still longer. While the medic, who came from the local hospital at Whipps Cross, examined the body, I sat with Mr Lee, Edward and some of the other Gypsy men outside Mr Lee's tent. From inside came frequent bouts of sobbing from Mrs Lee and Lily's many younger brothers and sisters.

Although from time to time Edward tried to raise the subject of the 'crime' he had committed with Lily, and the possible appearance of Rosie's unquiet spirit, Mr Lee cut him off: 'What you and Lily done was wrong,' he said, to the young man, 'but even if Rosie's *muló* did come it didn't kill Lily – on All Hallows Eve or any other time. They loved one another. Rosie never killed Lily. If you'm telling the truth, Edward, Rosie let you lie with Lily when her illness meant she could not do so any more. Rosie's *muló* could not be disquieted about what it already knew. No, the killing was done by a human hand. You foreigners, you're that feared of the world unseen . . .'

'But she, Lily, she saw Rosie's *muló!* She told me, our little lady – it is what we, Lily and me, called Rosie, our lady, ours . . .'

'Lily may have seen Rosie's *muló*, but then maybe she did not,' Mr Lee said, as he sucked hard at his blackened briar pipe. 'A lot of people have ideas about what my Lily might have seen.'

But what Edward had said might make sense. Whatever Lily had seen, she might have interpreted as a ghost.

It was, I reckoned, about four a.m. by that time and, because winter was almost upon us, it was still very dark. But even through the gloom we could see people moving about beyond the MPs' cordon. There had been a raid early in the evening on the previous day so it would have taken a lot of folk a long time to fall asleep. When Lily died it was possible that quite a number of people, apart from Williams, were up and about. As I watched various indistinct figures walk up and down in front of the Gypsy camp I wondered what those who had come to the forest for Lily's visions would make of it once the whole of London knew that the girl was dead. Would it shake their faith in the Virgin Lily had seen? Would hundreds, maybe thousands, descend into despair now that the connection to the divine had gone?

'Mr Lee,' I said, as I lit up a smoke for myself, 'have the coppers asked you what Lily was doing last night?'

'Yes, and I told them, honestly,' he replied. 'We put her tent back up yesterday and after she'd eaten with us, she went back to it to sleep. She was alone, and that was the last time we saw her.'

From the space behind the tent I heard the low growl of Bruno, the bear, waking up. In the comparative silence of the grieving Gypsy camp it had a menacing edge.

'What about the Head?' I asked. It seemed barmy to ask in such a mystical way about something I knew had to be just another Gypsy bloke – albeit one I had never seen. But from past experience I knew that they all wanted to keep the illusion going – or, rather, I hoped they did. David Green, worthless as he was, had made me think with his story about the Arab in Alexandria and his 'real' disembodied head. The memory made me shudder with superstitious fear.

'Oh, the Head was with her,' Mr Lee said.

'What? In her tent?'

'Yes.'

'So maybe the Head was, or could've been, the last person to see Lily alive. Have you told the police?'

Mr Lee shook his head. 'The Head ain't of this world.'

'Yes, but if he, it . . .' I took my fag out of my mouth and said, 'Mr Lee, I don't want to upset your beliefs but the Head isn't real. It is, I know, an illusion.'

I spoke into silence. All of the Gypsies regarded me with hard, unforgiving eyes. Suddenly I felt very, very alone.

Mr Lee leaned towards my ear and said, '*Gauje* shouldn't talk of what they don't understand, undertaker. The Head is magic, special magic that came from far away and settled on my Lily. Now that she has gone, so has the Head. There is no point in trying to speak to something that is no longer here.'

I did wonder, and I could have asked, where the Head might have gone, but I didn't. I couldn't see anyone who looked like the Head I'd seen in Lily's tent – I'd never seen anyone like that in the camp. Maybe the Head was magic, as they'd said, as the Arab's head had been. But Lily had rested to one side of the Head, just as the trickster David Green had . . . I was trying to smile to myself about the barminess of all these thoughts when Captain Mansard came over to us and crouched next to me.

'Dr Craig would like a word, Hancock,' he said.

Mr Lee, who was sitting next to me, said, 'What is it? What's going on?'

'Nothing yet,' Mansard replied haughtily. 'Hancock?'

'I won't be long,' I said to Mr Lee.

I stood up and followed Mansard back to the clearing where Lily's body had been discovered. The corpse was covered with a tarpaulin. The doctor from Whipps Cross, a short, red Scotsman, stood at its head.

'The girl was certainly murdered,' he said to me, without so much as an exchange of normal niceties. 'I think she may have been violated and then killed, but I will need to confirm that. The indigent and those in entertainment were ever vulnerable to such outrages. I'll have to take her body to the mortuary, if I can find some space for it. You can't have her yet.'

'You should tell her family,' I said.

'I will also have to take the body of Sergeant Williams,' the doctor continued. 'I have to see whether the wound to the girl's throat could have been made by the knife in his hand.'

I turned to Mansard. 'Do the Gypsies know about Williams?' I certainly hadn't said anything.

'No,' he replied, 'and nor should they. Sergeant Williams was a good chap. I don't want his reputation sullied at this stage. And, besides, if the Gyppos think one of my men might have been involved there could be trouble. We all know what these travelling types can be like.'

'Do we?' I said.

Mansard looked me straight in the eye and said, 'Lazy, dishonest, superstitious and violent covers most of it. That girl duped thousands up here with her religious nonsense, and her people have got more than a few quid off it into the bargain. Williams didn't kill her any more than some ghost did! If anyone did it was probably that brother-in-law of hers. By his own admission he'd slept with the girl. And he's ignorant enough to expect us to believe in ghosts. Or maybe it was one of the "faithful" come to camp here from somewhere down your neck of the woods, Hancock.'

The implication that the killer had to be either an East-Ender or a Gypsy made me mad. 'Sergeant Williams had a fancy for young Lily, you know!'

Mansard threw a hand dismissively into the air. 'Absolute rot! Williams has a smashing girl in the WRNS.'

'Be that as it may,' I said. 'But it isn't just me as thinks he was sweet on Lily. Ask her father.'

Mansard moved slightly away from me and hooked one hand into the lanyard across his chest. 'What kind of person are you, Hancock? A Jew?'

'No.' I didn't say any more than that on the subject. I thought, *Let the bastard guess*. 'I'm not against Sergeant Williams, Captain Mansard,' I continued, 'but someone wanted something from Lily she wasn't prepared to give. Sergeant Williams was supposed to have been sweet on her, but maybe others had ideas of that nature too. That, or maybe there was another reason that none of us knows about.'

Mansard frowned. 'What do you mean? What other reason?'

'I don't know,' I said. I didn't. The brief conversation Hannah and I had overheard between Lily and some man had been too short and indistinct for me to form any judgement on its meaning. 'But with so many people, including the Military Police, up here for all sorts of reasons, anything could have been going on.'

'Well, it will all be checked out in the fullness of time,' Dr Craig put in matter-of-factly. 'Sergeant Ives?'

A middle-aged civilian copper, almost as thin as I am, came into the clearing and said, 'Doctor?'

'Your men can move this body and the other one now,' Dr Craig said. 'The sooner we get them to the hospital the better.'

I turned to Mansard. 'We'll have to tell the girl's parents,' I said. 'Her mother at least will want to go with her.'

'To the hospital?' Mansard shook his head. 'Impossible.'

'It's their custom,' I replied, as calmly as I could. 'They mount vigil once a loved one has passed on.'

'Well, they can't mount vigil in a hospital mortuary,' Mansard said. 'It won't be allowed.'

'Yes, but—'

'There's a war on, *Mr* Hancock. People can't just do as they feel. Good God, man, by the time the doctor gets back to Whipps Cross we could have had another raid and the whole building might be in flames!' He put his hand up to his cap and, despite the coldness of the night, wiped sweat off his brow. 'Come daylight, somebody, probably me, is going to have to tell all of these nutcases looking for a miracle that the girl is dead. We might have riots up here, you know! And I've got to keep my eye on the Gypsies. So do please forgive me, Mr Hancock, if I do not unduly trouble myself with regard to the Gypsies' customs. All of us have quite enough to do—'

'Oh, for God's sake!' Dr Craig stood away from Lily's body while the civilian coppers picked it up. 'If a family member wants to come to the hospital and keep vigil, that will be fine,' he said. 'If it's the mother, she will have to sit outside, but . . .' He turned his hardened gaze on Mansard. '. . . vigils are important, Captain.' Then he headed out of the clearing.

Mansard regarded me coldly before he took off after Dr Craig. This left me alone with Sergeant Ives and the other civilian coppers, who'd come from their station down in Walthamstow. One of them, a fat-faced elderly geezer, said to me, close and confidentially, 'Comes from the Hebrides, see.'

I frowned.

'Craig,' the copper explained, 'comes from the Hebrides Islands in Scotland.'

I didn't understand what he meant by this comment so he said, 'In them islands up there they go in for all that vigil business, sitting with the body and what-have-you.' Then, by way of explanation, he added, 'Me mum come from up there, Lewis. When me dad died some years ago she sat with him, talking for days. My sister wanted to call out the doctor but I said no, because I knew it was their way.'

Which, whether the copper was right about Craig's background or not, was good for the Lee family. Whatever the reason, at least the doctor had understood – unlike Captain Mansard. But, then, as he had said himself he had a pile of trouble of his own round the corner, which would distract a man from the niceties of life and death. What would the great crowds who had come to see Lily after her sighting of the Virgin Mary make of her death? Would they take it as a sign that she lacked holiness or would they want to find and maybe harm whoever had taken Lily's life? And what of Edward and his story that the love he and Lily shared had been approved by his dying wife? I remained with Mr Lee and the other men, including Edward, until well after sunrise when we – *gauje*, Gypsies and policemen – found out what those who had believed in Lily's visions felt about it all.

Chapter Ten

'Here, you can have this for your daughter,' the young woman said, as she placed a red and gold scarf on the ground in front of Mr Lee. 'Go lovely with that red dress Lily wore. She was such a pretty girl!' She began to sob. 'Whatever are we going to do without her?'

The Gypsy didn't reply. The woman's gentle reaction was so unusual.

When Mansard had announced to the crowd that Lily Lee had died, almost everyone leapt to the conclusion that she had been murdered. Many had seen her fit and apparently healthy the day before, and some had seen the coppers come and go in the early hours of the morning. When a rumble of fear or disbelief passes across a big group of people it is truly terrifying. I can remember hours and days in the trenches when the blokes around me were so strained their hands would go for their weapons if you so much as looked at them in the wrong way. Captain Mansard sweated heavily as he watched men and women approach the cordon around the Gypsy camp to find out more or at least say their bit. Shots, only in warning but shots nevertheless, were fired.

I heard only snatches of conversations:

'Nazis in the forest done away with her. Them MPs, they've been looking for Jerries.'

'Holy Mary, Mother of God . . .'

'. . . can't have seen the Virgin. If she had, why'd the Holy Mother let her die?'

'We'll die now, all of us.'

'I still ain't packing up and going back to Silvertown!'

'If I find who done it I'll . . .'

Not that this had anything to do with me. I was still where I was for Lily – the Gypsies wanted to give her into my care as they had done with her sister. But with the body, accompanied by the girl's mother, at Whipps Cross there was little I could do so I made ready to take my leave of Mr Lee.

'You off to the hospital?' he asked, as I extended my hand to him.

'Dr Craig will let me know when it's time for Lily to come to my shop.'

Mr Lee took my hand and shook it. His palm was as dry and rough as sandpaper. 'I think there's going to be some trouble,' he said.

'You've got the Military Police to protect you,' I replied.

He looked at me so knowingly that I was convinced someone had told him about Sergeant Williams. I was almost on the point of pressing him when I came to my senses and said, 'Well, Mr Lee, shall I speak to the Reverend Sutton about the funeral or do you want to—'

'Give her a good send-off.' He gripped my arm tightly between his iron hard fingers. 'You will.'

'Yes, of course,' I said. 'I'll do whatever you want. I'll speak to your wife. She's welcome to stay as last time . . .'

Not that this was going to be easy. It hadn't been easy the

first time, with Rosie. But now we had Cousin Stella staying with us, deranged and demented Cousin Stella . . .

Mr Lee gave me another look, which, this time, was completely unknowable, then disappeared into his tent. I can honestly say that at that point I had no idea what he and his family were going to do next.

I left just before the first person, who was the bloke I'd met at Rosie's wake, Nobby Clarke, tried to break through the cordon to get at the tree Lily had stared at when she had her visions. He'd wanted, he told the MP who wrestled him to the ground, a souvenir for his missus. I followed the gentle woman who'd given Mr Lee her scarf out of the camp and on to the Snaresbrook Road.

The Duchess had had a bad night with her arthritis and her cough, and was now confined to her bed. It can be damp down in Anderson shelters, which is another reason why I won't have any truck with ours. That the blessed thing makes my mother feel more secure is not bad in itself, but what it's doing, night after night, to her poor bones, not to mention her lungs, worries me a lot. But she was pleased to see me and I spent some time in her bedroom telling her something of what had gone on up in Epping Forest the previous night. The counterpane over her eiderdown was covered with a thin layer of brown dust. Sometimes when bombs go off close by, the vibrations from the explosions shake some of the distemper off the walls and on to whatever might be below.

'That poor girl!' she said, when I told her of Lily's death. 'And her poor mother! To bury two children . . . But, Francis, who would want to hurt a young girl like that?'

'No one knows,' I replied. It wasn't a lie: Dr Craig hadn't

called or sent a message, which meant he was still examining the two bodies and trying to work out if or when they'd been together.

'Oh, but the people!' my mother continued. 'The people who have come, for the miracle . . .'

'I think they'll have to go back to where they came from,' I said. 'You know, Duchess, Lily's visions were—'

'If you are going to say that what Lily saw was not real you can save your breath,' she said, as she pointed a finger sternly at me. She coughed. 'You don't know that.'

'No, I don't. And I wasn't about to say they weren't real, Duchess,' I said. 'What I was going to say was that, now Lily is dead, the visions are quite unfathomable. I believe she saw something—'

'She saw the Virgin Mary.' I looked up and found myself staring into the face of my cousin Stella, for all the world a recovered woman. 'Auntie Mary read the story to me from the *Sketch*,' she said. 'It's a sign.'

I turned to my mother and said, 'A sign?'

'That Pop is alive!' Stella said joyfully. 'And that the war's going to come to an end too, of course.'

The Duchess lowered her gaze, then said, 'I read the story to Stella because I thought she might take comfort from it. I never dreamed it would do this . . .'

'Oh, well,' Stella said, 'I'd better go off and make a pot of tea. You can have Ovaltine, if you like, Auntie Mary. Pop'll have tea, of course, and he'll have my guts for garters if he turns up and there's no cuppa for him.'

And then, with a truly eerie giggle, she left.

'Uncle Percy's dead,' I said, when I was certain that Stella was out of earshot. 'I know there's no body as yet, and as time goes by that becomes less and less likely, but Percy is dead for all that. He—'

'Yes, I know you've said before about people vaporising,' the Duchess cut in. 'I'm so sorry, Francis, I never, ever . . . If I had known she would interpret Lily's story as a sign her father was alive I would never have mentioned it to her.'

'It's all right,' I took one of her hands and made myself smile. In truth, I was miffed at the way the Duchess had exposed Stella to what at best must have been some sort of mental condition in Lily and at worst a load of, well, God alone knew what. But, then, my mother is a religious woman so she'd seen no harm in any of it. 'I'll take a stroll up to the police station later and ask if they know any more about Uncle Percy. Maybe they've found something now,' I said.

I wasn't just talking for the sake of it. Sometimes bodies or parts of bodies don't come to light for days. And although if a limb or a foot was discovered we could never be certain it had belonged to Uncle Percy, at least it'd give me something tangible to bury. Christ knows I've put less into a coffin and called it Harry, Mavis or Grace in my time. And if she had a coffin with Percy's name on it, Stella would have to recognise that her father had passed away and mourn normally for him. If Lily's visions had done this to her, when she had never ever been up to the forest or seen the girl and her miracles, what they had done to all of the people actually up round Eagle Pond was something I recognised as being very powerful. Now that they knew the Gypsy was dead many disappointed and unhappy people would soon be dragging their few possessions back to Canning Town, the Isle of Dogs and Silvertown. The war wasn't ending for them any more than it was for heathens like me. But I could have told them that.

Just before I left her, the Duchess suddenly said, 'Oh, Francis, you don't know where I might buy the herb called coltsfoot, do you?'

'No.' I frowned. 'Why?'

The Duchess seemed a little sad. 'Well, that young Lily did say that coltsfoot tea would do my cough good, remember? I never did take her advice, but perhaps I should.'

'I'll see if I fall over some of it on my travels,' I said. 'Maybe some of the other Gypsies might be able to help.' But I didn't think they would. I didn't think I'd have the opportunity to ask them. I couldn't, after all, talk about coltsfoot at Lily's funeral, which, I believed then, would be the last time I saw the Lees and the rest of the group.

It was just after one when Dr Craig finally called.

'Here, Mr H, it's the telephone!' Doris yelled, as she ran out into the yard to take me away from car cleaning. 'Quick! Before the line goes! It's a Dr Craig.'

I know that most people don't have a telephone so I really shouldn't moan, but the line being up one minute and down the next drives me crackers. You never know whether someone who said they'd ring you will be able to and even when you have a line you never know for how long. I ran inside and whipped the receiver out of Doris's hands.

'You can come and get Lily Lee now, Mr Hancock,' Dr Craig said. 'I've concluded my investigations into her death.'

'Oh, thank you, Doctor,' I said, not even thinking to ask what his conclusions might be – doctors never tell you. 'I'll be over to get her presently.'

'Good.' And then, unprompted and unexpectedly, he proved me wrong about his profession when he added, 'The MP,

Sergeant Williams, killed her in my opinion. But that is just for ourselves and the police. I'm not telling the Gypsies yet.'

'No.'

'That is the job of the police, God help them,' he said. 'You know, it's chaos up in the forest as it is, Mr Hancock. People are demanding to know who is responsible for the death of the "elect of the Virgin" or standing in front of that confounded tree and shouting for Mary to come forth and save them. Wicked, idolatrous . . .'

The line went dead. A lot of Jocks are out-and-out puritans not at all happy about statues, pictures and relics. I could only take from this that Dr Craig had to be one of their number.

I put the receiver back on to the cradle and said to Doris, 'I'll be taking the motor hearse out in a bit. Betty Lee'll be back with us for a while.'

Doris, whom I'd told about Lily earlier, frowned. 'Poor lady,' she said. 'Just buried her other girl . . . I know some people ain't got too much time for Gyppos, Mr H, but if you've got any heart you've got to be sorry for that woman, haven't you?'

'Yes,' I said. 'Yes, you have.'

'Well, we'll all muck in to look after her,' Doris continued. 'Got to do your bit, ain't you, Mr H?'

This war has made me appreciate how lucky I am to have people like Doris around me. I'm what some would call a 'queer fish' and what others would say was 'off his rocker'. But those who are close don't care. They manage my strangeness without complaint, and the waifs and strays who cross and sometimes recross my path.

It took several hours to get up to Whipps Cross. It's to the north of West Ham, beyond Leyton, on the edge of the forest. Normally in a car it's about thirty minutes away, but as usual half the roads I would normally use were closed. One reason for that is, there's no way of knowing where damaged buildings are going to collapse: sometimes they fall into the road. But there are almost endless other reasons too – burst water mains, ruptured sewers, unexploded bombs, gas leaks. Everywhere is covered with rubble and everything stinks. I try not to sift out the various smells in my mind most of the time, but some whiffs just get to you – mainly those associated with my job. As I drove up through Stratford and into Leyton I thought about Uncle Percy and the possibility that somewhere, maybe, a bit of him was stinking to high heaven and beyond. But I didn't think about him for long, not once I'd found myself inside the great crowd of what looked like refugees coming down Leytonstone High Road. Crestfallen and weary, these people carried or pushed in carts often huge amounts of belongings and were accompanied by what seemed like hundreds of children. I didn't recognise anyone but, unless something particularly bad had happened up in this part of the city, something along the lines of a huge gas main rupture, I imagined they had come from the forest. Some were certainly muddy, while the sadness and lack of hope on their faces could have been put there by the ending of their religious dreams. And no one was speaking. East-Enders rabbit – we're famous for it. Bombs drop, water goes off, lights snuff out, but we always talk – even if it's only a load of cobblers. No, these people were dealing with more and worse than war. They were suffering from the death of their hopes.

'Where's Lily's mother?' I asked Dr Craig, when I eventually got to the hospital and found him in the corridor outside the mortuary. Betty Lee was usually very visible as well as audible.

But only little Charlie, Lily's younger brother, was in evidence now. He was sitting guard over a bag of Lily's clothes, dry-eyed and silent outside the blood-smeared door to Dr Craig's mortuary.

The Scot shrugged. 'I've no idea,' he said wearily. 'We've had one of those mornings when we've been unable to move for the dead. We've taken some from down by the docks for storage, but we're running out of space.' He shook his head. 'My job isn't to provide a storehouse! Ach, the woman probably left early this morning. The boy's been here watching the raw meat of war pass by since dawn. Do you have the hearse at the back?'

'Yes.' I looked over at Charlie, who lowered his head rather than meet my eyes.

'I'll have my porters make the corpse ready for you to take,' Dr Craig continued. 'If you go out to your vehicle . . .'

'I need a minute to talk to Charlie first,' I said. 'I'd like to find out who's coming back to the shop with me.'

'If you wish.' The doctor sniffed. 'But whoever it is had better keep their head down on the journey back.' He leaned in close to my ear and said, 'You've seen the crowds on the roads, from the forest?'

'Yes. Took me quite a while to get through.'

'Well, if any of them recognises anyone in your hearse, or even the vehicle itself, you might have trouble.'

'I didn't coming here,' I said. 'No one took any notice of me or the car.'

'Even so, the MPs are saying that some less moral types have been grabbing "souvenirs" from the Gypsy camp ever since the girl's death was announced. Care will be needed. Imagine what they'd do to her body.'

I tried not to. People can be beastly sometimes. If we didn't have this side to human nature there wouldn't be all the looting that takes place so much of the time. People wanting to make a quick quid at someone else's expense or, as in this case, people trying to hold on to a shred of hope with a lock of hair or a piece of clothing as a good-luck charm. Yes, it's ghoulish, but I could understand it. Lily's 'followers' knew as well as I did what would happen after her death. The end of a dream – after all the reports of happy people in the forest – wasn't going to make either the papers or the wireless. The big tragedies don't – the direct hits involving hundreds or even thousands, the end of people's hope. Bad for morale.

'I'm going to recommend we tell people that the girl's body is to be taken back to the Gypsy camp,' Dr Craig continued. 'Then the more insane among her admirers will have a fictional area to focus on. Also, the MPs will be able to mount guard on the whole camp.'

'That seems sensible,' I said.

'Oh, and I've had Captain Mansard in here,' Dr Craig said, as he made to leave and then stopped. 'He won't have it that Williams did away with the girl.'

'Williams was one of his men,' I said, as if that were explanation in itself.

Dr Craig whispered, 'Mansard thinks that one of the girl's own, a Gypsy, killed her. He intends, in particular, to pursue her brother-in-law, who, I believe, has spoken of having some part in the crime.'

'Edward? The only thing he did wrong was have an affair with his sister-in-law – with his dying wife's approval. Doctor, Edward believes that the ghost of his wife killed Lily,' I said. 'He didn't do it himself!'

'No, Williams did. He didn't assault her, though. In spite of appearances there was no sexual attack, but he did kill her.'

'You're sure?'

The doctor fixed me with a stern gaze. 'The knife in his hand was the murder weapon,' he said. 'That is my professional opinion.' Then he added coldly, 'When you've done with the boy, come and remove the corpse. I can't have it taking up space any longer.'

He went back through the mortuary doors then, leaving me alone with Charlie. I sat down next to the boy and watched as a couple of porters carried a bloodstained stretcher out of the mortuary and down the corridor towards the outside of the hospital.

'So where's your mum, then, mate?' I asked, once the pair had passed and the passage was relatively quiet.

'You got a fag, have you?' Charlie asked.

Like a lot of the Gypsies, the lad didn't have a clue as to his date of birth. I reckoned him to be about ten, twelve at the most. But in common with some of the other kids in the camp I'd seen him smoke alongside his elders and betters on several occasions. So I rolled him one up, then held it aloft as a sort of a bribe while I asked him again where his mum might be.

'She had to go back,' Charlie said.

'To the camp?'

'Yeah,' but he turned his head away as he said it.

I gave him the fag, which he lit, using a pungent-smelling lighter.

'So you'll come back with your sister and me to the shop?' I continued.

'She'd be frightened if I didn't,' the boy responded simply. 'You know.'

I nodded. Of course, alone among the *gauje*, Lily's spirit would be in constant discomfort. Whatever she had done, including sleeping with her sister's husband, she was still a Romany woman and was deserving of respect for that, if nothing else.

As if reading my thoughts, Charlie said, 'You know that Lily and Rosie loved each other, don't you? Lily wouldn't never have done nothing to hurt Rosie, nothing Rosie never wanted.'

I'd heard it more woefully, from Edward. 'You're saying you know about how Rosie and Lily and Edward had an arrang—'

'I don't believe she saw Rosie's *muló*.' Charlie turned his face full on to mine. 'Don't believe she saw no Virgin neither.'

'Then what,' I asked, 'do you think she did see, Charlie?'

'A devil,' he answered. 'There's devils everywhere now and they kill Romanies and Jews, and they worship that bloke Hitler.'

'Charlie,' I asked, 'how do you know about such things?'

Gypsies were not often, in my experience, abreast of the news and, besides, knowledge about the hounding of the Jews and the Gypsies in Europe wasn't known to everyone – it still isn't believed by a lot of people even now.

'I do a lot of listening,' he said.

'To who?'

'People.'

'What—'

'You do a lot of asking questions for someone who ain't a copper,' Charlie said.

His face, though not beautiful like those of his sisters, Rosie and Lily, was handsome in a serious way. His large, well-made features were more adult in character than childlike and I wondered whether Charlie was considerably older than he at first appeared. I also wondered whether he was as good at play-acting as he was at avoiding my questions. After all, so far, I'd only ever looked at Gypsy men in relation to Lily's mysterious Head illusion.

'Charlie,' I said, 'Lily's Head—'

'Gone. Now she's gone, the Head's gone.'

'Yes, but I think that the Head may have been the last person to see Lily alive, apart from whoever killed her . . .'

'Head don't know nothing!' Charlie said. 'The Head's magic. It don't do with things in this world.'

Mr Lee, his father, had said much the same.

With the kid, however, fairly or unfairly, I decided to push it. 'Oh, come on, Charlie,' I said, 'you're a bright boy, you must know who did that illusion with your sister!'

'No, you're wrong.' He turned away quickly.

'What about the Head being a bloke made up to—'

'You don't understand!' He stood up and began to pace the corridor in an agitated fashion.

I stood, too, and this time I assumed a very serious air. The boy was obviously disturbed by this part of the conversation so it was up to me to convince him that what I was talking about needed saying – urgently. 'Listen, Charlie,' I said, 'Captain Mansard of the Military Police has got some idea about a man of your people killing your sister. Everyone, especially your brother-in-law Edward, will need to have what is called an alibi, someone to vouch for where a person was at the time of a murder. Now, the Head must have been with Lily just before she set off into the trees to—'

'I've told you, the Head's gone!' he said. 'I won't—'

'Charlie, Gypsy men could be arrested!' I said. I'd taken to heart what Craig had told me about Captain Mansard and his opinion of the doctor's beliefs about Sergeant Williams's involvement in Lily's death. Military types like him are all the same. In the Great War you got accustomed to it. Officers rarely accept that their men are involved in crimes or acts against civilians – it damages their pride too much. Mansard, I knew, would fight hard to clear Williams and, by association, his own name too. I also knew that the truth of what had happened wouldn't matter to him when the pride of the regiment was at stake.

However, before I could say any more, Charlie fixed me with his winter black eyes and said, 'That won't happen. No one will be arrested.'

'But, Charlie,' I said, 'you don't know people like Captain Mansard.'

'No.' He still held my eyes with his.

Dr Craig put his head round the door then, the noise of the squeaking hinges breaking the spell between Charlie's eyes and mine. 'Mr Hancock,' he said sternly, 'can you come now, please?'

I apologised and made Charlie sit in the corridor while I went to collect Lily. I didn't think it would be good for him to see her in the state I know bodies can be in after doctors have investigated a death. As it was, there wasn't a lot to see, but I loaded the body into a shell and a couple of Craig's men helped me carry it out to the hearse. Before I left I asked the doctor what would be happening now and he told me that that was up to the civilian police.

'If the MPs don't like it, that's too bad,' Dr Craig said, as I retrieved Charlie from the corridor and began to walk with him towards the exit. 'If a man is guilty, he's guilty. No friendship or regimental loyalty can change that.'

Once outside, Charlie said to me, 'They think Sergeant Williams killed our Lily, do they?'

'Well . . .'

'He never,' the boy said.

I held the passenger door of the hearse open for him, then went to the driver's side and got in. 'How do you know that, Charlie?' I asked. 'Do you know who did kill your sister?'

'No. But it weren't Sergeant Williams.'

I started the engine. 'How do you know?' I said.

'I dunno.' He shrugged. 'Just don't sit right.'

I didn't know exactly what he meant. I couldn't know precisely what was inside Charlie's head. But something in what he'd said made me feel uneasy, so after I'd taken the body back to the shop and settled Charlie with a plate of Nan's scrag-end stew, I went over to Plaistow police station. I didn't know whether the boys over there would have any information about the investigation into Lily's death, but it was worth asking and, besides, I still had my own business to follow up on too.

Chapter Eleven

'If we'd found so much as a finger you would've been the first to know,' Sergeant Hill said, as he shook his head regretfully. 'I'm sorry, Mr H, but I think your uncle Percy just disappeared. You know how it is.'

Yes, I did. As I had always believed, Percy had vaporised, split into a million million atoms and gone back into the earth and sky whence he had come.

'Your Stella still in a two and eight about her old man, is she?'

'Sort of,' I said. 'Although it's different now. She reckons that the "miracle" up in Epping Forest means her dad might still be alive.'

Sergeant Hill sighed. 'Poor old Stel,' he said. 'She must be disappointed about the turn of events up there.'

'Yes.' It was the perfect lead-in to what I'd really come to talk about.

I told him how I'd been called out by the Gypsies to Lily's body and about what was likely to happen now. I also told him that when I'd returned to the shop with Charlie Lee I had tried to explain what was happening to my cousin but without success. 'Stella just skips about with a soppy grin on her face,' I said. 'Shock's a funny thing, isn't it? So many people are going to have problems with this forest business.'

Although the station was quiet, which was a bit strange in itself, Sergeant Hill took my arm and led me through into one of the back offices. As he shut the door behind me he motioned me towards one of the chairs, then sat down. He offered me a Woodbine and took one for himself.

'You know a lot of my fellows are up the forest, don't you?' he said, as he leaned in towards me. 'There's a lot of trouble.'

'With the Gypsies?'

He looked over one shoulder, then the other. 'Mr H, this is very hush-hush,' he said. 'People ain't supposed to know about such things.'

'About what?' I asked.

He pulled his chair so close to me that I could almost have smoked his fag instead of my own. 'Things bad for morale,' Sergeant Hill whispered. 'Since this girl died, there's been violence up there, people wanting to know who killed her, people threatening to find who it was and do him in. Not the Gypsies, the bloody *gauje*! Walthamstow and Leyton divisions called on us for help to calm it all down! No matter what's happened and who done what to who, the MPs have still got their job to do. We and, I've heard, some plainclothes from Scotland Yard have to make sure they can carry on doing it.' He put a hand on my arm and said, 'But this is hush-hush, remember. You can't tell no one.'

I understood, all right. No one with an ounce of intelligence takes at face value everything the government does or doesn't tell us. Like a lot of people round here I can remember the official silence back in September when South Hallsville School in Canning Town bought it. A direct hit, people killed, hundreds made homeless, but it was nothing – in the national news. Here, things were different. Here we watched the victims carrying on as usual, suffering in silence for the sake of their pride as well as the sake of their country. Such events, should they get out, would destroy morale, so it's thought, and let the Nazis into people's heads. I'd rather know the truth myself, but I'm a madman, which means my thoughts cannot be relied upon.

'What went on up in the forest was a nice little miracle with a nice little Virgin keeping, thank Christ, schtum,' Sergeant Hill continued.

'Count your blessings that Lily's Virgin didn't predict the end of the war or the death of Hitler or anything, eh?'

'Bloody right!' the policeman said. 'Imagine if she'd told all them up there to go and march on Downing Street or something! Don't bear thinking about!' He shivered. 'But then again, all of them up in the forest left unsatisfied don't sit that much better. They want to know why the Virgin come to the girl and what punishment heaven or whatever is going to pour down on humanity now that Lily Lee's gone. Don't you go telling too many people you've got the girl's body up your place, will you? They'll all be down camped outside if you're not too careful!'

'I know,' I said. 'Dr Craig up at Whipps Cross warned me about that. He's going to recommend people are told the girl's body is going back to the Gypsies.'

Sergeant Hill looked doubtful. 'Could be trouble with that,' he said. 'Could have people trying to get into the Lees' *tan* – er, their tent.'

'Could be trouble whatever's done.'

'That's true.' He cleared his throat, then asked me about the funeral and I said, quite honestly, that I didn't have a clue about when it might take place. I hadn't seen either of the girl's parents about it yet and I could hardly ask young Charlie. The only thing I did know was that the service, in all probability, would be performed by Ernie Sutton.

'Well, you let me know when it's going to be, won't you, Mr H?' Sergeant Hill said, as he rose to indicate that our conversation was over. 'Elaborate dos, Gypsy funerals. All sorts of traditions have to be kept. Anyway, we'll need to be there to hold back the crowds we hope won't turn up.'

'I don't think that the Lees will want people outside their group . . .'

'They might not have much choice,' Sergeant Hill replied. 'Not if so much as one of them buggers up Epping gets wind of it. And they will. Things like this can never be secret, can they?'

He was right, of course: there are few real secrets in life. Most things unknown are simply suppressed. I expect that most of London knows about what happened at South Hallsville School, but I'd lay money that few ever talk about it. That would make it real, and a horrible event is much easier as a half-truth. To face the reality would be painful, and people have enough of that in their lives as it is. When you don't have any coal to heat your home in winter and all your blankets are wet with damp, that's enough for anyone.

I left the police station in a bit of a dream. I'd seen people leaving Epping Forest earlier and in what appeared to be good order. But if coppers had been called up to Epping from this far south, not to mention from Scotland Yard, then things up there had to be serious. Hysteria, this time not of a religious kind, was taking hold . . .

'Watch where you're going, for Gawd's sake!'

I came to and found myself staring into a broad, heavily

scarred female face. Mrs Hinton, a proper street-fighting woman if ever there was, and one of the 'girls' my sister Aggie worked with down at Tate & Lyle.

'Oh, it's you,' she said, as she recovered herself and gave me what passes in Mrs Hinton for a smile. I'd buried her husband, Jack, back in '39 and she'd shown her gratitude by trying to run me up her stairs to her bedroom before poor old Jack was even cold. Naturally I'd been nervous of Mrs Hinton ever since. Now here she was with one hand inside her green gabardine coat – at chest height. I prepared to close my eyes.

I raised my hat politely to her. 'Hello, Mrs Hinton.'

'Hello, Frank Hancock.' Her toothless old gums shone up at me like a row of pink limelights. Thankfully, she soon closed her gob, then looked quickly over both shoulders, like Sergeant Hill had back in the police station. There were scores of people going about their business before darkness and the Nazi bombers came. But this didn't seem to deter Mrs Hinton, who just dug her hand deeper into the top of her coat.

Christ, I thought, *I had enough of a look at what she had when she chased me up her stairs!*

''Ere y'are,' as she said, as she pressed a small, still-warm chicken into my hands. 'Get that in yer coat and don't say nothing!'

Now it was my turn to look around wildly, mainly at the police station behind me.

'Mrs Hinton! If this is knocked off . . .'

'Quick! Put it away, you daft ha'porth,' she said, as she bundled the brown-feathered chicken under my coat. 'Course it's knocked off. Who has a chicken for his dinner, these days?'

140

'But . . . you . . .'

'Oh, don't worry about me,' she said, with yet another of her horrible smiles. Then, pulling her coat to one side, she revealed three more chickens pressed to her heavily drooping and very bare right breast.

'Bet you don't see one of them every day, do ya?' she said, as she scurried off down the Barking Road in the direction of Green Street.

You can call behaviour like hers madness, the result of a mind gone barmy from the bombing, but it's also an act of great spirit. Europe is tearing itself apart at the behest of monsters like Hitler and Mussolini. A person could easily fall into despair. But while an elderly woman is prepared to hide knocked-off chickens against her bare chest, then give one to a man she fancies outside a police station, there has to be some hope. At least, that was how I saw it as I chuckled my way home under the eyes of an equally amused old constable who, on his way back to the station, had seen the whole barmy thing.

Even before I opened the door to the shop, I knew that something was different. In the hours of daylight it's always noisy out in the street – women trying to get a bit of shopping before the next raid, newspaper sellers shouting their smoke-dried bark, encouraging people to buy papers that will tell them nothing, kids running about picking up whatever they can find to sell, pawn or eat. And in the shop, these days, it's rarely silent, as it used to be in the more peaceful and respectful twenties and thirties. There's far too much death, far too many people needed to help me, for that. But as I pushed open the shop door in what was becoming the half-light of dusk, all I could hear from within was silence and all I could see was Doris standing in front of the candle-lit desk gazing somewhere that I knew I had never seen her gaze before.

I took my hat off. 'Doris?'

She said nothing. I approached her, but not too closely. I didn't feel it would be right. 'Doris, what's happened?'

Still she didn't answer.

'Doris?'

And then, suddenly, her eyes met mine, so quickly it was almost as if she had snapped them into place. 'My Alfie's dead,' she said baldly.

Although people die suddenly every day, I was stunned. Alfie was a mate. 'Oh, Doris . . .'

'Midday. There was an unexploded bomb at the end of our street. Some disposal boys come to blow it up, but it went off in their faces. They all died. My Alfie too. The blast was so close, it stopped his heart. He had a dodgy ticker, as you know.' There wasn't a tear in her eye, not a crease of grief upon her face. And yet she was suffering. She had loved her husband, Alfie. He had worshipped the ground she walked on. Doris tossed her head backwards and said, 'He's out the back, if you want to go and have a look. He ain't got a mark on him.'

I put out a hand to touch her arm, but she flinched away from me. Alfie Rosen, her husband, had been a bus conductor. It was well known that he'd had a weak heart, which had been made worse when his father was interned. He'd found that time a tremendous strain. But for Alfie to die from the effects of bomb blast, even with his weakened heart, was still difficult to take in. Alfie had been a cheeky, cheerful soul, unlike me, very full of life. It wasn't fair. It never is.

'The Reverend Silverman says he can bury Alfie up the

cemetery in West Ham tomorrow. Can you do tomorrow afternoon for my Alfie, Mr H?'

'Doris . . .' My eyes stung with tears for Alfie, for Doris and for this terrible manifestation of ice-cold grief she was suffering.

'Half past three, the rabbi said,' she continued. 'I mean, I know I don't have to tell you, Mr H, that Jewish people have to be buried quick, so I apologise for hurrying you up like this . . .'

'Doris, of course I'll conduct Alfie's funeral!' I said. 'There's nothing in this world that could be more important than—'

'I'll pay,' she said, raising her small round face to mine. 'And I'll be back to work the day after—'

'You will not,' I said, as calmly as my rising panic would allow. I know what we used to call 'shell-shock' when I see it. 'You will not pay me a farthing and you will only come back to work when you're fit to do so. Doris . . .'

She backed away from me. 'I don't want no charity!' she said. Only now did she seem close to tears. 'I don't want nothing!'

Behind her I could see my mother and Alfie's father, Herschel Rosen, standing just inside the black curtains at the back of the shop. They looked first at Doris and then at me, their faces clouded with grief and concern.

'Doris . . .'

'No!' She backed to within an inch of my mother's arm. Then her face screwed up and she shrieked, 'Alfie! I want my Alfie! That's all I want! I don't want no money or— Stuff it! Stuff you, Mr H, and your fucking free funeral and—'

Before she sank to the floor, Herschel and the Duchess caught her in their arms. The weeping and the weakness of grief had rendered Doris incapable and she sat on the floor in the arms of the old people at the end of all of her strength. She's only a young woman, Doris, in her early thirties. Alfie, with whom she hadn't had any nippers, had been her world.

As I bent down to Doris who was now begging my forgiveness for shouting at me, I put my hand on old Herschel Rosen's shoulder and said, 'I'm so sorry, Mr Rosen.'

The old man shrugged.

'Arthur and Walter have laid Alfie out ready for you, Francis,' the Duchess said.

'Thank you.'

So now I had two bodies to prepare for the grave – one a young girl barely into adulthood and the other a friend and sometime employee. Alfie Rosen had done a few good turns bearing for me alongside Arthur and Walter. I would miss him, but more than that I would miss the light he had put into Doris's eyes when she married him. You see so many young widows now – girls with downcast faces and dead eyes. I tried not to imagine how she would do without him.

As I went through to the back of the shop to see Alfie Rosen, I saw my cousin Stella cleaning the stair banisters with beeswax polish, humming cheerily to herself. Young Charlie Lee, who was at the bottom of the stairs, was staring at her with ill-disguised confusion. But Stella was the very image of a complete basket case. God knows, I understand what that's like, but suddenly I snapped.

'Stella, you know that Doris's husband has died, don't you?'

She gazed at me with vacant eyes and smiled. 'Yes, but the Virgin will make sure he's safe, Francis,' she said. 'The Virgin will bring Dad back to me eventually.'

I lost my temper. 'Christ Almighty, Stella,' I said, 'the girl that "saw" the Virgin is lying out the back here awaiting burial, and Uncle Percy is not coming back here or anywhere else. He's dead!'

There was a tiny pause and then it was as if all the magic and stories that had sustained her blew off Stella's face and out of her mind all at once. 'Francis!' she screamed. 'No!'

'He's dead, you're an orphan, and God, the Virgin and all the saints are off on a beano to somewhere the other side of heaven!' I stretched up towards her now weeping face. 'Because they certainly aren't here, are they? Because this is hell and those types don't come to where the devil is, do they?'

'Oh, Francis!' she wept. 'Don't talk like that! Please!'

I knew I was being cruel and part of me wanted to be. But poor Stella's face and her ruined dreams threatened to make me hate myself so I pushed past Charlie Lee and went out the back to Alfie. Already in the tailcoat and stiff white shirt he had been married in, Alfie Rosen lay in the coffin the boys had found for him, as if he was asleep.

I sat down beside him as I had a hundred times before and lit a fag. I talked for some time, apologising for the loss of my wand and other nonsense, before I'd built up enough courage to take one of his ice-cold hands in mine and squeeze it, like a mate.

I'd asked Charlie Lee several times without success about what his parents intended for their Lily. I'd even telephoned Ernie Sutton to find out if he knew anything, but he was as clueless as I was.

'We can't keep your sister here for ever, you know, Charlie,' I said to the boy, after we'd all finished what had passed for our evening meal. Although Doris and Herschel Rosen had now been taken home by Rabbi Silverman, Hancocks was still a morbid and subdued place to be. Everyone had known and liked Alfie, and the knowledge that his dead body lay just one floor below our parlour was not comfortable. Nobody had so much as glanced at the chicken I'd got from Mrs Hinton, and that included me.

Charlie didn't answer. My sister Aggie, however, who, it has to be admitted, is a sight more forceful than me, or most men come to that, said to the boy, 'Are you listening to what my brother's asking you?'

Charlie looked up into Aggie's powdered and rouged face with undisguised dislike. 'Yeah.'

'Well, why don't you answer him, then?' Aggie said. 'You can see what a hard time we're having here. We've just lost a good pal.'

'Agnes, the boy has lost his sister,' the Duchess put in, as she placed a calming hand on Aggie's shoulder.

'Yes, I know, but—' Aggie lit a fag, then sprang to her feet and agitatedly left the room. 'To bloody hell with everything!'

We all heard her sobbing as she ran up to her room. But no one followed her. What she was doing was only natural. People you know die all the time in war – the butcher over the road, a cabbie my old dad used to talk to up on Green Street, some old girl who always got drunk in the Abbey Arms – and it isn't pleasant. But when those close pass away, like Uncle Percy, like Alfie Rosen, it's different. It hurts physically as well as in the mind. I don't eat, but everybody's different. As Aggie howled on, we all felt that extra bit depressed as the gas went down in the parlour when she put her light on up in her bedroom. But then the fact that we had any gas at all was, we all knew, a mercy. Ever since the shop windows had been boarded up, downstairs had only been bearable when we'd had gas. Otherwise we were forced to meet our customers and do our business by candlelight. Even for an undertaker who's seen most things and believes in little, the shapes and shadows that candlelight can throw, particularly in a dusty old place like this, can be unnerving at best. Now, however, as darkness had fallen some hours ago, we were all occupied with waiting for the sirens. Alfie was dead and it hurt, but there was still that feeling of moving on that one gets after a close death these days. An uncle or cousin lies dead, but your ears still strain for the wail that tells you to get down to the shelter or run for your life. And you do.

But it wasn't the sirens that broke the silence that hung over my family, Charlie and me that evening. It was the shop doorbell.

'Who's that?' Nan said, as she always does when people call after hours.

'Perhaps it's the fire-watchers,' the Duchess said. 'Mr Deeks from the bank and his boys.'

Nan put her knitting on the floor and stood up. 'Well, what would they want?'

'It's a cold night and they'll be out there for hours,' the Duchess said. 'Maybe some tea or blankets . . .'

'Yes, but they bring things with them and that and—'

'Well, if you don't go to the door, we'll never know, will we?' I said, through gritted teeth. Like a lot of East-End women, particularly those of middle age and beyond, Nan can't half go on about nothing sometimes. She glared at me before she went downstairs.

A moment later, Charlie said, 'I'd best get down and be with our Lily.'

'You know that when a raid's on I'm going to make you go down into our Anderson,' I said. 'No arguments.'

'Mum said she stayed with Rosie when she was here and German planes come.'

'Your mum's a grown-up. She can do what she likes,' I replied.

The Duchess looked at me at crossly. She's always hated the way I won't go down the shelter with the rest of them. But she was never in a trench with ten tons of mud above her head, threatening to bury her alive at any second. It's not a thing I can tell her too much about either.

I set about to change the subject back to my original conversation with the boy. 'Charlie,' I said, 'about Lily . . .'

I was interrupted by the thunderous sound of many boots running up our stairs. Charlie, alarmed, cast his eyes around the room as if searching for a way out. But there is only one door into our parlour so when Captain Mansard and two of his Military Policemen stood in it they cut off this exit to all of us.

'Where are your parents, Charlie?' the captain said to the boy, without so much as a word to me or my mother. 'Where's Edward?'

'At the camp,' the boy said.

'No, they're not!'

Charlie shrugged.

'Your parents, Edward whatever-his-name-is and your brothers are nowhere to be found,' Mansard said. 'Your sisters are not exactly forthcoming and Bruno the bear appears to have been given to some old man with a wooden leg. What's going on?'

'Maybe Dad's gone on the *drom* again,' Charlie replied. 'I don't know.'

'On the *drom*? What nonsense is that?' Captain Mansard

reached down towards the boy and said, 'You're coming with us.'

'*Drom* means on the road,' Charlie said, as he tried to pull Mansard's hand away from his neckerchief. 'Ow!'

'Er,' I said, 'Captain Mansard, aren't you supposed to be guarding the Gypsy camp? Aren't you telling people that Lily's body is there? If they find out it's here . . .'

'The adult Lees have left the campsite,' the captain said, with what seemed to me a lot of anger in his voice. 'The other Gyppos are still there but the Lees have gone.'

'Well, I'm sure they'll be back because of Lily,' I said. At the same time I tried to catch Charlie's eye but found I couldn't. That Betty had left her daughter down at the mortuary had been strange, I'd thought at the time. Now I was inclined to think that Charlie might know why that was. However, why any of it was important to the MPs was beyond me – unless, of course, Mansard was still intent on clearing Sergeant Williams's name.

'Captain Mansard,' I said, 'why are you so worried about the Lees?'

His eyes blazed. 'Why, Hancock, are you asking that question?'

'Well . . .'

He moved in close to me, an action that caused the Duchess to walk over to my side.

'Our main job up in the forest is to find deserters and those foreigners attempting to avoid internment,' he said. 'With regard to the latter, we discovered a couple called Feldman some days ago, but there is still one German missing.'

The Gypsy, Martin Stojka.

'And because this "person" is one of their kind, we

understand that some native Gypsies might be helping him,' he continued. 'The Lees have been in my sights for some time.'

'But you haven't found this person with them?' I said.

'No. But my fear is that they have used the tragedy involving their daughter to cover up this individual's escape.' He leaned forward. 'Williams didn't kill that girl. They did, the family, that brother-in-law . . .'

'That's nonsense! Why would the Lees kill their own daughter?'

'I don't know,' he said hysterically. 'They're Gypsies – who knows?'

'But Dr Craig has said—'

'Williams was set up by the Gypsies!' Mansard stared down, wild-eyed, at a very frightened Charlie. 'You're coming with me,' he said. 'You're going to tell me where your family and Stojka are or I swear—'

'He's only a boy!' the Duchess cried, roused to anger.

'He's a filthy Gypsy, is what he is!' Mansard said, as he roughly grabbed one of Charlie's wrists.

'Oi!' I put my hand across Mansard's, an action greeted by one of his blokes aiming a revolver at my head.

'Hancock, this is a matter of national security,' Mansard hissed, as he pulled the boy towards him.

'Mr Hancock!' Charlie cried.

I tried to keep a hold on the lad but Mansard wrenched him out of my grasp.

'Where are you taking him?' I asked, as I watched the boy being dragged towards the door.

'Mr Hancock, come with me!' Charlie pleaded. 'Let Mr Hancock come with me!'

'Christ Almighty, boy, I'm only taking you back to your camp!' Mansard told him.

'Well, let me go with him, then,' I said. The captain obviously thought that Charlie had information about the whereabouts of his family and possibly this Martin Stojka too. I was afraid he wouldn't be too careful about how he got to it. 'Captain Mansard?'

He turned back to me with cold, hard eyes. 'This is not a job for a civilian,' he said. 'And we don't need an undertaker – at least, not yet.'

As the MPs propelled Charlie towards the top of the stairs, he caught hold of Nan's apron. 'Miss Hancock, please!'

Nan, who hadn't been comfortable with what she had seen so far, now reacted to the fear in the boy's eyes. 'Oh, come on,' she said, 'he's only a kid. Could be a raid any minute! Where's your Christian hearts?'

Captain Mansard pushed the boy away from her and said, 'Probably quite near my Christian lungs.' And then he raised his cap briefly to my sister while his men picked up Charlie and carried him down the stairs.

The last thing I heard the child say was, 'Mr Hancock, don't let our Lily be alone, will you?'

Even before I heard the front door of the shop close behind them I was chastising myself for not having done more to protect the child. Whether or not Mansard was right about the Lees shielding Stojka was immaterial. Charlie was too young to be guilty of anything beyond doing what adults wanted him to do. And although I knew that what Mansard was up to had a point, and was probably quite right, I was worried about the methods he might use. He obviously didn't like the 'Gyppos' and would not, I felt, be anything like gentle with young

Charlie or any of the other Romanies the Lees had left behind to go God alone knew where.

But within seconds the sirens went, and other considerations took hold. Stuttering, as I do when a raid is on, I picked up and took my mother down to the Anderson in the yard. Closely followed by Nan, we both called to Aggie, whom we still couldn't hear moving about up in her bedroom.

'A-A-Ag,' I shouted. 'C-c-c-come . . .'

'Agnes!' Nan yelled. 'Get here!'

Our feet made a thundering noise as we pounded down the stairs, followed after a while by Aggie, muttering, 'All right, I'm coming, keep your bloody hair on!'

Once all three, plus Stella, who had been brooding in the shelter ever since I'd shouted at her earlier, were settled and I'd satisfied myself that the horses were securely tethered in the stable, I went back into the shop as the first set of explosions lit up the sky above the Royal Docks. All the treasures of the Empire, it is said, are in those warehouses around those vast bodies of water. I thought of them on fire – of great hands of bananas, enormous sacks of sugar and grain, and of the rats that fed on all that, cracking and screaming and disappearing for ever into the mouth of the flames. It made me want to run. Oh, God, did it make me want to run!

But I didn't. I went into the room at the back of the shop where Alfie Rosen was now hidden inside his coffin and where Lily Lee still lay uncovered. There I, a *gaujo* and really not worthy, had a go at batting back the bad spirits from Lily for Charlie. But the dark shapes I saw in the corners of the room were familiar rather than the exotic things I imagined the Romanies had. They were the endless screams of men whose heads flew off as soon as they put them over the tops of the trenches, they were horses' legs cracking under the weight of the Flanders mud like twigs. They were things that were devilish because they were so horribly human.

As the bombing reached its height about an hour later and the ground shook beneath me in an endless earthquake, I bent down low over Lily Lee and whispered, 'I – I w-won't let them g-get you, Lily. Y-y-you will be s-safe with me.'

And then I placed the coffin lid over her lest the ceiling should come down and damage her.

Chapter Twelve

There is a very sad story associated with the Jewish cemetery on Buckingham Road, Forest Gate. Known as the West Ham cemetery, the site is enhanced by a large, round mausoleum that was built to take the body of a young woman called Evelina de Rothschild. Married to Ferdinand, of the famous banking family, poor Evelina died in childbirth in 1866 and was mourned by her husband for the rest of his life. The mausoleum is a testament to Ferdinand's grief, which apparently turned the poor man into a recluse. It was a rather fitting place for a young and much-loved person like Alfie Rosen to be interred.

There must have been hundreds of mourners. My lad Arthur, whose aunt Flo works in the heart of the Jewish East End at one of the sweat-shops on Fashion Street, reckoned that almost every tailor and seamstress in the area had downed tools to come out for Alfie Rosen. At half past three on a winter afternoon, with Jerries expected any minute, that was quite something.

Once I'd got Doris, her mum, her sisters and Herschel Rosen to the cemetery and lowered Alfie's coffin into the hole, I stood with my lads by the Rothschild mausoleum. After all, once Rabbi Silverman began his prayers we'd all be at sea, not having any grasp on Hebrew. All I knew was that once it was all over the male congregants would fill in the grave as opposed to the Christian custom of paying others to do it for us. The only non-Jews in the thick of the congregation were my mother and sister Nan. The Duchess held on to the arm of Doris's mother, Sadie Mankiewicz, another long-standing widow like herself. Only Aggie didn't make it, not because she didn't want to but because she had to work. If you're in munitions or food production, like Aggie, that's a reality of your life. Nothing can interrupt the war effort.

'Poor Doris Mankiewicz,' Hannah whispered into my ear, when she reached my side to stand next to me.

I looked down at her and said, 'What you doing here?' My girl knew Doris a bit on account of their both coming from the same area, and through me, of course. But with Hannah and things Jewish, there is and always will be a problem.

'Weren't Sadie Mankiewicz and her family cut me off when I went with that boy,' she said. 'That was my parents and the rest of the *frummers*. This lot here ain't like that.'

Hannah's parents were, and always had been, very religious or *frum* Jews so her going off with a Gentile had effectively separated them from her. Doris and her people were not religious and therefore not nearly so scandalised. Alfie Rosen, like a lot of young Jewish men, had been totally anti-religion, and a considerable number of his mates in the congregation carried Communist flags.

While the rabbi did his stuff I watched Doris. White and, for once, thin-looking, she was being literally held on her feet by one of her younger sisters. There are no flowers at Jewish funerals so there's little to look at except the other mourners – and the awful coffin down its dreadful hole.

155

'Doris wants to come back to work tomorrow,' I whispered to Hannah, 'but I said no.'

Hannah shook her head. 'Well, I wouldn't expect her to sit *shiva*, not being *frum*, but even so.'

'It's the shock,' I said. 'She can't see any other way to carry on except the normal one, as if Alfie was still alive.'

'We put our dead away too quickly,' Hannah said. 'People can't tell whether they're on their heads or their heels.'

'It's traditional.'

'Yeah,' she said, I thought with some bitterness in her voice once again. 'Yeah, it's traditional.'

And then the men, starting with a weeping Herschel Rosen, began to shovel earth on top of Alfie's coffin. It's a terrible thing to bury your child. My dad, who'd seen most things in this business in the course of his life, never got used to it and neither will I. After the oldest of Doris's brothers-in-law had taken his turn with the shovel I went over to pay my last respects and gladly take my place at filling in the grave. Arthur and Walter did their bit and, as I watched them, I said goodbye and 'Thanks, mate' to Alfie in my head. He'd been a good sort and as I turned to Doris yet again, that fear for her future gripped me in the way it had when I'd first been told of Alfie's death.

I went back briefly to Herschel Rosen's small flat in Spitalfields for the subdued thing that passes for a wake among the Jews. But I couldn't stay – or, rather, I didn't want to – so I left the horse-drawn hearse with Walter so that he could take the Duchess and Nan home and made off in the car. Hannah had bade farewell to everyone at the cemetery but we had arranged to meet on our own back at the shop. Just occasionally, usually when someone close to me dies, I have a need to feel alive again, just for a while. There's only one way I know of, I'm ashamed to say, that I can do that. But, then, in my own defence, not just any woman will do. I have to feel passion. Just to do 'it' would be disgusting. But that's never the case with Hannah.

Not daring to go inside the empty home of my fathers, I took Hannah into my arms in the pitch-black darkness of the back-yard. I began to feel myself becoming excited when suddenly I heard a voice that was neither mine nor Hannah's.

'Mr Hancock!' it hissed. 'Mr Hancock!'

It was a child's.

'What is it?' Hannah said, as she felt my body move away from hers. 'What's wrong?'

Suddenly I felt excited in a different way. 'It's—'

'Mr Hancock, it's me!'

'Charlie?'

I couldn't see him but the yard was very dark and Charlie Lee, like me, is a dusky person.

'Yes!'

Two startled eyes came out of the gloom towards me.

'What's going on?' Hannah asked.

'It's Charlie, Lily the Gypsy's brother,' I said. 'He's—'

'Come out of nowhere at an important time, H,' Hannah said, a little tetchily, as she smoothed her skirt down towards her knees. I began to wonder, as Charlie got closer to me, whether I was still disarrayed myself. But hearing his voice so suddenly had done much to cool my ardour.

'Charlie, did Captain Mansard let you go or—'

'I run away,' the boy said. Now that he was very close I could see that his clothes were even more dirty and torn than usual. He smelt strongly of damp and earth.

'What about your mum and dad, your brothers?'

Charlie looked quickly at Hannah, then back at me.

'It's all right Charlie,' I said, 'Hannah, Miss Jacobs, she's a friend.'

Even through the gloom I could see that he was giving me a right old-fashioned look. Whether he'd seen us out together before up in the forest I didn't know, but I was well acquainted with the fact that Gypsy boys are rarely little innocents, even at Charlie's time of life. He'd known what we'd been doing.

'So, your mum and dad and your brothers . . .' I pressed.

'Safe. I see 'em. But I never took that *gaujo* captain to 'em,' Charlie said proudly.

'So they're . . .'

'Mr Hancock, what the *gauje* soldiers say about the Romany from Germany ain't true.'

'Martin Stojka?'

'Sssh! Sssh!' Charlie hissed. 'Don't know who might be listening!' He lowered his voice still further. 'The Germans are killing our folk. The Gentleman, as we call him, he's on the run.'

I didn't know what he meant, really. After all, whether Stojka was a Nazi or not, he was only to be interned, as far as I knew. He wouldn't be sent back to Germany and, as horrible as internment no doubt is, all this trouble was hardly in proportion to what would happen to him in the end. I took Charlie and Hannah inside the shop and made us all a cup of tea. I know it doesn't solve anything, but I'm a Londoner and making tea at times of crisis is what we do.

'Mum and Dad have got him hid,' Charlie said, as he rolled himself a fag on the kitchen table. 'I know where they is but they ain't told me about the whereabouts of the Gentleman. The less I know the better, they say.'

Had Mansard been right about the Lees and their involvement with Stojka all along? I wondered. 'So why are you here?' I asked, taking in the somewhat sour expression on Hannah's face.

'They want to get the Gentleman out of the forest and out of London,' Charlie said. 'A car does it quickest, my dad says, and you're the only person we know with one.'

Hannah, who had been shaking her head for some seconds, said, 'Are you soft in the head, boy? Blimey, if the MPs are out looking for someone there'll be roadblocks all over the shop!'

'Dad said you could put the Gentleman in one of your coffins,' Charlie said to me. 'Only you folk have cars as can take body boxes. Them don't get stopped by the coppers.'

Mr Lee had obviously thought this through without, however, considering that I might refuse my assistance. Hannah was right: with the MPs after him, Stojka was unlikely to get away and if I were to be found with him I could be tried for treason. 'No, Charlie,' I said, 'I can't do that. It's far too risky.'

Charlie's face screwed up into a scowl. 'But the Nazis are after him, Mr Hancock!'

'No, the Military Police—'

'They'm sent by the Nazis, my dad said!'

'But, Charlie, the Nazis aren't here, leastways not yet.'

'No, but there's traitors ain't there?' Charlie said. 'Traitors sent them soldiers after our Gentleman!'

'What? Captain Mansard? I know he's not always very polite, but—'

'He'm a murderer!' Charlie said.

'What?'

'Weren't Sergeant Williams what killed our Lily, it were him – Captain Mansard,' the boy said.

'Look, Charlie,' I said, 'I don't know what your mum and dad are doing or what they've said to you, but Dr Craig told me he was certain that Sergeant Williams had killed your Lily. I know it's hard to bear because Sergeant Williams has himself passed on—'

'H!'

There was real fear in Hannah's eyes as she gazed at something over my shoulder towards the kitchen door. I turned and saw my old mate Horatio Smith.

'Hello, Horatio,' I said, then stopped when I saw what he had in his hands. It was a *kukri* knife, just like the one some Gurkha bloke had given my old dad up in northern India. Where the Gypsy had this one from or why he had it, I couldn't imagine.

'You're a good man, Mr Hancock, and it would pain my soul to hurt you, but I will if I must,' Horatio said, as he stood in the kitchen doorway with the *kukri* knife outstretched. 'We need your hearse car for our Romany brother.'

'Give it to him, H,' Hannah said, her eyes bright with fear. 'I don't know what any of this is but just give it to him!'

'If it were that easy we wouldn't've been disturbing you, Miss. We'd have just took the thing ourselves,' Horatio said baldly. 'But we don't drive, leastways not motor cars.'

'Horatio,' I said, 'I don't know what's going on here so I'm not prepared to drive – at least, not with Hannah, Miss Jacobs.'

I knew, of course, that despite our many years' acquaintance he would put that *kukri* up to my neck, and he did. Every man's loyalty is greatest when it is to his own, whatever and whoever that might be.

'I'm sorry and all that,' Horatio said, as he moved the knife away from my neck, 'but you have to help us. On your feet now.'

As I stood up I said, 'I just hope you're right about this Gypsy "brother" of yours not being a Nazi.'

Horatio and Charlie exchanged a look.

'Oh, he ain't no Nazi, Mr Hancock,' Horatio said. 'Can't tell you no more'n that, but he ain't a German, I can tell you.'

It didn't make me feel any better but at least whatever I was going to be asked to do was something I was almost entirely ignorant about. Whether or not that would save me from a traitor's death, should the police catch us in the act, I didn't know.

Horatio, standing in front of me, said, 'Let's go.'

I paused to draw breath, and Horatio dropped, suddenly and dramatically, unconscious to the floor in front of me.

'Stella!'

When you haven't always lived with people you don't always remember that they're there. This applies particularly when said people are a bit barmy.

'He was gonna stab you!' Stella said, as she placed the large saucepan with which she'd hit Horatio on the kitchen table. 'I couldn't have that.'

'Stella, thank you,' I said, still shocked at such violent action from my timid spinster cousin. 'Thank you very much.'

Hannah, who had rushed over to the Gypsy as soon as he'd fallen, said, 'Well, he's alive.' She handed me the *kukri*, which I put down on the table a long way from both Horatio and the boy.

Charlie Lee, who was standing behind me, now looked

terrified. 'You won't hand us over to the coppers, will you, Mr Hancock?' he asked nervously.

Hannah's arms were around Horatio. When our eyes met she shrugged. I had that feeling I often get with Hannah that she knew what I was going to say and agreed with it. 'I want to know everything you know about this foreign gentleman of yours,' I said. 'If you tell me the truth I may well help you in spite of what has happened here tonight. If he isn't a Nazi, well . . .'

'I know he's important, the Gentleman, to Romany people, 'specially those what come from where Mum come from,' Charlie said. 'I know that if Hitler gets a hold of him again then that's bad.'

I frowned. 'Gets a hold of him *again*?'

'Shall I put the kettle on now?' Stella said. Of course, she didn't know anything much, beyond the death of Lily Lee, about this situation so I had to get her away from us or vice versa as soon as I could.

'Yes, thanks, Stel,' I said, as I stared fixedly into Charlie's big, dark eyes. 'Can you get the water from down in the yard?'

'Oh, is the tap—'

'It's off, love,' I said. 'You'll have to fill up from the water butt.'

I didn't know whether the water was off or not, but we do have a butt in the yard for rainwater. Stella picked up the kettle and left. I said to Charlie, 'Well?'

The boy put his head down. 'The Gentleman was made to work for Hitler in Germany,' he said. 'Hitler wants the magic, see, our magic.'

'And Mr Stojka gave it to him?' I asked.

Charlie shook his head. 'It weren't like that. Hitler would've killed the Gentleman's *chavies* if he hadn't done what he wanted. Gentleman got them away and then he ran.'

'So he's here with his children.'

'No, they'm dead,' Charlie said. 'The German soldiers found them. Mum says that the Gentleman is the most important Romany in the whole world.'

I heard a groan from the floor.

'I think this mate of yours is starting to wake up,' Hannah said.

I passed the saucepan Stella had used on him down to Hannah and said, 'If he starts again, use this.'

She took it from my hand with a frightening smile. 'Gotcha.'

'Charlie?'

'Mr Hancock, I don't know no more,' the boy said. 'All I know is that the Gentleman can't go back to Germany but that there's people here trying to take him back there.'

'What people?'

'I dunno. But if the army coppers get their hands on him he could end up being give over to traitors, so our dad says. Not saying the coppers is Nazis . . .'

'You talked about Captain Mansard . . .'

'He killed Lily.'

'You know, I still think I've seen that MP captain somewhere before,' Hannah said. 'I can't . . .'

'Yes, love,' I said, not wanting her to go into whether she might or might not have seen Mansard 'professionally'. 'Charlie, why do you think that Captain Mansard—'

'Dad told me he done it. Said it had been seen, the murder. I don't know why the captain done it but Dad don't lie, leastways not to our people.' That was something I understood to be true, that Gypsies don't generally lie to their own, unless

Charlie was lying to me. But I didn't think he was. After all, to rope a settled Gypsy like Horatio into such an adventure as the one proposed meant that whatever was going on had to be important. But 'magic', just like 'miracle', is not an easy word for me to take seriously, and these Gypsies had used both in the past few weeks.

'Charlie,' I said, 'if I did help you, I'd be taking an awful risk.'

'Mr Hancock,' Charlie said, 'if Hitler gets a hold of our Gentleman there ain't no hope for none of us. That's what my dad says. If he gets hold of our Gentleman the Germans'll win. We have to get him out of London. We have to.'

So that was my mind made up for me.

Chapter Thirteen

I 'd wondered how Horatio had imagined I'd able to drive around completely unnoticed for some time. But when he told me it was obvious – just wait for a raid to begin. In the meantime I thought about the Duchess and Nan and why they weren't home yet. If Walter brought them through on the hearse into the yard, as he probably would to stable the horses, I didn't know what I would say. But as soon as the sirens started up we all, with the exception of Stella, got into the car and set off. I didn't, I confess, say much to Stella about what was going on, except that she was to tell my mum not to worry. A stupid thing to say at the beginning of a raid, I knew.

Beyond thinking we were mad to be out and about, no one would bother us during a raid – or, rather, that was what I and Horatio thought. The Gypsy, who was now conscious but with a sore head, told me to drive as if we were going back to Eagle Pond. But just as I drove on to Leytonstone High Road there was a massive explosion down by the railway lines and a copper came out of nowhere to tell me to pull the car off the road and 'get under bleedin' cover, you daft bastard!'.

I said, 'I'll – I'll just g-g-go up a bit. I've r-r-relatives up further.'

I saw him struggle to understand my stutter, but then he said,

'Okey-doke, mate, whatever you say. Just keep your head down,' and off we went again.

Although we did go north, we didn't go anywhere near to the encampment at Eagle Pond. Where we went, away from what wasn't, on this occasion, a heavy bombardment of the docks, was a far deeper and denser part of the forest. It's difficult enough to see your way driving in the blackout – the covers you have to have on your headlights don't so much lessen the light as block it out completely – but among trees and in what is really the country, it's almost impossible to see anything. Without Horatio telling me left then right then forwards and so on, I would probably have ended up, accidentally, of course, putting the poor Lancia into a ditch. But he and Charlie knew where they were going and eventually I was told to stop and get out.

'You wait here with the lady and we'll be back presently with our Gentleman,' Horatio said, as he and Charlie trudged off into nothing short of endless blackness.

When they'd both gone, I put an arm around Hannah's shoulders and whispered in her ear, 'I wish I knew exactly what this is really about. All this talk about Hitler and magic . . .'

'I wish I knew why you're whispering,' Hannah replied, in a normal voice. 'Middle of bleedin' nowhere here. Christ knows where we are!'

'Horatio and Charlie know,' I said.

'Oh, well, that's just fine, then, isn't it?'

'Hannah.'

'Well,' she said, 'load of old mumbo-jumbo.'

'I don't know,' I said, and I didn't. But, then, who does? We see things like Lily Lee's Head and assume it's an illusion. But we, or at least some of us, see that same girl talking to thin air that she calls Our Lady and we see God Almighty.

'I know that some people say the Gypsies have special powers,' I said, 'but I wouldn't have thought that old Adolf would have been much impressed. Strikes me he has nothing but disregard for anyone who's not a German.'

Hannah shook her head. 'I don't hear much, not where I am now,' she said, referring to her present place in Canning Town, 'but when I do see Yiddisher people they all tell the same story.'

'What's that?'

'That Hitler don't just hate the Jews, he wants what they have too. And I don't mean their houses and businesses and suchlike. He wants what the old rabbis and the *frummers* know about God and religion and that. He wants our . . . All right, I know I said mumbo-jumbo, but he wants our "magic", if you like. I'm not talking about what Davy Green does neither. I don't rightly know what I am talking about, but some of the old *frummers* could, it's said, do impossible things. My parents brought me up on such stories.'

'Oh, yes,' I said. 'My dad told me a story about some rabbi who walked through a wall – in Poland, I think it was. And the Gypsies . . .'

'They're also supposed to be able to do things other people can't too,' Hannah said. 'Still bloody mumbo-jumbo, in my opinion. But Adolf's greedy, I think. He wants to be able to do everything, he does.'

'Well, I s'pose if you're trying to conquer Europe you have to take all the help you can get,' I said.

It was a light reply, and Hannah didn't much like it. 'You know he's killing people and we ain't doing nothing?'

'We're at war with Germany, Hannah,' I said.

'H, Jews and maybe Gypsies, too, were dying for a long time

before this country decided to give Adolf Hitler what-for. People who got out, them in the internment camps, them like the Feldmans, they'll tell you.' She paused briefly to light a fag, then said, 'I may not believe in magical mumbo-jumbo meself but if wanting it makes Hitler kill people it needs to be kept away from him.'

'So you think I was right to help Charlie and Horatio and this Gentleman – this Stojka bloke – of theirs?'

'I don't know,' she said. 'Not really. But if you believe them, H . . .'

Suddenly through the deep black undergrowth Horatio returned with a bloke I recognised walking in front of him. Even in the gloom and without the makeup I could tell – I never forget a face, living or dead. He didn't look a bit like the photograph Sergeant Williams had shown me.

'Hello, Django,' I said to the man, who had once been known as the Head.

Martin Stojka smiled and said, 'You, Mr Hancock, are doing much more for this war than you will ever know.'

An owl hooted in one of the great trees over our heads. Owls are messengers of death, some say.

'I want some answers before I go anywhere,' I said.

Martin Stojka smiled his enigmatic Head smile. He was thin – not like me: thin as if he'd been starved. 'Then maybe I will drive the car myself,' he replied, as he pulled open the driver's door. Then, after a moment's pause, he shut it again and laughed. 'But I don't drive, do I? I had a car, once, but I had a driver too. The Führer was very generous to me – in a way.'

He was a good-looking bloke in what Aggie would have called a 'foreign' way. Like me, he was very dark with a sallow face and long, slender nose. But he was also, as so many Gypsies are, much shorter than the average man. I reckon he had to be five feet three at most.

'We need to get on, Mr Hancock,' Horatio said. 'We don't know where the coppers might be.'

'I need to know where we're going and why,' I said.

'Get in the car, Mr Hancock. Please.'

'Horatio . . .'

'Bloody hell, it isn't half brass monkeys out here!' Hannah said, as she threw her fag down on to the ground, then rubbed her hands together for warmth. 'Why don't you fellas do your talking in the car, eh?'

I looked down at her, frowning. Suddenly her attitude seemed far too casual in this situation.

'Don't have to drive yet, do you?' she said.

And, as usual, she was right. She was also, from the look I now saw in her eyes, playing for time on my behalf. She didn't trust anyone or anything any more than I did. We got into the car with Martin Stojka sitting beside me at the front. In profile he reminded me again of myself or, rather, of my mother. It's easy to see the Indian connection in some of the Gypsies, like this bloke. But it wasn't India he talked to me about now: it was Germany.

'My family have been settled in the city of Berlin for three generations,' he said, as he took, with a nod, the Woodbine I offered him. 'I have had education – I speak English, as you see – and I was, like my father, a maker of jewellery. Stojka is well-known jewellery shop. Very creative Roma people – what you call Romany or Gypsy, we say Roma – making fabulous things for big Jewish bankers, for generals, for the wife of the Kaiser.' He laughed. 'And also for rich Roma families, "aristocrats" from

Rumania and Constantinople. Because Stojka, although *in* the *gauje* world, has never been *of* the *gauje* world. Pure Roma every one of us and something else too,' he leaned in closely towards me, 'something special.'

I felt all of the hairs on the back of my neck stand up. Something rustled in the trees outside but I – like Hannah behind me, I later discovered – was mesmerised by this man with his guttural accent and deep, very wide eyes. And I do mean mesmerised. I'd never been in what you'd call a trance before and I haven't been in one since, but those few moments with Martin Stojka were, I swear, genuinely strange.

'The family Stojka are guardians of the Fourth Nail,' the Gypsy said. 'My father, my mother, my brothers and my wife all died before I would show it to Hitler – he so wanted it – but with my children . . .' His eyes filled with tears, he put his head into his hands and began to sob. Released from his gaze, I felt myself again and, even though I didn't know what he was going on about, I made as if to touch him in sympathy.

But Horatio tapped my shoulder and said, 'Best drive on, I think, Mr Hancock.' He looked at Stojka as he spoke and I wondered, from the strain on his face, whether Horatio felt the Gentleman had said too much.

As I turned the key in the ignition I remembered something that, if Stojka really was a fugitive from whatever, had to be important. 'I thought you wanted Mr Stojka to get into that coffin,' I replied, pointing to the shell we'd loaded into the hearse at the shop.

'We can do that once we're out of the woods,' Horatio said.

'Yes, but where—

'Just get back on to the road and then we'll see.'

'I showed him, Hitler, the Fourth Nail. I showed him in

return for the lives of my children,' Stojka said, as he raised his head and stared at me with his wild, violent eyes. I looked away. 'But he didn't touch it. I told him, "Later", I would let him touch it later. He believed me for a while.'

I was about to put the car into gear but I was too distracted now by what this man had said. I didn't have a clue what he was talking about and I said so. 'You've lost me, pal,' I said. 'I don't know what you're going on about.'

Martin Stojka sighed. 'You know it is said that when Christ was crucified one of our people fashioned the nails that held him to the cross?'

'You, or rather the Head, told me something about that,' I said. 'In Lily's tent.'

'It's not true.'

So what was all this about some important nail then, I thought, and why was it the fourth that was so special?

Martin Stojka had an answer, of sorts. 'But what is true is that a Roma brother long ago took one of the nails when the Saviour was brought down from the cross,' he said. 'It was the only one not used to nail Christ to the tree. It lay at his feet, bleeding his own blood for the shame of its fellows used to kill him. The Nail is power. It bleeds with the blood of God and it can do anything in this world and in others. And that Roma brother who took it, he was my ancestor, and that is why I have that Nail to this day.'

'You have a nail from the Crucifixion?'

'Yes. If you remember in Lily's tent, that day again, Mr Hancock, the Head raised the words the "Fourth Nail" to your charming mother.'

I did remember now and I looked at Stojka sharply.

'It is a very holy thing,' Stojka said. 'Truly so.'

I felt myself shudder. Years before, I'd taken Nan and the Duchess up to Westminster Cathedral to see some relic or other paraded for the faithful. I'd stood outside having a fag. But the women had been impressed – Catholic, superstitious women. Now here I was in the middle of the night with a dodgy Gypsy bloke and, apparently, another bit of superstitious junk that had not one iota of meaning for me. Suddenly I felt angry. I turned to Horatio and said, 'You brought me out here to rescue a fucking holy relic?'

'Mr—'

'H, calm down!' Hannah said. 'Hear this Mr Wotsisname out. Remember what I said about Hitler and what people say about magic.'

'The lady is right. Hitler is very interested in magic,' Stojka said. 'I know, Mr Hancock, that to you this seems stupid. But Hitler is wanting everything – bones of saints, books of spells, the Holy Grail and the Fourth Nail of Christ. The Nail can be used to get power, it is said. Hitler wants power over everything. Roma people do not want power, which is why we keep it. But then comes Hitler. He has these people, magicians they call themselves. They want to do spells on the Nail, they take my children—'

'Mr Stojka—'

'No, listen to me!' He raised a hand. 'If Hitler gets the Nail it will give him even more power! When I ran away from Berlin and took the Nail with me, he sent men for my children and he killed them! My heart is dead!' His eyes shone with tears and grief. 'But I cannot give up the Nail to him or any of his people. I cannot!'

'What sort of power does it have, this Nail?' I said, not really believing any of it but asking anyway. 'What do you mean?'

Stojka sighed, as if defeated. 'I do not know,' he said. 'As with all holy relics it has to be made to work so if you do nothing with it it will do nothing. I am not worthy of its power, no man is. Mortal people can only use it badly because we are all in sin. It bleeds only. It is always covered with blood.'

His face was so devastated – which a man's face would be if all his family had been murdered – that I put what I felt to one side and took the handbrake off. His eternally bleeding nail didn't have to be 'genuine' for either him to protect it or Hitler to want it. After all, if the Lees, and principally Lily, had taken the trouble to hide this bloke inside an illusion, what he represented had to be important to them. The car rolled forwards into the darkness.

'And the Lee family?' I asked. 'How do you know them?'

'I escaped to Britain,' Stojka said. 'I went to Whitechapel, London. Then I hear, the Jews say, that the British are looking for me. All Germans are to be interned in prison camps. I am a German with German papers. Everyone is looking for me, I think! I run, I don't know where. I want to find Roma people.'

How did you end up in the forest?' I asked.

'I heard of a fair there. I thought, If my people are anywhere they will be at the fair. I meet Zinaida – Betty Lee. She speaks the same Roma language as me. She knows who I am, what I am, what I have. All her group are excited and afraid. She takes me to Lily and the husband of her sister, another Roma from Europe. They were performing this illusion with the Head.'

'So you took over from Edward.'

'Not quickly, no,' he said. 'I just hide. Only when the Military Police come looking for me do I do the Head. To hide where all the world can see. It is Lily's idea. She was a good magician.'

When he'd spoken about the nails of Christ to me and the Duchess back in Lily's tent, he'd taken what I felt had to have been a stupid risk. I told him this and then I said, 'That was a bit reckless of you, wasn't it?'

He smiled. 'Undertakers and priests do not talk,' he said. 'Only to the dead.'

I wanted to ask him whether, in the case of priests, he included God and the saints in 'the dead'. But this nail he claimed to have was of God so he couldn't not believe in God's existence, or so I felt.

'You know they only want to intern you,' I said. 'Put you in a camp for a bit. It isn't pleasant, but you do get fed and attended to if you're ill.'

From behind I heard Hannah sniff in disgust. Using the word 'only' with 'internment' is like swearing to her, and she does have a point. But it isn't as if internment means death.

'They want to kill me,' Stojka said. 'Whether here or back in Germany, they want my blood. Hitler, he wants to take the Nail and use its power. Because I run away he will kill me. He has people here to kill me. You have to believe it!'

'Who do you mean? The MPs?' I knew the word 'spy' had been mentioned by Sergeant Hill in reference to Stojka, but as far as I was concerned, the Gypsy was being sought with a view to his being interned, not executed. And, anyway, even if I were to believe every word that Stojka said, I couldn't think it possible that people over here would kill him.

I peered into the darkness ahead. It seemed as if I'd been driving for a lot longer than it had taken me to get from that track Horatio had called a road to wherever it was we'd ended up taking Martin Stojka on board.

'The captain of the Military Police killed Lily because she would not tell him where I was,' Stojka said.

'No. Sergeant Williams—'

'I saw it happen.'

So it was from Stojka – or, rather, from him via Mr Lee – that Charlie had got that story. I turned to Stojka, whose face was blank now.

'And you didn't help her?' I said. 'She helped you.'

'I saw only the end. I heard some voices. I ran over towards them. He stabbed her, she was dead, there was nothing I could do. I ran away.'

'Nothing you could do?' Hannah, who has strong views about violence to women, sounded more than displeased. 'Too busy protecting that bleedin' nail was you?'

I looked all around me and realised I didn't recognise anything.

Suddenly Martin Stojka exploded with rage. 'These policemen will take me to people who will either kill me themselves or send me back to Germany! They will not intern me! They will take the Nail! Hitler will use it, something that is ours, to give himself more power!' He turned to me again and said, 'You do not believe this, do you? You are going to give me to the police!'

Tired, confused and still suffering, if I'm honest, from the recent death of Alfie Rosen, I put the brake on, turned the engine off and spoke to a nervous-looking Horatio: 'I don't know where I am and I don't think you do either,' I said. And then I said to Stojka, 'As for you, I don't know what to believe. You and your lot say one thing, the police and the MPs say another—'

'They are not telling you the truth!'

'So you say,' I said. 'Show us this nail and—'

'The Nail is not something people can just ask to see. You must do so with prayer, with pure things in your heart.'

I wasn't believing this bloke any more. It was all beginning to sound like so much tosh. But suddenly – it was Hannah who spotted the light behind us first – we were all in a much more dangerous situation than I had ever imagined.

Chapter Fourteen

Captain Mansard had only three of his blokes with him, but they were all armed so the Lee family, who with Edward and the three young boys numbered six all told, were very much at their mercy. Betty Lee and the younger of Charlie's two older brothers cried and shook with fear as Mansard and his men drove the family roughly in front of them.

'Ah, Mr Stojka,' Mansard said, as he put his head into the car with a brief smile in my direction. 'Want to ask your passengers to get out, Hancock?'

I didn't know whether I was relieved to see him or not, but I did as he said and Stojka, Horatio and Hannah got out and stood with me to the side of the vehicle.

'Well, I don't know what you're doing all the way out here in a hearse in the middle of the night, Hancock,' Mansard said, 'but if you were, as I believe, trying to assist Mr Stojka's escape, I should tell you I take a dim view.'

I said nothing.

'Assisting a Nazi spy is a treasonable offence,' he said to me. 'You could hang for it.'

'The Gentleman is not no Nazi!' Betty Lee screamed. 'You know what he is!'

Mansard tipped his head at one of his men, who smacked

poor Betty's face with the butt of his rifle. It was to me an over-use of force and something that would have outraged even the most hardened soldiers.

'Steady on!' I said, while Hannah shouted, 'Oi!'

Mansard turned his full and violent attention on my girl and said, 'Shut your filthy mouth before I shut it for you!'

There was something almost personal in his outburst and I said, 'You'll do no such thing!' as I attempted to put myself between him and Hannah. 'My ladyfriend hasn't done anything except come along with me. She knows nothing about any of this!'

'This being?' he snapped nastily.

'Well, this situation, with Mr—'

'Assisting a Nazi—'

'Mr Stojka is only a German citizen, as far as I know,' I said. 'You can say I assisted someone in avoiding internment, if you like, but him being a Nazi is not something I know anything about.'

Mansard shrugged, then leaned up against a tree and lit a cigarette. 'If you're telling the truth, maybe that could change things,' he said. 'I don't know what stories he has told you but I imagine that, true to his . . . inclinations, he was quite persuasive.'

Whether he meant Stojka's inclinations as a Gypsy or as a Nazi, I didn't know. I looked across at Hannah who didn't see me, her still furious eyes firmly fixed on Captain Mansard's face.

'Well, whatever Mr Stojka may or may not be, I think you should let Horatio and the Lee family alone,' I said. 'They did what they did because they thought it was right.'

'Came out with some poppycock about being a poor refugee, did he?'

I didn't answer. I didn't know exactly what Stojka had said to the Lees and I didn't want to talk about my own recent conversation with him. I'd had enough chats about strange and impossible things over the previous few weeks to last me a lifetime.

'I saw you kill Lily Lee,' Stojka said to Mansard. 'You and this other man.' He looked over at the captain's sergeant.

'What utter tosh!' Mansard laughed. 'Although it pains me I have to accept Dr Craig's opinion that Williams did it. I didn't want to accept it, but—'

'But you know that is not true.'

Under cover of his three men's pistols, Mansard moved in on Stojka. 'Williams was besotted with the girl, I don't know why. He had a lovely girl in the WRNS. But, anyway, he raped this Lily. Williams's fingers were curled around the knife that was used to kill her afterwards.'

'Because you put it there,' Stojka said, 'after you and your man murder him. I saw you.'

I felt my heart jump in my chest. Mansard had killed Williams? Why?

Mansard crossed his arms over his chest. He didn't seem in the least upset by any of this. 'And why did I do that, Mr Stojka?' he said, echoing precisely my own thoughts. 'I liked Williams. He was one of my chaps, totally loyal. And anyway, if you saw me commit all these crimes why didn't you try to stop me?'

'Sergeant Williams did not just like Lily Lee, he understood her heart,' Stojka said. 'For a time he knew she knows something about me, but she would not tell. She told him she could not answer his questions and he respected her because he loved her. But he believed your lies about me. He believed you almost up until the time you killed her.'

'Oh, when the scales fell from his eyes?'

'He did not know you were a bad man at first but then he did find out and he dies for that.'

But Lily Lee, I remembered Dr Craig saying, had not been assaulted. It had just looked as though she had. The Lees as a group began to get restless. Charlie, afraid but wanting to get closer to Stojka, moved towards him.

'Get back, you little bastard!' One of Mansard's blokes poked Charlie's chest with the butt of his pistol. The other two watched the rest of the family nervously.

'Leave him alone!' Hannah cried.

'I've told you before!' Mansard screamed. 'Shut up!'

'He killed my daughter, Mr Undertaker!' Mr Lee pointed at Mansard. 'He wants to know where our German Gentleman is so that he can take the Nail away from him! He's working for Hitler! Prob'ly going to give the Nail to some bloke high up to take it to Germany. These Nazis, they all work together! The Nail has so much power—'

'Christ Almighty, not this again!' Mansard said. And then, turning to me, he continued, 'Did any of them tell you their silly story, Hancock?'

I gazed at him as blankly as I could.

'About their sacred nail? The one the ancestors of this rabble supposedly stole from the site of the crucifixian? God, what a load of tosh! Only Gyppos would boast about stealing anything. Not shown it to you, I suppose, has he?' Again I didn't respond. 'No. Well, something that doesn't exist can't be seen, can it? Everything about this man is a lie! If he saw me kill both the girl and Williams, why didn't he do anything about that, eh? With his miracle-working nail why am I still alive?'

'The Nail is powerful. My first duty is to protect it always! You know nothing of it. I cannot show it—'

'Oh, Mr Stojka – or Django the Head, as we now know you were – you and Lily Lee made quite a pair, didn't you? She saw the Virgin Mary and you live with the nail that bleeds for Jesus Christ! God Almighty, if you hadn't made such a fool of me with your tatty little fairground illusion I might have let you avoid internment. You are pathetic! Like Williams, like all of these pitiful Gypsies here. Or, rather, you would be if you were not working for the Third Reich, Mr Stojka.' He paused, then looked directly at me. 'You have to ask yourself what a German national is doing in this country, don't you? Hiding out, disguising himself . . . Our friend here may well end up being interned but he will be questioned about his activities first – at some length.'

The Gypsy looked at the ground and I thought I caught guilt on his face. I had started to believe him but . . . but this made me unsure yet again.

'Mr Stojka?' I asked.

He looked up at me with violent eyes. 'Believe what you like,' he said, 'I do not care!'

'If there were more of us I'd offer to escort you back in your vehicle, Hancock,' Mansard said, as he took Stojka's arm. 'But as it is . . .'

'I thought you'd want to do us for aiding someone you believe to be a Nazi,' I said. 'You said yourself I could hang for such a thing.'

'I'm feeling generous and you're not a bad chap. It's easy to be taken in by these exotic types.'

And I was, I admit, ready to take his kind 'offer'. There I was, in the middle of the night with my ladyfriend in Epping Forest and a suspected Nazi sympathiser – it didn't look healthy. But suddenly I was being given a way out. There is a coward in me as well as a man who just wants to protect his lady.

And thank God for that lady, who pointed at Mansard and said, 'Now I fucking know where I've seen you before!'

'You pushed me into the road, you bastard!' she said. 'You and all your Fascist mates!' Even through the night-time gloom I could see that Hannah's face was distorted with rage.

For once, Mansard did not respond to Hannah's outburst by shouting. 'I don't know what you mean,' he said quietly, as he passed Stojka to one of his other chaps and attempted to take Hannah to one side. She shoved him away from her.

'Brick Lane,' she said. 'Nineteen thirty-four. You and your pals pushed me in the road, nearly under a car! I've never forgotten it. You pushed your face right into mine and then you called me a Yiddish pig!'

'I think you're mistaken—'

'I thought I knew you and now I know I do! Them days are burned into my brain.'

There was a moment of silence.

'Hannah,' I said, 'what's going on?'

She turned to me, but Mansard pulled her face around to his once again. 'You're—'

She spat at him, full in the face. 'He's a Fascist, H,' she yelled. 'Him and his mates all in black shirts, following that bastard Mosley!'

He slapped her hard across the mouth. Mr Lee and I sprang forwards in her defence. The sound of guns being turned against us brought us both to a standstill.

'They used to come down to our manor terrifying poor Jews,

right up until we kicked them out in 'thirty-six when the whole East End stood up to Mosley in Cable Street,' Hannah said, as she wiped blood away from her mouth. 'I'd gone back to see if my mum and dad were still alive, if someone like him hadn't thrown them through a shop window!'

'Shut up!'

Hannah had reckoned she'd recognised Mansard some time before. But I'd given it little thought – apart, of course, from wondering whether he'd been a customer of hers. I was relieved he hadn't, but I was frightened too. Mr Lee had given his opinion that Mansard was working for someone higher up who wanted to get hold of Stojka and his nail. And now, if Mansard was or had been one of Mosley's Blackshirts, there was a possibility that he and the three lads he had with him were doing that job directly for Adolf Hitler. There was something else to take into account too, something about Hannah.

'Hancock?' Mansard raised a questioning eyebrow. He began to appeal, I felt, to my good sense. 'Are you going to take this "lady" out of the forest? I suggest that's for the best. What do you think?'

'The problem I have, Captain Mansard,' I said, 'is that Hannah doesn't lie. She doesn't get on with her mum and dad, and if she went back to Spitalfields it must have been for a serious reason. I remember all that trouble back in the thirties, and nineteen thirty-four was the height of it, Blackshirts everywhere. Hannah said you were a Blackshirt then.'

'If I had been a Blackshirt, how the hell would I have got into the MPs? God! Do use your intelligence!'

'I don't know how Mr Stojka got here from Germany,' I said. 'Seems like a bit of a miracle to me, but he did it.'

'He's here because he's one of their fucking agents, as I told you!' Mansard yelled.

I looked at Martin Stojka, the Head, the keeper of the Nail of Christ or whatever it was. He was dirty, cowed and breathing heavily through fear. His story was ridiculous and he could easily have been a Nazi spy. But just as I knew that Hannah was telling the truth about Mansard, I knew that Stojka, whatever he might be, was no Nazi spy. After all Sergeant Williams had had no reason to kill Lily Lee, and I couldn't accept that the spirit of the girl's dead sister had done it.

'Hitler wants to kill all of our people,' Martin Stojka said softly, to me. 'He wants our secrets and then our deaths.'

Mansard turned his gun on him.

The other three men positioned themselves, two in front and one behind the rest of the Gypsies. The travellers out-numbered the MPs, but sometimes those shot for desertion in the trenches were executed in groups. More than once, those we killed outnumbered those of us who had been ordered to do the shooting. I still see those things in waking nightmares. I had a feeling so bad it was almost as if my bones were melting.

'Captain Mansard,' I said, 'I believe you are an enemy of this country, and I also believe that you have to be stopped.'

'And you're going to stop me, are you?'

'No,' I said truthfully. 'I don't have anything to stop you with. But if you want to stop me telling people about what you've been doing here in the forest with these people you'd better kill me.'

'H!'

'I'm sorry, love,' I said to Hannah, 'but I can't just let him execute these people.' I looked at Mansard. 'Because you will, won't you? I don't know why you want Martin Stojka so much—'

'I told you!' I heard Stojka say. Then I watched, with everyone else in that clearing, as he put his hand into his jacket pocket and brought something very bright out into the darkness.

I heard Mansard click off his safety catch.

'He wants this,' Stojka said, as he held what looked like a dart of light up before him.

There was a gasp and then all of the Gypsies got down on the ground and hid their faces in their hands. The light from the thing, which was white and bright, made their deep black hair seem to shine.

'The Fourth Nail,' I heard Mr Lee say. 'The Nail of Christ!'

I don't believe in anything supernatural. I don't think that such things are possible, but whatever Stojka had in his hand lit the scene in front of my eyes so brilliantly that I could now see the hard lines of hatred on Captain Mansard's face. Addressing Martin Stojka, he said, 'Give the Nail to me.'

I wanted to say something about his not believing in this thing, but by that time I was speechless. As Stojka held it out to Mansard I motioned for Hannah to get out of it sharpish. But she was as fascinated by what was going on as I was. Her eyes looked almost as if she were seeing inside herself rather than staring at what was happening outside. There was probably half a second of the deepest silence this side of the grave. I turned my attention from Hannah to Stojka. But now the scene had changed. There was nothing bright and ethereal in Stojka's hand any more and Captain Mansard was screaming.

'Oh, Christ!' Mansard yelled. He was lying on the forest floor, rocking, holding his face and shouting.

I'd seen nothing happen, yet Mansard was tearing at one blood-filled eye. Martin Stojka, who had embedded the nail in Mansard's face, watched impassively. Even when Mansard's sergeant hefted his rifle and shot Stojka, the Gentleman Gypsy did not move. In fact, it wasn't for some moments that I realised Stojka had been shot. Then, slowly, like a tree that has been felled, he dropped forwards on to the ground, the wound in his back pouring blood, his eyes wide open and seemingly without life. The nail in Mansard's face had ceased to glow and we were all where we had been before Stojka had removed it from his jacket, caught in the gloom of Mansard's boys' torches.

'Help me!' Mansard shouted, as he clawed and shredded his face.

'Fucking hell, Sarge,' one of the younger MPs said, to the man with the stripes on his arm in front of him.

Rosie's Edward and her mother lifted their heads from the ground, only to be shot by the other equally terrified young MP behind the Gypsy group. He did it as reflex, a deadly reaction to fear.

'Betty!' Mr Lee lunged across towards his wife's twitching body.

'Stay where you are!' the sergeant MP warned him. He took his eyes off Mr Lee and turned to Mansard. 'Captain?' he said.

But Mansard was speechless. Gasping for breath, his fingers lost in a bloody hole inside his face, he rocked on the ground in the grip of an agony I could only imagine. I made to go over to him to see what I could do. We're all human, aren't we, and he was a human in great pain? But as soon as I moved I found myself looking down a gun barrel.

*

'Kill 'em all, and then we'll think about what we're going to say later,' the man with his gun in my face said to his younger colleagues.

'There ain't half a lot of 'em,' the young lad who had shot Edward and Betty replied, as he surveyed the remaining wailing and bloodied Gypsies on the ground before him. 'What about Captain Mansard?'

'I'll deal with him,' the sergeant replied. 'You do what I tell you.'

"Sarge." He swung his machine-gun down from his shoulder again and clicked off the safety catch.

The man in front of me bent down towards Mansard as Mr Lee tore himself away from his wife's body and shouted, 'No!'

"Sarge" looked at his younger colleagues and said, 'Now!'

I saw one of the kids swallow hard before he fired, but both he and his mate still did it. I could hear Hannah screaming behind me and I feared she might run forward in an attempt to save the Gypsies. But she didn't move any more than I did. Whether we were rooted to the spot with fear or whether we didn't feel the Gypsies were worth our own lives, I will never know. But the fear that it might have been the latter haunts me. I felt pain when I saw little Charlie Lee's life shot out of him, but that doesn't do anything to lessen my guilt. In the end, if you're there you do something, and in that moment I did nothing.

Once the shooting had finished there was silence. People imagine that after an execution like that some of those only wounded will groan and cry out in their agony. But it doesn't always happen, and it seemed at the time that the young MPs had been thorough. All I could hear was Hannah's weeping and the pounding of my own blood inside my head.

'You,' Sarge said to me, as I stood trembling with terror in front of him, 'get the nail out of Captain Mansard's face. I think he's almost dead now.'

'No,' I whispered, my throat almost closed by terror. His voice was so far from humanity it made me want to be sick.

Sarge moved towards me. 'Now, you listen to me, you dirty little wog,' he said. 'The Captain, Jonesy, young Hanson over there and me, we've had 'ard time getting hold of what these bleedin' Gyppos have. We've lost the fuckin' war anyway, so why not give old Adolf what he wants, eh? Captain would've done it for love of the Fatherland, but I'm quite happy with the ackers and the chance to carry on living meself.'

Mansard had now stopped clawing at his face and was just twitching in a way that the dead Gypsies were not doing. The nail, long, dark and thin, stuck way out and up from inside his bloodied, smashed-up eye-socket.

'Don't do it, H!' I heard Hannah cry. 'We haven't lost this war! We can't have lost this war!'

Sarge's face moved up into a sneer. 'What the fuck do you know, love?'

I wasn't going to do a thing to help him.

'No,' I said, more strongly this time. 'You want it, you get it.'

'I'll fucking shoot—'

'You're going to shoot us anyway!' I said. 'No, you do it yourself.'

The youngster still standing behind the great heap of dead Gypsies said, 'Sarge, it's getting light!'

I would have done what Sarge did, which was glance up into the lightening sky, but my eyes were on something that was moving at the edge of my view. It was a man and, though bloodied, he did not appear to be hurt.

'If you touch the Nail with bad intent it will do you harm,' Mr Lee said, as he picked himself up from among the bodies of his dead children.

'Jonesy!'

But the lad was frozen, his eyes riveted to the gory, weeping figure that had emerged from the massacre.

'The Gentleman, Mr Stojka, was keeper of the Nail. It will let me, as one of his own, for a while, take it now,' Mr Lee said.

Sarge moved his pistol away from me and pointed it at the Gypsy. 'If you think I'm going to let you have what we've taken months to find, then you've another think coming! You ain't doing to me what that German done to the captain!'

Mr Lee stood very still, then raised his arms slowly into the air.

'Now, look here,' the MP said, 'unlike the captain, I ain't no Nazi. Hitler must be a bloody madman to be offering ackers for something like this. I just want the money.'

'You've killed all these people for it!' I said. Until I heard him talking so calmly about money the true horror hadn't really hit me. A man, a woman and children had been wiped out for something I would've put in the same box with Lily's visions – something from the mind. Relics were just bits of old wood, metal and bone that people said were powerful because there was a story attached to them. They weren't real. But all of us, Sarge included, had seen that nail glow when Stojka took it out of his pocket. And if Sarge was so confident he didn't believe in its power, why had he asked *me* to pull it out of Captain Mansard's face? Why hadn't he done it himself?

'Yeah,' Sarge replied, 'and if you try to stop me and Jonesy and Hanson, we'll kill you an' all.'

I glanced across at the other two and caught just the briefest hint of doubt flash between them. They were young and, as I knew from my own experiences, killing doesn't always become a habit with blokes who take oath for King and country. There were four of us – Horatio, Mr Lee, Hannah and myself – and only three of them. They had less to lose than us, but they had the weapons we lacked. Not that that superior situation had saved Captain Mansard. Something else had happened to him, something I still can't explain. It did make me think, though. 'Well, Sarge,' I said, as I fixed Mr Lee with what I hoped was a meaningful stare, 'we certainly don't want that, do we?'

'You don't.'

'No. So why don't you take the nail yourself and—'

'It's in the Captain's eye!' The watery early-morning sun had risen considerably now and by its light I could clearly see Sarge cringe. 'I ain't pulling that out!' He pointed to Mr Lee. 'He can do it. Seems he wants to.'

'And then have you take it off him and kill us all anyway? No, Mr Lee,' I said, 'don't do it. Don't—'

The muzzle of a pistol jammed against the side of your head will generally shut you up and Sarge's weapon had the appropriate effect on me.

'You ain't giving the orders here, Mr Hancock,' Sarge said. 'That's for me to do.'

'Leave him alone!' I heard Hannah squeak.

But no one took any notice of her. 'Get the fuckin' thing out of the captain's face, Gyppo!' Sarge said to Mr Lee. 'Then lay it on the ground so I can pick it up meself.'

'And if I won't?' Mr Lee was looking at me in a way that told me he had understood what I'd wanted him to do, which was to confound and confuse these already edgy men by playing on their squeamishness, and their distrust of him – another Gypsy with his hands on that nail.

'Sarge, this is all going wrong!' the lad called Jonesy said, panicking.

'Shut up, Private! Let me think,' Sarge said now, visibly sweating with the strain.

'Jonesy's right,' Hanson chipped in, his voice shaking with what sounded to me like terror. 'We can't kill all these people and get away with it! Captain said all we had to do was get that nail thing for him and he'd give us money. No one said nothing about killing.'

'Oh, don't be such a bloody baby, Hanson! You knew that the Captain killed the girl and you weren't too upset about that. You even knew about Williams.'

'Ah, yes, Lily and Sergeant Williams,' I said. Sarge's gun was still jammed against my temple but I felt I had to carry on keeping him mentally off-balance. Also, I was curious. Mansard had never explained why he'd killed the Gypsy girl and his sergeant. 'Why did the captain kill them?'

'Why do you want to know?'

'Why do you not want to tell me if you're going to kill me anyway?'

Sarge wiped some sweat off his brow, then said, 'Fair enough.' He cleared his throat. 'Williams found out the girl knew about Stojka, heard her talking about him to her brother-in-law. So, anyway, the girl, she fancied Williams a bit, talked to him and that. He was a good-looking bloke, he got close. He convinced her he was in love with her, playing her, like. You know how it is with red-blooded geezers.'

'He was in love with her,' I heard Mr Lee say. 'He was.'

'The girl liked him and told him Stojka was special, but she wouldn't tell Williams where the German was. He told the captain as much as he'd found out – he trusted him then – and the captain told Williams to try and find out more. But then Williams heard me and the captain talking one day, about the nail and Hitler and the money we was going to make. Couldn't hide how cold he was towards us after that, so we followed him. He went to see her first, Lily, to warn her. After that, we heard him say, he was going to the coppers. Left us with little choice. Captain killed the girl, I killed Williams, and then the captain put his knife in Williams's hand. It weren't difficult.' He took the gun away from my head now and said to Private Jones, 'Get that nail for us, will you?'

The boy didn't answer, just stood there with a dead white face. A few birds were singing.

'Christ!' Sarge sighed, then reached into his battledress pocket for a fag. 'Don't you blokes want to make some ackers?'

Neither of the two privates, still with their guns trained on us, answered.

'You'll have to come with me, whatever we do,' Sarge said. 'So you might as well put your backs into it and help me make some money. You've just killed some people, for Christ's sake! Now, lets get this fucking thing Hitler wants and get out of here!'

I sensed, rather than saw, the two privates make up their minds to do as he asked, so I said, 'But how are you going to get it to Hitler?'

'Oh, don't you worry about that,' Sarge said, and gripped me hard around my throat. 'Captain had that all arranged.' He let go of me and said to his men, 'All right, Jonesy, you drag the captain's body into that hearse and we'll deal with his eye later.

Must be dead by now, musn't he.' He looked back at me. 'Handy coffin in the back we can put him in, ain't there? You,' he said to Horatio, 'help Jonesy.'

Private Jones and Horatio picked up Captain Mansard's body and loaded it into the shell in the back of my hearse. Sarge went on about how 'handy' it was to have my motor at his disposal, while Hannah, Mr Lee and I looked on with, in my case, mounting anxiety. As soon as Sarge and his blokes had put the captain away, the four of us would be of no use to him. Not a ruthless man in the way I think Mansard had been, but I recognised Sarge's type of pitiless greed. He came, I imagined, from Canning Town or the Island or some other place where kids walk about in Salvation Army jumpers and the only uncle they know is the one who lives in the shop with the three brass balls over the door. Not that I think poverty can be an excuse for killing, it can't, but it can and does explain some people, like Sarge.

Once Horatio was back with us again, we were all made to go and stand by Mr Lee, whose dead wife, children and son-in-law were on the ground behind his back.

'Making a neat pile?' I asked Sarge, as he and his two colleagues stood before us with their weapons at the ready.

'It ain't personal,' he said, 'but if you live we might not have time to get to the coast.'

I wanted to make some sharp comment about Sarge meeting Hitler in Brighton for a walk around the Pavilion and an ice-cream from the stop-me-and-buy-one man. But I knew that even if I did have to die, I could try to save Hannah. Sarge and Jonesy took aim.

I put one hand out in front to try to stop them. 'Let Hannah live!' I blurted. 'Take her with you!'

'H? No!'

'If you get into difficulty with the police you could use her as a hostage,' I said. And then, laughing hysterically at the madness of what for me was the last clutched straw, I added, 'Take her with you. Use her . . . She . . . let her live . . .'

'No!' Hannah said. 'Go with them? I'd rather die!'

I began to weep. 'Hannah, this is nothing to do with you. You must live . . .'

'I don't want to!' Her eyes were full of tears too, smudging what little remained of her carefully put-on funeral makeup. 'Not without you!'

I saw in her eyes what I had always known anyway, but I wanted her to say it to me before one or both of us died.

I put out my arms to her. 'Say it, Hannah, that you love me.'

'I . . .' She moved into my grasp but was violently jerked away from me. Private Hanson dragged her out of the firing line by her neck and pushed her toward an amazed Sarge. 'I—'

'Bloody hell, Hanson!'

'I can't kill a woman!' the private said. He was little more than a boy, really. Then he just smiled weakly at Hannah.

'You didn't have a problem with that Gypsy!' Sarge snapped back, referring, I imagined, to Hanson's part in the death of Lily Lee.

'No, I know, but . . . Well, that was a Gypsy and . . . Sarge, maybe the undertaker fella's right about a hostage . . .'

As I've said before, Sarge wasn't exactly an evil man, so I knew he didn't take pleasure in killing us. I saw him think about what Hanson had said and then, perhaps in spite of his better judgement, I saw him shrug and say to Hanson, 'Well, put her in the hearse, then. But if she gets lairy she's all yours.'

'You fucking—' Hannah spat and cursed as the young boy

dragged her towards the car. 'H! H!' I turned my face away from her now and sighed with something like contentment as I heard the two remaining MPs take aim at us. I knew this routine of old.

First Mr Lee dropped in an explosion of blood, followed by Horatio, who died in the selfsame way. Not a word or a look passed between any of us, not even an expression of friendship, comfort or goodbye. We were simply things to be slaughtered so others could get money. It wasn't personal or cruel or even really that frightening. My only regret, as everything went black around me, was that I hadn't heard Hannah say she loved me.

Chapter Fifteen

In all the time I'd spent in Flanders not once had I ever been shot. I was gassed, twice, and wounded with a bayonet to the left-hand side once, but until that moment in the middle of Epping Forest I had never taken a bullet.

It hurt. Once I'd come round from what must have been a faint, the pain smashed into me like a tank. I couldn't scream, though. I couldn't make any sound until the hearse had driven away, and for several endless seconds Sarge and his boys hung around. Although I thought of nothing at the time, I imagined later it was because whoever was driving had had to work out how to operate the Lancia before he took it on the road. But eventually it went, and when I was sure I couldn't hear it any longer I let out a long, low growl.

In a way I was angry with whoever had shot me for not finishing me off. Surrounded only by the dead, I looked at the place where the pain was coming from, which was on my right-hand side, just under my ribs. It would match up with my left side now, I thought grimly, provided I survived, which didn't look possible. I'd been shot in the stomach, the same as Horatio, who was clearly dead, and unlike Mr Lee who had obviously been shot in the head. Why the different methods, I neither knew nor cared. I just felt the pain, which had sent even all thought of Hannah from my mind. There was blood everywhere. If I'd tried to stand I would have slipped over in it. I remember that I looked at the hand with which I'd attempted to cover my own wound once and found that as soon as I took it away I could hear my blood leaving my body in a powerful stream. I felt dizzy and sick, and I knew, with a certainty I'd never experienced in the Great War, that I was going to die. There, on that leafy forest floor, surrounded by dead Gypsies. I wondered, as the lights went out in my head, what people would make of the scene and whether what had really happened there would ever be discovered.

I went into that darkness in silence, but a voice brought me – I have to say reluctantly – back into the watery light of dawn.

'Oh, my, he ain't *mullo~*!'

It was a woman's voice and to me it was just nonsense. Only when I could see again did I think I knew what was going on.

'Lily.'

Lily Lee had come to greet me as I made my journey into the land of the dead. It just went to show that heaven was nonsense. I, an atheist, was there with Lily Lee, a girl who had, to some, mocked God, Jesus and the Holy Virgin.

'No, 'tain't Lily,' the very Lily-like girl said. 'I'm Beauty.' And then she began to cry.

I thought how appropriate that word was for her when I began to sink again. The last thing I heard was a man's voice: 'We must get him to *drabalo* Mary. Ain't no time for crying.'

As a rule I don't get drunk. There's quite enough going on in my head without adding booze to the mixture. But drunk was how I felt as I gazed up into the face of someone so old and dry they could have been either male or female. I even had the taste of booze on my tongue: brandy.

The person said, 'It's going to hurt, *gaujo*. There's nothing except the brandy that I can do about that.'

And then it was as if my right-hand side melted into flames. In fact, there was a strong glow from firelight dancing on the roof of the tent I had somehow come to be in. And because this time I didn't seem capable of passing out I soon saw other things in that dank little space. As I said, there was a fire and a person I could now see was a woman, but there was a man too, whom I recognised from Mr Lee's fireside gatherings. I tried to speak to him, to tell him it wasn't me who had killed his friends and neighbours, but he said, 'You be quiet now and without worry. We'm know what you done and what you never.'

My eyes were fixed on two big buckets of steaming hot water when the pain came again. I screamed.

'Here, bite on that,' the old woman said, as she wedged a large clothes peg into my mouth. ''Twon't help with the pain but it'll give you summat to do.'

There wasn't always anaesthetic available in the first lot. If supplies were low, our MOs would have to do things in what they called 'the old-fashioned way'. If a bloke came in with his leg shattered or if a chap had taken a bullet, any surgery was done under booze if he was lucky, and nothing if he wasn't. The woman the Gypsies called *drabalo* 'doctor' Mary had been kind enough to give me booze for which I will always be grateful. But not at the time. As she hooked that bullet out of me with what felt like red-hot tongs I called her every name under the sun. To be fair, she swore back, but it took her such a long time to free me from that evil metal plug it's hardly surprising.

Although I was screaming silently into my peg for most of the time, I was occasionally aware of other things outside myself. I knew, for instance, that the Lily-like girl called Beauty poked her head around the tent flap from time to time.

'Yes, you look at the girl if it do make you feel better, my *rais*,' Mary said, when she spied me staring at Beauty. 'You look anywhere so long as it keep you living.' And then she plunged something horrible inside my body and this time I did pass out.

When I came to, I found myself looking up into Beauty's, rather than Mary's, face.

'We have to get him to a *gaujo* doctor now,' I heard Mary say, through her phlegm-heavy throat. 'He'm need to have blood and *gauje* medicine.'

In spite of the pain, I felt light and slow.

Beauty smiled at me and I thought, *I'm going to die.* This lovely young girl is smiling at me with pity in her eyes because I'm going to die. I opened my mouth to speak, but found it impossible. But by that time someone else, another man, was at Beauty's ear, and as soon as he had finished speaking, she jumped up and walked over to Mary.

'His car's been stopped,' she said, as she tipped her head in my direction.

I thought, rather than said, Hannah.

'I'll have our Joe take him to the hospital,' I heard Mary growl.

Beauty made as if to leave the tent, but Mary caught her with one of her thin, leaf-dry hands and said, 'You be careful, girl. Don't you go . . .'

'I'll do what I have to,' the girl said, and left the tent without another word.

Although light-headed, I knew that the blood I could smell

was probably my own. If I looked down I could even see it – a great red blanket covering most of my shirt, right down my trousers to my boots. These days, I'm not as well off for suits as I used to be. Most of those I haven't shrunk out of have been ripped by flying glass or, in one case, nibbled by the rats that have come out of the damaged sewers and into people's houses. I began to ask Mary about the whereabouts of my jacket but she shushed me and said, 'My boy Joe's gonna take you down the hospital so you can get some blood. I can't do no more for you now, my *rais*. Your jacket will be fine wherever it might be now.'

And from then on it was as if a light was switched on and off by turns inside my head. My journey was fractured because I was dying. It is in the nature of what I do that I have some – second-hand admittedly – experience of what those around the dying have observed. Putting aside the stories old ladies tell about loved ones walking towards bright lights or Christ-like figures opening their arms in greeting, those near to death do seem to come into and go out of this world for quite some time. Loved ones are recognised one minute and forgotten the next, places, if my own experiences are anything to go by, have no real meaning, so how Joe, a young lad of no more than fourteen, took me to Whipps Cross I still do not know. All I was certain of at the time was that I was taken in a horse-cart in the middle of what seemed a dreadful commotion of people, horses and noise. That so many were destined to be off somewhere quite different from Joe and myself was only vaguely known to me then. Later I would remember more. But at that moment . . . I am told that by the time I reached the hospital I had stopped breathing altogether.

*

Nobody woke me. Nobody pushed their face into mine to rouse me from my sleep. Coming back to the land of the living, in contrast to leaving it, was a gentle, slow affair that occasionally allowed me a view of a woman with very blonde hair. She sat in a chair beside my bed smoking a cigarette, and although I couldn't make out her face in all its detail, I knew she was connected to me. There was that feeling you get when family and loved ones are close at hand.

'Ag?' From my dry throat it sounded like the caw of a crow.

My sister stood up, smoothed her skirt and then, stroking my hair with one hand, leaned over to smile at me. 'God help us, Frank,' she said. 'What have you been doing?'

My throat was bad and I was far too tired to talk. I was in a bright, empty room, whose walls were painted green. The sheets I lay in were very, very white, and there was a metallic tray with a syringe and a glass of water on top of a cupboard beside the bed.

'You're in Whipps Cross hospital, Frank. They told me a Gypsy boy brought you in,' Aggie said, and added, with confidence, 'Charlie.'

Even if I'd had a voice I wouldn't have known where to begin.

'It was Stella told us you'd took off with Charlie and some other Gyppo and, er, Miss Hannah Jacobs,' Aggie said, stammering a little over Hannah's name. Aggie knows what Hannah is, and although she never says anything, I know she doesn't find it easy to bear. The mention of my girl's name made my heart jump. Hannah. Last time I'd seen her she'd been pushed into my hearse by that MP Private – Private . . . I couldn't remember his name! What had become of her?

'Hannah?' I croaked.

Aggie looked across to where I now saw a man standing by a door. He was about forty and wore a long dark raincoat and a trilby hat. Even in the state I was in I could tell he was a copper. They have a way of standing, with their hands behind their backs and their feet turned out, that is unmistakable.

'Frank, the coppers need to talk to you,' Aggie said. 'About all this, what you've been through. This is Inspector Richards from Scotland Yard. He don't want to talk now, though, you're still sick and . . . But in a bit, you must . . .'

I ignored her. 'Hannah!' I said, and attempted to push myself up in the bed, only to find that my whole right side was on fire again. There was a sharp pain in my right arm too. I slumped down again but as I did so I signalled to Aggie that I'd like her to give me the glass of water. Not that I could drink from it myself: Aggie had to hold it for me. The copper by the door watched with interest as I gazed at him over the rim. He didn't look as if he was about to tell me anything awful – but, then, who does, these days? There's only so many times a person can look genuinely distressed, and with people being blown to bits every day it becomes too ordinary for real emotion. Even, I with my mad brain, can't be upset or enraged all the time. No one has the energy for that.

With my throat now lubricated I said to the copper, 'You want to talk to me?'

I saw Aggie glance at him with strain on her face. 'You've lost a lot of blood, Frank,' she said. 'Maybe talk to Inspector Richards later, eh?'

It was obvious they were keeping something from me so I asked him outright. 'Is Hannah Jacobs all right?' I said. 'It's all I want to know.'

'Mr Hancock . . .'

'Frank, you have to hear the whole story or you won't understand,' Aggie said. 'And you ain't really able to do that yet, are you? You need to sleep.' She stroked my head again, then said, 'Mum and Nan'll be up later.'

I looked across at Inspector Richards with, I knew, tears in my eyes. I was weak, I was tired, but I knew I wouldn't sleep without knowing what had happened to Hannah or passing on what I knew about Sarge, Jonesy and . . . and *Hanson*. Yes, that was the name of the other private, the one who had taken Hannah away from me.

'I want to know now, Ag,' I said. 'I've things to say to this copper.'

'Frank—'

'No!'

'If your brother is happy to speak to me, Mrs Groves, I'm very pleased to oblige,' Richards said. He spoke stiffly but well, in that sort of accent some people who have come from the East End and moved out a bit, into Essex usually, tend to have. He also used my sister's married name, which, for a moment, I didn't recognise. In general, these days, except for official purposes, she's gone back to being Agnes Hancock.

Aggie went back to her chair. 'Well, Frank,' she said, 'if you must, I can't stop you but,' she looked at Richards, 'you'll have to ask that matron before you carry on. If she says my brother can't . . .'

'Mrs Groves, if you'd like to leave the room now,' the copper said, with what even I could see was a sudden, almost frightening coldness.

'Yes, but—'

'Mrs Groves!'

He opened the door, and outside I could see a uniformed

copper leaning against the corridor wall. Aggie sat for a moment finishing her fag. Then she stood up. 'Frank, if you get tired you must say so,' she said.

I told her I would and then she made to leave. As she drew level with Richards she said, 'You know, I will tell Matron, and when I get home I'll tell Sergeant Hill up at Plaistow about this an'all.'

Richards smiled. 'You can do that, Mrs Groves.'

'Yes, well, I will.'

'I'm sure my guv'nors at the Yard will be very interested in what your Sergeant Hill might have to say to them.'

'Yeah, well, they ought to be!' Aggie said, with a lot of well-acted pride. 'Ain't right what you're doing! Taking advantage of a sick man! He needs his rest, my brother does, not endless questions!'

She marched out with her head held so high she was almost looking over her shoulder. Beyond Sergeant Hill, who is approachable for a policeman, Aggie has no love for coppers – not because she's a bad girl, she just doesn't like anyone in any sort of authority. In that she's like most of our friends and neighbours in West Ham.

Once Aggie had gone, Richards walked over and took her seat. 'Okey-dokey, Mr Hancock,' he said. 'Let's find out what's been happening to you.'

Chapter Sixteen

Richards told me little, except that no one answering the description of Hannah Jacobs had been involved in any trouble – as far as he knew. There had been, however, what he called an 'incident' involving my hearse.

'At just after seven o'clock this morning,' he said, 'officers in Leytonstone were called to a fracas on the High Road. Your hearse was at the centre of it, Mr Hancock, and a right strange sight it was too,' he said, with a piercing stare. 'Four corpses was what greeted those officers who looked inside, all Military Policemen.'

'There was no woman with them?' I asked.

Richards shook his head. 'No. Just two young lads in the back, one more at the wheel and the other in a coffin. I can tell you, Mr Hancock, it was an eerie sight. But, then, it was the end of what had been a most funny morning.'

I imagined that the corpse at the wheel must have been Sarge. I assumed he had driven off from the forest in my vehicle. I couldn't think he'd've allowed anyone else to do that for him. But how had he and the others died? And then I remembered how Captain Mansard had died and felt very cold.

'But then again I say that one of the corpses was at the wheel when what I should say is what was left of this poor character was at the wheel. He'd been torn to pieces by something.'

I looked up into Richards's thin slightly grey face and I heard him say, 'Do you know anything about this, Mr Hancock?'

I told him everything, which he wrote down in his notebook. It took a long time because I was exhausted. Once a large woman in a matron's uniform came in and asked nervously how I was. Whatever Aggie had said hadn't worked. Matron had been told to keep away. I wondered, even as I was telling Inspector Richards about Mansard and his boys, how much the coppers had known about the captain and his politics. Not that he commented on any of what I said. He just kept writing it all down grimly. Only when I came to talk about the Nail did he look up.

'So you're saying,' he said, 'that the Gypsies were hiding this Stojka fella to protect a nail s'posed to have been used to crucify Jesus?'

That wasn't exactly how the Nail's history had been told to me, but I said, 'Yes. Mansard wanted it to take to Hitler. That was where Mansard's true sympathies lay.'

Inspector Richards, although I could hardly blame him for it, was looking doubtful. 'In Germany?'

'Yes. He'd been a Blackshirt. My, er, Miss Jacobs remembered him from back in the thirties, with Mosley and his lads. She's a Jewish lady, Miss Jacobs.'

'This is the lady we've not come across yet? The one you say the MPs took?'

'Yes.'

'And where does Miss Jacobs live?'

I paused a little before I replied. For obvious reasons Hannah doesn't like coppers knowing where she lives, but if she was missing I didn't have any choice. 'Rathbone Street, Canning Town,' I said.

Inspector Richards wrote down this, to me, notorious address without a flicker.

'I don't know where in the forest the Lees' boy Charlie took us, so I can't tell you where to look for the bodies of the Gypsies,' I said.

'We'll find them,' Richards said.

I could, of course, tell him when Mansard had died. I also knew how many of the Lee family, Horatio and Stojka had met their ends. But I couldn't explain how Mansard had died – I still can't, if the truth be told. Stojka must have attacked him in the half-second, or whatever it was, when I looked away, but I can't always convince myself that that is the case. Sometimes, even now, I imagine the Nail floating off and attacking him of its own accord. Clearly that's rubbish, but it still crosses my mind. Richards, on the other hand, was more certain.

'So this Gypsy Stojka attacked Mansard with the nail and pushed it into his eye?'

'Yes . . . Well, I think so.'

He nodded, paused briefly to light up a smoke, then continued, 'So where did he, Stojka, go with this amazing nail after he'd attacked Captain Mansard with it?'

'He was shot by one of the captain's men,' I said. 'He didn't have time to get the Nail back.'

'So who took it out?' Richards asked.

'No one.'

'Not Sarge or,' he glanced at his notebook to remind himself of the relevant names, 'or Privates Hanson or Jones?'

'None of them would touch it,' I said. 'They were squeamish

about it, as I was. But they were afraid too. Mr Lee, Lily Lee's father, warned them not to touch it.'

'Mmm. Mumbo-jumbo.' Richards shook his head. 'We've had quite enough of all that round here from those Gypsies, with their visions and virgins and God knows what.'

I coughed. 'It isn't their fault that Hitler wants this thing,' I said. 'They—'

'Well, anyway, there wasn't any nail in Mansard's face when we found him,' Richards said, 'so someone must have taken it. Maybe one of those barmy types who attacked your vehicle.'

'What do you mean?' I said.

'We still don't know who stopped your car, not for certain, but some people say it was a group of Gypsies. This was up here on the Whipps Cross Road. What happened we don't know. When we got the call about your vehicle it was in Leytonstone High Road, up by the Underground station, with four corpses inside. It was surrounded by people who had recognised it as yours and were looking for the body of Lily Lee. Wanting to pay their respects, they said.' He smiled. 'Got a bit of a shock when they saw what was inside. We've got all those we could lay our hands on down the station. They all say the same thing. The hearse was parked by the station and rumour went round that the girl's funeral was happening today. Where that rumour come from, especially at such an early hour of the morning, I don't know and neither, apparently, does any of those involved. The hearse with your name on the side of it just appeared in the smog.'

I didn't remember any smog that morning but I'd been rather far away and busy dying at the time. Things came into my head now in what felt like a jumble.

'The men who shot me, the MPs,' I said, 'they were making for the coast.'

'And why were they doing that?' Richards asked.

'I don't know,' I said, 'but I think they were going to carry on with whatever plan Mansard was following. Maybe they were meeting other traitors . . . Mansard was going to take the Nail to Germany, which I suppose would make sense of wanting to go to the coast.'

Richards nodded. 'You don't know where on the coast, do you, Mr Hancock?'

I knew how important this question was so I racked my brains to find an answer for him, but I couldn't. We're told the coast, particularly here in the south, is very well defended by a string of heavy gun emplacements, pillboxes and anti-aircraft batteries. If a boat or a plane had been coming from Germany with the intention of picking Mansard up, its pilot would have had to know what he was doing. Then again, maybe Mansard had meant to deliver the Nail to someone else, another Nazi, who perhaps lived near the coast. I didn't know, and as time was going on I was feeling more and more tired and in pain. Richards, who had been, I think, largely oblivious to anything outside his investigation now gave me a strange look.

'I'll call the matron,' he said, got up quickly and moved towards the door.

'What?' The room was spinning now in a queasy fashion.

'Matron!' I heard him call down the corridor.

Then he rushed back to me and took one of my hands in his. 'Mr Hancock?'

A thought occurred to me. 'You know,' I said, 'if some Gypsies stopped my hearse in the first place, they might know where Hannah is.' I felt very, very sick and there was blood again, although I couldn't tell whose it was.

'He's talking gibberish,' I heard Richards say to someone. 'God, I hope I didn't put too much strain on the poor chap!'

I couldn't make out the reply to this, except that the voice was female, elderly and quite cross.

I went to sleep then and dreamt of the old crone *drabalo* Mary, and how, just after she'd taken the bullet out of me, a great gang of Gypsies had gone off somewhere.

For what I later discovered was almost another whole day, the doctors at Whipps Cross tried to stop the bleeding from my side but couldn't. As quickly as they transfused blood into me – on one occasion from my sister Aggie – it just poured out again. There was a raid that night so I was moved with a glass bottle of blood to the cellars. Not that I remember anything about that, thank Christ. A nice young nurse told me about it later. I don't even remember my dreams except that they were not about Hannah, my family or anything of importance in my life.

Everyone came to see me. My mother, my sisters, Arthur and Walter, even poor Doris. Then they called Father Burton. He was on his way to give me the Last Rites when *drabalo* Mary's grandson Joe bade farewell to Hannah at the front of the hospital and she asked one of the nurses where I was. She was dirty and damp, as if she'd been sleeping in the open, but the copper still stationed outside my room let her come in to see me. I remember her calling and crying, leaning on the bed to shout into my face.

'H! H! For Gawd's sake, fight!'

I can only imagine how scandalised the Duchess and Nan must have been by such behaviour. And even though Hannah's reappearance marked a turning point in my condition I didn't know about any of it until some time later, when Father Burton had visited and been sent on his way by a doctor who hoped he was right that I seemed to be recovering. To me it was a dream until early that evening when I opened my eyes to see my family and Hannah ranged around my bed with grey, concerned faces.

I would have liked to come to calmly, for their sakes as much as my own, but I was rocketed back into my life with a single thought. I gripped Hannah's arm and said, 'The Gypsies! I've got to tell the coppers! The Gypsies were going somewhere when *drabalo* Mary took the bullet out of me!'

'Sssh!' Hannah smoothed her hand across my brow. 'Don't worry about that now, eh?'

'Yes, but—'

'H, don't go worrying about no Gypsies now. You just get yourself well again.'

'Hannah,' I said, 'how did you get out of the car? My car with the corpses and . . .' I tried to pull myself up in the bed but the pain in my side was still so great that I slumped back on to my pillows.

'Francis,' I heard my mother say, 'Miss Jacobs is right. You mustn't worry about anything now.'

I looked from Hannah to the Duchess and saw that my mother was weeping. I tried and failed to reach out to her.

'Oh, rest, will you, please, Francis? You nearly died,' the Duchess said, in a voice so broken it was painful to hear. 'I called Father Burton. Francis, I nearly lost you!'

She got to her feet, came over and kissed every inch of my face. I cried, I admit it. Then I realised something I'd often thought about before: I owed it to them to live. Sometimes I don't want to carry on. Even with Hannah in my life, what I've done and what I've seen outweigh everything. But that isn't the fault of my mother or my sisters, and they should never have to suffer because of me. So for the time being I didn't ask any more questions, and didn't get any more answers, until Hannah came to see me on her own the following day. This time she was her usual smart-as-a-pin self, complete with hair-do and perfume.

'Listen, H,' she said, as she sat down beside my bed and lit me a Passing Cloud, 'you mustn't say nothing to the coppers about the Gypsies.'

This seemed to be worrying her considerably. I took the fag from her, drew in, then coughed, which made my side hurt like hell. I hadn't smoked for a few days so I had to push through the pain to get used to it again. 'But, Hannah,' I said, once I could speak properly, 'the coppers think the Gypsies may have had something to do with the death of Sarge and the others in the hearse. I heard them, the Gypsies, all go off somewhere when that girl took me back to the camp. It must've been about the same time as—'

'Well, it can't have been,' Hannah said. 'I never saw no Gypsies.'

'So how did you get out of the car?' I asked.

She shrugged. 'They pulled over. Near here, it was. I opened the door and ran.'

'Didn't they run after you?'

'For a bit, yes,' she said.

'And they didn't catch you?'

I couldn't believe that three fit young MPs would allow a middle-aged woman like Hannah to get away from them. I could understand why, out of the forest, they wouldn't want to shoot at her, but I was pretty sure they'd have been able to catch her.

'No . . .' Hannah turned away. My stomach churned sickeningly.

'I know you're lying,' I said. She didn't contradict me. 'If you'd really got away, you would've come looking for me. But you didn't turn up anywhere until yesterday. Why are you lying? We don't have any secrets. What's going on, Hannah?'

'Nothing.' She glanced down at her hands. 'It's the truth,' she said. 'I got away and I never come looking for you. Sorry. I'm not as good a friend as you like to believe sometimes.'

I still wasn't convinced and I told her so. The previous day she had been desperate to see me, worried sick. Now, suddenly, she wanted me to believe she didn't care. I wondered, not for the first time, whether she'd met someone else. But when or how she could've done that, I couldn't imagine. It didn't make any sense.

'The Gypsies saved you,' Hannah said, as she got up to leave. 'Remember that.'

'How do you know the Gypsies saved me?' I asked. 'You and me, we haven't spoken about that.'

Hannah sighed. 'You talked about some Gypsy Mary woman when you was in your fever. And, anyway, one of the nurses told me,' she said, with more than a little impatience in her voice. And what she said was quite true: the nurses did know that the Gypsies had saved me. 'Look, H, if you want to say you heard some Gypsies going off somewhere when you was at their camp, you can do that. That's up to you. But they never come after your hearse. You ain't to say that they did, because that ain't true. I don't know how them horrible soldiers died, but it wasn't anything to do with no Gypsies.'

'Have you been to see the coppers?' I asked. I knew they had been keen for her to contact them.

'Well, of course I have!' she said, again tetchily.

'And you told them what you've told me about how you got away from the car and—'

'Yes!'

'So did they ask you where you were between escaping from the hearse and turning up here yesterday?'

'Yes.' She was studying her hands again – so different now from the scruffy vision I had seen the day before. Unusually for Hannah, she had actually been dirty.

'And what did you say?'

She looked me hard in the eyes before she replied. 'I told them I was working,' she said, 'which I was.'

'But you didn't go home. They would have found you there if you had because I told them where you live,' I said. 'I was worried!'

'Well, I was making meself a few bob up in the forest,' Hannah said. 'You were dead, as far as I knew, and I didn't have a farthing on me to get home. Now that a lot of those religious people have gone there are plenty of sorts going about all types of business up there needing a little company among the trees.'

I stubbed out my fag in the ashtray beside my bed. I was trembling with anger now. 'I don't believe you,' I said. 'Going with gangsters up against trees? With me not even cold, as far as you knew? You couldn't be so heartless. Did you tell the coppers about Mr Lee and Horatio and me getting shot?'

'I was scared,' Hannah said. 'I went off and did what I do and hoped it might all go away!' Her eyes filled with tears. 'That's how it was, and if you don't believe me, well – well, stuff you, Francis Hancock!'

214

And with that she left. In tears and with a face as red as a tomato and me not knowing whether to feel hurt, confused or just plain angry. She had, after all, provided I did as she said, put me in a difficult position with the police. What she wanted me to do, while not actually lying, was leave out a detail they might find useful. The Gypsies *had* left to go somewhere in a hurry at just about the time that the hearse stopped on the first occasion. Someone on Whipps Cross Road had even seen some Gypsies around the car at the time. Yet Hannah wanted me to say I had no knowledge of this. Well, I did and so did she. I thought about these things a lot in the hours that followed, and it wasn't comfortable. Being hurt in your mind or your heart is far more painful than being hurt in your body. This time was really the darkest period of the whole affair for me.

Chapter Seventeen

I was sent home from Whipps Cross the following day. I could hardly walk, so they laid on an ambulance to take me back to the shop. Like most people, these days, I wasn't strong enough to leave hospital, but the nurses and doctors can't cope with any more than the most serious cases. Every night brings new casualties so once you're reasonably well they let you go. But, then, our family is lucky in that we have a doctor and the wherewithal to pay him. I'd only been home for half an hour at most before Dr O'Grady came to inspect my wound and talk to me about how it was to be cared for.

'You will need to rest, Frank,' he said, 'and you will have to go down to your shelter.'

'No,' I said firmly, smiling as I did so because Dr O'Grady is a good man and always means well.

'I'm going to tell Arthur to help you get down to the shelter before he leaves for the night,' the doctor continued, ignoring me.

'Doctor—'

'Frank, for the love of God, will you think of your mother and sisters for once?' the doctor roared. 'Go down to the shelter for their sake!'

I knew that he was aware of why I didn't like going down the Anderson and that he had some sympathy with me. But Dr O'Grady, like everyone else, was tired. He left without another word while I tried not to think about going down the shelter, even though his words had convinced me that I had to try to do so.

Against my instructions Doris had been allowed to come back to work and, a little after the doctor had left, she knocked on my bedroom door and brought in my appointments diary. Her face, though made up as it usually is, was as dry and white as a clean sheet of paper.

'Mr Cox has been covering your bookings since you've been ill,' she said. Albert Cox has an undertaking business down in Canning Town and, although he was getting paid what should have been my money for taking over, he was doing me a real favour.

'Yes, he's a good mate,' I said. I noticed that Doris had lost still more weight. Poor sad girl, it didn't do her any favours. 'Doris . . .'

'Mr H, if this firm don't do no work, you and your family are going to go hungry.' Her eyes filled with tears, as much, I felt, for her poor dead husband as for me and my family. 'I can't bear to think of Mrs H suffering.' She wiped a hand across her eyes. 'So I've been thinking and it seems to me that the best thing you can do is give Arthur the chance to do your job.'

Arthur is sixteen years old, thin as a rail and full of spots, poor lad. I must have looked thunderstruck to say the least, but then Doris held up her hand to me. 'Hear me out, Mr H,' she said. 'I know he looks like a plum duff and he ain't always the brightest lad in the world, but he would like the chance. He's seen you conduct a hundred times and he knows what to do.'

He probably did. Whether he'd have the necessary gravity was another matter. I didn't even have my wand to pass on to him! Without it, I felt sometimes that *I* lacked gravity. I was honest with Doris and told her my feelings.

She said, 'Look, Mr H, nothing's right at the moment. You're up here, and we're . . . well, we're several bearers down.' She averted her eyes for a second, remembering, I had no doubt, the times when Alfie had occasionally done that job for me. 'But I've spoke to my uncle Wolfie, who's said he'll come and do a turn bearing for you. We've only got the one hearse.'

'What?'

'The coppers have still got the motor car,' Doris said. 'They still don't know who killed them boys.'

'No?' I hadn't said anything to her about what had happened to me, but I imagined that the Duchess and the girls would have told her what they knew.

'No.' But she had no more need to discuss what had happened up in the forest than I did. 'So that just leaves us with the horse-drawn,' Doris continued. 'But we managed with the horses until very recently, didn't we?'

'Yes.' Except that until September 1940 death wasn't as popular as it was by November, not even in this poor manor.

'We'll be all right,' Doris said. 'I'll go and speak to Uncle Wolfie tonight, and if you have a word with Arthur we can do the funeral that's down for eleven o'clock tomorrow morning. Look.'

She showed me the booking in her neat hand. It said, 'Queenie Ramm, 11 a.m., Haig Road to East London C'try'. It didn't look like a difficult job – I knew it wouldn't be a big do. Queenie had died the previous week after a long struggle against TB. She'd been in her eighties and left only a widowed daughter, who was childless.

'Well, all right, then,' I said, after a bit. 'Send Arthur up, and if you can speak to your uncle Wolfie . . .'

'Smashing!' She actually smiled. If nothing else came of this plan, it was all right by me if it made Doris smile. 'I'll go and tell him right now.'

She went to take off downstairs like a rocket but I managed to stop her. 'Doris!'

She turned back, her face tense and grey again.

'Nothing,' I said, with a smile. 'Thanks, Doris.'

'Thank you, Mr H.' And then she was gone. People react to tragedy in so many different ways it's impossible to say what they will or will not do. Doris was dealing with her loss by throwing herself into her job. She didn't want to be at home and she didn't want to talk about Alfie. That I had wanted to speak to her about him was more to do with me than her, and I was glad now that I hadn't.

I waited for Arthur to appear, all six foot odd of him, and lit up a Woodbine to pass the time. I still wondered about him. I looked into the little fire Nan had lit for me in my fireplace and found myself worrying again that I had no wand to give the boy. And this time it wasn't a niggle as it had been before: it was a deep, superstitious worry that lack of the wand could only spell disaster for Hancocks. After all, ever since my grandfather, Francis, had started the business back in 1885, the wand had been with whoever had conducted. Just knowing it was no longer around made me feel naked. It was then that I began to think about the Nail the Gypsies prized and where it might have ended up. In a way the Nail and the wand were the same: relics with meaning and therefore power over those who believe in them. That the Nail had no significance for me didn't mean I couldn't feel something of it. I'd felt something when Lily had had her first vision; I'd felt terrible superstitious fear when Stojka had used his relic to murder Mansard. I just couldn't connect any of that to God. Like my wand, such things should be free of any explanation or reason. That they just *are* is a mystery, and maybe that's the whole point.

But I was far from at peace with what had happened to me, and the whole affair was not to be put completely to rest just yet. Even with a war on, our police still have a duty to solve murders, and the Epping Forest Business, as I believe the thing is called these days in copper circles, had brought them a lot of dead bodies, eleven in total, that had not been killed by bombs. They took it very seriously indeed and, as I was soon to see for myself, just because I'd been shot it didn't mean they wouldn't come back to me for further explanation.

It wasn't Arthur who walked up our stairs after Doris had gone but Inspector Richards.

'Well, Mr Hancock,' Inspector Richards put his trilby hat on his lap as he sat down in the chair at the side of my bed, 'what can I say?'

There was an edge to his manner that I didn't remember him having when he'd seen me up at Whipps Cross. Maybe I was only noticing it now that I was so much better. Or maybe it was new, and if it was, what lay behind it?

'Mr Richards?'

'I have succeeded in discovering the bodies of the Gypsy Lee family, Horatio Smith and some other character no one seems to want to talk about,' Richards said. 'They were in an area of the forest known as Woodford Wells. Apparently, the Gypsies had already found them.'

'Yes,' I said. 'The Gypsies found me there. That's why I'm alive.'

'Yes, I know,' he replied. 'Some Gypsy kid brought you in to Whipps Cross. The Gypsies didn't try to hide the site from us. Didn't exactly tell us about it either, though.'

'I'm sorry I wasn't able to tell you in the hospital,' I said. 'I couldn't think straight then and, anyway, I had no real idea about where I was at the time. Woodford Wells is news to me. But the Gypsies didn't tell you?'

'No, the poor bloody coppers had to work it out for theirselves yet again.' He shook his head. 'Gyppos – I'd already asked them to tell us what they knew and they'd shook their heads like they was all Mutt and Jeff. Then when the bodies were found, there are the selfsame Gyppos sitting around looking at them!' His speech was much more London than it had been before. 'Would you credit it?'

I explained, as far as I could, the Gypsies' views about dead bodies and how greatly they feared them.

When I'd finished Richards said, 'The Gyppos, they say, know nothing about what happened to the Lees and the others. I asked them about this Stojka fella you told me about and they all said they didn't know what I was talking about.'

'The unknown body is Stojka,' I said. 'The MPs were looking for him in the forest. Ask what's left of Mansard's group.'

'Oh, I've already done that so I'm in no doubt that the body is Stojka's. It was obvious the Gyppos were lying. But there are some other problems, Mr Hancock. I'd be telling an untruth to you if I said that there weren't.'

He offered me a fag from his packet of Players Weights, which I took.

'You see, you are the only person who's said anything to us about this mysterious Nail of Christ article. You're also one of only two people who survived whatever happened up there in the forest.'

'Yes, Han— Miss Jacobs survived,' I said.

'Yes, and Miss Jacobs has told us how brave you were, Mr Hancock, in trying to stop Mansard and his men arresting Stojka. How you prevented the MPs keeping the Gypsies, who were hiding him, at bay. She didn't put it like that, of course.' He leaned towards me and said something that came as a shock to me, 'Mansard was doing his duty. Stojka was a Nazi.'

'No! No, he can't have been! That's not right.'

'Sergeant Williams came and told you about Martin Stojka and why he was wanted by the authorities.'

'Sergeant Williams was killed by Captain Mansard. That other sergeant of Mansard's told me. Williams found out that Mansard and his sergeant were Nazi sympathisers and went to see Lily Lee to tell her to be on her guard and not let on about Stojka's whereabouts to Mansard. Williams was going to come to you, the police, but before he could do that Mansard and his men killed Williams and Lily to silence them. Mansard put the knife into Williams's dead hand to make it look as if he had killed Lily Lee.'

'Did he? Dr Craig – I believe you've met him – has given his opinion that the killer of Lily Lee had to be Williams. He wanted relations with the girl, she wouldn't have it, so he killed her. Then he killed himself.'

'No . . . No. Dr Craig needs to look at his evidence again and in the light of what that sergeant told me.'

Richards shrugged. 'Maybe he does, although the doctor is certain Williams killed the girl, Mr Hancock. That's what's

222

written down in black and white for all to see. Dr Craig even thinks that Captain Mansard was trying to protect Sergeant Williams – or, rather, his memory. The captain himself seemed to think, or wanted to think, that one of the Gypsies had killed the girl.'

I was feeling shaky now, so as soon as I'd put out the fag he had given me, I immediately took one of my own. The story of what had happened in the forest, what had been said and believed, was changing in front of my eyes. It made me wonder whether I had got all my facts right, whether I had had *any* handle on what had been real and what hadn't.

'Mr Hancock, I think you've been taken in by these Gyppos,' Richards said. 'Miss Jacobs has told us there was a lot of talk about some superstitious rubbish between you and the Gypsies. She says you weren't completely took in, in her opinion, and to your credit. She saw Stojka attack Mansard and one of his boys shoot the Gypsy in his defence.'

'Mansard's boys shot the Lees,' I said. That absolutely was and had to be true. 'They executed those people!'

Richards was beginning to give me the kind of look people gave our Stella just after her house was bombed out. 'No, no, Mr Hancock,' he said. 'The Gypsies were threatening the Military Police. There was no execution. Dr Craig has inspected the site and the bodies, and he is convinced that the Gypsies were killed with just cause. The MPs had no choice.'

My heart was pounding. 'It wasn't like that,' I said. 'The Gypsies were unarmed! How could they have hurt anyone? I was there! Is Dr Craig mad or—'

'Mr Hancock, Military Policemen have been murdered!'

'Gypsies have been murdered!'

'How many more times?' he shouted. 'The Gypsies were

hiding a Nazi! These people killed our boys – some of them in your car!'

'Does Miss Jacobs, who was in the car, after all, say that the Gypsies killed the MPs?' I asked. Hannah had asked me not to talk about any Gypsies going out to pursue or intercept my car when I was back in the hospital. I wondered, with good reason, what she was saying about it now.

Richards was brought up short by this, or so it seemed. He paused for a moment, taking a deep breath. Then he said, 'Well, no, no, she didn't say anything about Gypsies. She ran away before anything happened. I think she knows it was wrong now.'

'Why?'

'The MPs were only trying to help her.'

'No, they weren't,' I said. 'I told you, they took her captive!'

'We believe they took your car to go and get help for you.'

'They tried to kill me. Miss Jacobs knows. Ask her!'

He didn't answer. Whatever Hannah may or may not have said, I knew she had to have told the coppers she'd been taken against her will by the MPs.

'They shot me, those "boys",' I said. 'And that is something that can't be argued with.'

'Can't it?'

I stopped breathing temporarily. Now I was frightened. I knew what he was going to say next and it terrified me.

'You aren't always aware of what's going on, Mr Hancock,' Inspector Richards said. 'Not that I'm criticising. I was in the Great War myself and I saw a lot of men go through . . . what you go through. It's . . .'

'I'm not mad, Inspector Richards,' I said, as calmly as I could. I was gazing at the statues of the saints on top of the tallboy in the corner of the room now to distract myself from the copper.

'No one is saying you are, Mr Hancock,' he replied. 'But you know that accusing our boys of anything treasonable is a serious business. We have to be very sure.'

'And you're not sure, are you?'

I heard him sigh. 'Mr Hancock, I am only anticipating what others will say. Your story, you have to admit, is fantastic, and that you and Miss Jacobs are telling it, well . . .'

A madman and a whore. No it didn't look promising, and in our new world of censorship in the name of morale, I could see his point. After all, how reporters on the *Daily Sketch* would tell the country about Nazis in the King's armed forces I didn't know. But the point, of course, was that they wouldn't, because they, like the rest of the country, would never know.

'Don't you want to find out who killed the four MPs?' I asked.

'Well, of course I do,' Richards said. 'I'm not giving up on those Gypsies, you know.'

'But why would *they* kill the MPs, eh?'

'Because, like it or not, we have to accept that one of the MPs, Williams, killed the Lee family's daughter. And, anyway, we've witnesses saw some Gypsies in Whipps Cross Road.'

'Yes, but Hannah said she *didn't* see any Gypsies on Whipps Cross Road, didn't she? And she was in my hearse.'

'Well, either she's lying or the Gypsies came along after she had gone. I'd ask her again if I knew where she was.'

Now I looked at him.

'Miss Jacobs left her digs in Mrs Harris's house in Canning Town yesterday afternoon,' Richards said. 'According to Mrs Harris, she left no forwarding address. We're searching for her now.'

I felt as if I'd been kicked in the chest. 'Are you sure?'

'Why would I lie?' he replied. 'She paid all her rent up to yesterday, then left. She took a suitcase with her. She didn't tell Mrs Harris where she was going, except that she was staying outside London.'

'No.' I shook my head. 'No, that's impossible.' Hannah didn't know anyone outside London. Beyond Dot Harris and the other 'old girls', as she calls them, in the house in Rathbone Street there was only myself and her family. But she didn't get on with her parents so she couldn't be with them. I was panicking now and couldn't think straight to imagine where she might be.

'You'll have to give us a proper statement soon, you know, Mr Hancock, especially if Miss Jacobs doesn't reappear, so I'd think carefully about what really happened that night,' Richards said, as he rose to leave. 'We all need to pull together for the good of the war effort, don't we? Can't have no frightening stories – might make people nervy. Anyway, I'd best let you rest now.'

He left, and I stared into the fire once again. I suppose I was looking for comfort. But I didn't find any. Hannah had gone and I didn't know why, not for certain. Gypsies had to be involved somewhere because she'd been so insistent that I fail to mention them to the coppers. They'd had a hand in the deaths of Sarge and the others, but not for the reason that Richards thought. The Gypsies were not Nazi sympathisers – that was ridiculous. Unless I was wrong. I did, I admit, begin to wonder about what I had seen and done in the forest. I know I don't always see and hear what others do, yet the fact remained that Sarge and the others had talked about that Nail, they had shot me and taken my motor car. However much Richards wanted the 'boys' to be innocent, they weren't. And as for making people 'nervy', surely if Nazis were active either in London or on the coast people needed to know. Well, I thought so anyway, even though I knew that the government view was probably quite different. What people know, even now, is laughable. It's just like the first lot in that respect. 'Careless talk costs lives' but so does no talk at all. Not talking means not knowing and that can be very dangerous.

For a while I racked my brains for any friends Hannah might have that I knew little about. But there was only the magician, David Green, and I was pretty sure she wouldn't be with him. But, then, even if I had known where she was I couldn't have gone after her in my condition. Every movement still gave me pain and I was very weak.

There was a knock then, and Arthur popped his smiling head around my door.

Chapter Eighteen

Inspector Richards didn't hang about. The following morning he was back on my doorstep, demanding that statement of his. He wasn't unpleasant about it but Doris, who'd told me how impatient he'd been to see me on the previous day, wasn't inclined to hurry him into the parlour, which was where I'd chosen to be that morning. With Nan and Walter's help I'd got out of bed and was now talking to Arthur about his new temporary job as a fully fledged undertaker.

'The important thing,' I said to him, 'is to maintain the dignity of the occasion. If you slip over or fall into a hole left by an incendiary, then that doesn't matter and you just carry on as if nothing has happened. Letting go of the coffin, however, war or no war, is very bad. The deceased and his or her family don't deserve that, so you watch what the bearers are doing and if they look as though they might be in trouble, you go and help them yourself.'

'Yes, Mr H.' Arthur has always looked like a stick of liquorice in his mourning suit and topper. But in the past, of course, he's always been at the back of the cortège. Now he was about to be right at the front, all six foot God knows what of him, looking like an overgrown, badly dressed infant. Spots and boils are not what you usually associate with a funeral director but that was what the funeral of Queenie Ramm was going to be treated to and that was that. Or so I thought.

Aggie had slipped into the parlour without my noticing her. When I did, though, unusually, she was smiling. She also seemed to have something hidden behind her back.

'Well, Arthur,' she said, 'what a day, eh? Conducting a funeral and you not even twenty-one.'

I saw the boy's face whiten.

'Younger than you were, Frank,' she said to me, and she was right. I hadn't conducted a funeral until I was into my thirties, when Dad's malaria got too bad for him to carry on. 'And so,' Aggie continued, 'because we love you and because my brother is a very superstitious man, I've come to give you this.'

She whipped one of her hands around and held up a long cane, topped with an ornate, familiar silver handle.

'It's your wand,' she said, as she pressed it into my hands. 'Well, it's the top of it. Nan gave it to me. She said you was so upset and wondered if I knew anyone as could help. There's this bloke down the Abbey Arms, owes me a favour . . .'

I grinned.

'So give it over to Arthur, then,' Aggie said, in the sharp way she's always had with her. And then, smiling at the boy, she said, 'You'll be all right, Arthur, now you've got the wand.'

'I know,' he said, and in spite of his lack of belief in superstition I felt he meant it. Some things, whether you believe in their 'power' or not, are just important.

I gave Arthur my wand, then waved him off to his first shot at the 'top job'. 'I won't let you down, Mr H,' he said, as he left.

Once I was alone with my sister, I gave her a cuddle. 'So, who's this fella down the pub owes you a favour, then, Ag?' I asked. I was curious to know who had fitted the handle of the old wand, which itself had been damaged in the blast, so well on to the new cane.

'Someone with a girlfriend who has a sweet tooth,' Aggie replied, with a wink. Working as she does at Tate & Lyle's sugar factory, I knew not to ask any more. All sorts of deals are done in pubs, always have been, and our local is one of the only places Aggie can get any sort of relief from her long shifts at Tate's and her not-always-happy time at home with the rest of us. She's still quite young and pretty, in spite of the shortages we have to put up with – as well as the hard conditions down at Tate's – and I've lived in hope for some time that she might meet a nice bloke who'd really look after her. But there's been no luck on that score so far.

'Frank.' She came and sat down beside me, looking serious.
'Yes?'

'Look, I know you're still not well enough to do much but . . . there's a horrible smell out the back, in the room where . . . Frank, Lily Lee's still down there and I don't know what to do with her.'

My jaw dropped. I'd forgotten all about her. There had been so much death and I'd been so ill that she had entirely slipped my mind.

'Oh, Christ, she needs burying,' I said. 'But her family . . .'

'Well, that's what I thought,' Aggie said. 'From what you've told us they're dead, aren't they?'

They were mostly, although I knew that when the parents had disappeared into the forest to escape from the MPs and aid Martin Stojka they had left their young daughters at the Eagle Pond camp. Lily still had family of sorts, and there was her sister Rosie's grave, which could be reopened to take her.

'Ag, are you doing anything?' I asked. 'Because if you're not could you go and see Ernie Sutton and tell him I need to talk to him? I'd do it myself but . . .'

'Oh, don't be daft, the telephones are down. Of course I'll do it,' Aggie said. 'Can't have that stink, Frank, not for much longer.'

She stood as if to go. 'There's that copper of yours downstairs with Doris, the one who says he's from Scotland Yard,' she said. 'Doris has kept him out so you could speak to Arthur, but I suppose you'd better talk to him now. He's been downstairs so long he's even started chatting to Stella.'

'Yes . . .' She'd talked of Richards oddly, I thought. 'What do you mean he "says he's from Scotland Yard", Ag? He *is* from Scotland Yard.'

'Yeah, I know, but he gives me the heebie-jeebies. I complained to Sergeant Hill at our station about him when you was in hospital. I was afraid all his questions'd make you ill, and they did. Anyway, I just don't like him.'

'What? Because he's a proper copper? Not a sort of a mate like Sergeant Hill?'

'Some mate!' She laughed. Aggie has more than a few friends who buy and sell things they shouldn't. 'But you're right – I probably don't like Richards 'cause he's "proper".'

But she still seemed puzzled. I thought at the time that maybe she was angry with Richards – perhaps because he'd made a pass at her. A lot of blokes do and she's rarely flattered by it. But when she showed him up, there didn't seem to be any atmosphere between them so I just got on and gave him my account of what had happened in the forest again, this time in a formal statement. He told me that I could have the Lancia back the next day. I was pleased, but I'd already decided that, car or no car, I was going to get out of the shop sooner than that.

I couldn't take another night in that Anderson – it was a flipping leaky box just waiting to become my coffin. I hoped that Ernie Sutton would do as I was going to ask him.

Just before he left, Richards said, 'Oh, we've taken a couple of male Gypsies in for questioning about the deaths of Mansard and the others. I'd like to find the Lees' daughters but they've disappeared.'

'Have they?'

'Yes. If you hear anything you'll let me know, won't you?'

'It's not likely, with me stuck here, is it, Inspector?'

'I don't know, Mr Hancock,' he said. 'Maybe the Gypsies will come to you. It wouldn't be the first time and, I believe, you still have the body of the girl Lily on your premises.'

'Yes.'

'Well, keep me informed, won't you? As yet, it's still only you and Miss Jacobs who claim to have seen the miraculous nail. The Gypsies and the remaining MPs in Mansard's company know nothing about it.' He looked me straight in the eye but without even a hint of a smile. 'In view of Miss Jacobs's disappearance it would be better for you, Mr Hancock, if someone else could confirm your story about that night. The Lee girls, having lost their parents and brothers, have no need to conceal the truth, whatever it may be. We do need to find them.'

I returned his very straight gaze with one of my own and said, 'Yes.'

'Apart from anything else, I assume those girls will want some involvement in a funeral for their relatives,' he continued. 'If not, it'll be parish dos, won't it? Seems a shame to me that they could end up in paupers' graves when the girls could have them buried decently.'

I didn't answer him. He had an entirely different view of

what had happened to me from the version I believed. I resented having to prove myself, and what I'd been through, to him.

Richards stood up, smiled, then almost immediately frowned. 'By the way, Mr Hancock,' he said, 'you've a bad smell downstairs. Your drains damaged, are they?'

Stella let him out, babbling on about how Horatio Smith 'would've killed our Frank stone dead if it hadn't been for me', as she led him down the stairs and out into the yard. Later on, when she thought I was asleep, Stella came into the parlour and stared slack-jawed into my face. I didn't know what she wanted and she didn't utter a word. It was an unnerving, almost frightening experience.

'Ernie,' I said, as soon as he came into the parlour and settled himself beside me, 'can I borrow your motor car?'

Of course, I couldn't drive myself – I still didn't have my own car – so Ernie had to do that for me. I couldn't after all, ask the police. After Richards' visit I had some important reasons for wanting to speak to the Gypsies – if I could find them – without any help from any coppers. Ernie, too, had an interest in trying to find what remained of the Lee family.

'If I've no information to the contrary, I'll have to copy what I did for Rosie's funeral. I won't perform a pauper's do – I'd rather pay for it all myself than that,' he said, as he brought his car to a halt in front of Eagle Pond. 'But I'd like to make it more personal if I can, with chosen hymns and whatever, and it would be so much better if Lily's family could be there.'

The sun was setting and a thick, almost smoggy mist had fallen across the trees. Nothing, as far as I could see, was moving in the thick undergrowth or around the pond. It was silent too, which is not something easily associated with groups of people. But as Ernie pulled me, in some pain, out of his car, I was not downhearted. I knew how easily the Gypsies could hide themselves in the forest. I also knew that once they'd spotted me they would want to talk to me too, in all probability, if only to ask me what I'd said about their fellows in police custody. And from my point of view there was another reason. The Gypsies, I hoped, might be able to tell me what Hannah had done after she'd escaped from the MPs' car. By her own admission she'd gone back into the forest where they, or some of them, had been at the time.

As Ernie and I inched forwards into the undergrowth around the pond, I told him that Hannah had disappeared.

'Well, you know, Frank, that may not be such a bad thing,' he said, as he slid an arm under my shoulder and helped me to step over a fallen log. 'She's a very nice woman, Miss Jacobs, but she is, well . . . I don't have to tell you what she is, do I?'

'What do you mean?'

He had to know that Hannah was a Jew, but I'd thought he was ignorant of the other details of her life.

'Well, what she does, her . . .'

His words made me frown. I'd never looked on Ernie Sutton as a man to judge others. 'Do you mean because she's a Jew or because she's a tom?' I asked him, I admit harshly.

'Frank,' he said, 'I'm a vicar. I have to say these things. Where would we be if we all married outside our own religion, eh?'

'You forget, Ernie,' I gasped, as the pain bit into my side, 'I don't have a religion.'

He didn't answer but made me sit on a tree-stump. Apparently even the small amount of light coming from the evening sky showed that my face was green.

'Your Aggie was right,' Ernie said, as he looked at me hard. 'You shouldn't be out. Your mum'll have my guts for garters when she finds out I've taken you off into the wild blue yonder.'

Aggie alone, as far as I was aware, had known I was going out and she hadn't been happy about it. I told her I had to in order to sort out Lily Lee's funeral with her family. She had replied that, given a choice between my health and Lily Lee's funeral, she'd rather the poor girl stink the shop to the ground rather than me have one more second's worth of pain. She hadn't got her way and soon it would be dark. Being among the trees again brought back the feelings and fears I'd had when I'd last been in the forest – with Mansard and his men, the Lees and my Hannah. I felt my breathing go and not, for once, because a raid had begun. That particular horror was not uppermost in my mind. It would come much later.

Standing over me, Ernie shook his head and was about to say something when a voice called from somewhere to me: 'Mr Undertaker.'

I cocked my head to one side, thinking that perhaps I hadn't heard right. 'What?'

Ernie, too, was frowning now. 'Did you hear that?' he said. 'It sounded like . . .'

'It's a woman's voice,' I said.

'Yes . . .'

We glanced around, our heads moving in the same direction. When we looked ahead of us again she was there with a couple of young lads, both about her own age. Beauty.

Seeing her again was, for me, like an electric shock. I made noises rather than words.

'Last time we saw each other you was nearly dead,' she said to me. '*Drabalo* Mary saved your life.'

'And you,' I said, when I'd found my voice. 'You came . . .'

'I were there,' Beauty said, nodding her head of thick black hair at me. 'Me and old Danny Boy had gone up to see how the Gentleman was getting along and to take all of them up there some food. We saw them soldiers shoot everyone.'

'Well, maybe you ought to tell the police. They don't believe me,' I said. She didn't answer.

A dart of pain hit me and I had to wait until it had subsided before I spoke again.

'We've come to speak to Lily Lee's family,' I heard Ernie say. 'Mr Hancock and I need to make arrangements with them for her burial. Where are what's left of her family?'

Beauty, I now realised – more than even the first time I'd seen her – deserved her name. She was short, nicely plump and with features not unlike those of Mary Pickford, but she was as dirty and ragged as the two frightened boys who stood to either side of her.

Ignoring Ernie, Beauty said to me, 'We'll take you to *drabalo* Mary. She'll be happy you're alive.'

If I'd thought that was all we were going to learn from this meeting or that Mary was the only person we were about to see, I would have protested. But I felt there was more to it than that. As Ernie helped me follow the Gypsies into the forest I noticed that Beauty was scanning around her, as if to check that we were not being followed. Then when the sirens signalled the nightly raid her face reflected deep and abiding terror.

'You wasn't ready to die, I could tell,' the old woman said to me, as she hung her kettle on the hook over her fire. This deep into the forest there was no one to enforce or even care about the

236

blackout, or so it seemed. 'But you needed the *gauje* medicine to help you on your way. I knew that.'

'I – I owe my life to you,' I said, panting as I spoke. We'd walked for what seemed like hours and I was done in.

She dismissed my thanks with a tut and a wave of one thin, dark brown hand.

'We've come to find what remains of the Lee family,' I said, as I let Ernie help me down on to the ground beside the old woman's fire. 'We need to bury Lily, Mr Sutton and I.'

Drabalo Mary narrowed her eyes. 'You want money?'

'No,' I said. 'Her – her parents are dead. I just want to do what's right for her. I – I want to know what her family, her sisters, want me to do. Her parents and her brothers' bodies can wait, but Lily must be buried quickly now.'

To the south of us came the distant flashes and bangs of the East End taking another hammering. I tried not to think about my family.

'I – I also n-need,' I said, 'to know for myself whether you or anyone else from your camp saw my ladyfriend Miss Jacobs after all the shooting took place up at Woodford Wells.'

The old woman gazed across the fire at Beauty, who, some time before, had come to sit silently with us, and a couple of very young girls, who were also sitting on the cold, hard ground. The boys who had escorted us to the camp with Beauty had disappeared. But there were other tents besides those of Mary and Beauty, and other Gypsies too, men, women and children many of whom I recognised from the original camp. But by the light of their several fires, Mary's included, I could see that they were more nervous than before. Some of their number had died and more, according to Inspector Richards, had been taken away by the police. I was about to speak again, to plead with

Mary to help me, when I heard a low animal growl from somewhere rather too close for my comfort. Ernie, who had also heard it, gripped one of my arms.

Drabalo Mary smiled and said, 'Don't worry, my *rais*, it's only Bruno the bear. Old Eli have him now but he'm not so happy since his real master passed away. Bears is intelligent beasts. They know when things happen.'

'Yes . . . Mary . . . Look, about that night . . .'

She smiled. 'You know about the Fourth Nail, my *rais*. And I trust the Reverend as a man of God so we have to go right back to the beginning,' she said.

Ernie, frowning, said, 'Fourth nail?'

I hadn't told him about the Nail. I hadn't seen him for long enough to get into all that. To be honest, I'd had enough trouble telling the coppers and my family, in a much shorter version, about something that I knew had to be, in part, really just a story.

'Oh, Reverend don't know nothing?'

'N-no.'

So Mary told him. Had he been an ordinary Church of England vicar, I'm sure he would've laughed. If my understanding is right, they don't approve of relics and suchlike. They think it popish. But Ernie's church is what they call 'high', which means it's practically Catholic, so he was, I could see, very interested. And I must confess that *drabalo* Mary's telling of Martin Stojka's story sent a shiver up my spine, even though I knew it from before. It was, I suppose, confirmation to me that everything I had told the police was real.

The faces of old Gypsies frequently put me in mind of my own grandparents – the Duchess's mum and dad. Lined and dry and tanned to the colour of old wood. And with the firelight and the flashes from the explosions peppering the docks illuminating her face, Mary had the look of a creature not just living in the forest but belonging to the trees.

When she'd finished her story there was a moment of silence before Ernie said, 'So what happened to this Fourth Nail, after the military policemen drove away with Captain Mansard's body?'

Drabalo Mary didn't answer him. Instead she turned to me and said, 'My boy Joe took you up the *gauje* hospital that night and he left you to them.'

'Yes, I know. But Joe wasn't the only one away from the camp that night, was he?' I said.

Mary exchanged another look with Beauty.

'You'd seen what had happened to your Gentleman, the Lees and me, hadn't you?' I said to the girl. 'I saw you go off with some others. I heard you talk about finding my car. What happened?'

Beauty's lovely face folded in on itself and she began to cry.

'Victory and Betty Lee was her dad and mum and them boys was her brothers,' Mary said. 'With Rosie and Lily gone, she's the oldest now so she had the right. Took no pleasure in it, mind, as you can see.'

I'd thought that Beauty was a ghostly form of Lily when I'd first seen her. Now I understood. She was their sister. Now there was just her and, it seemed, the three almost identical little girls at her side.

'What do you mean, "she had the right"?' I asked. 'The right to what?'

Mary was rolling herself a fag now, totally involved in it. It made me want one so I put my hand into my pocket for my

Woodbines. I was about to light up when Ernie nudged me and put his hand out. I gave him a fag and lit it for him while Beauty dried her eyes. Then, without any preamble, she said, 'We killed them, the soldiers. They wouldn't give us the Nail so we – I killed them.'

I squinted at her, the better to appreciate her smallness. Sarge and his blokes had been big, armed men. 'But you're—'

'I killed them,' she repeated. 'Coppers come and took away Danny Boy and Righteous and Job, but they never killed 'em. It was me.'

I turned to a still-confused Ernie and said, 'She's saying she killed those three MPs found murdered in my hearse. They were bristling with guns.' I turned back to Beauty. 'It just isn't possible that you did that alone. The sergeant, so the coppers told me, was torn to pieces! Did you do that?'

Yet again Beauty and Mary exchanged a look.

'That isn't the whole truth, is it?' I said. When they didn't answer I decided to take a different tack. There was, after all, something of my own that I needed to know. 'What about Hannah – Miss Jacobs? What was she doing while you were killing those men in my car?'

'Job stopped your car,' Beauty said. 'Threw hisself on it, he did. Then the rest of us come, many of us, more'n the coppers will ever know.'

'Yes, but they had guns!' I said.

'Yep, and Beauty, she had Bruno,' Mary put in.

The girl blanched. 'Mary!'

'He has to know, girl!' the old woman said. 'He ain't no *muskero*.'

'Could get us *lelled*! Bruno put down!'

'Nah!' *Drabalo* Mary looked at me and said, 'You wouldn't

240

get old Bruno killed for what he done to them as took your lady, would you?'

I didn't answer. Sarge had been torn to shreds, according to Inspector Richards. I wondered whether the bear had somehow understood that his master had been killed or whether Beauty and the others had maddened him.

'Danny Boy brung your lady back to camp,' Beauty said. 'She didn't see no killing.'

'And then? What did Miss Jacobs do after that?' According to Hannah, she had done some 'business' in the forest after she had escaped from my hearse. But her version of what had happened and Beauty's account were already different from each other.

'She stayed here with us,' Beauty said. 'Till 'twas safe for her to go. She ask a lot of questions and we told her the truth.' Her big eyes narrowed. 'Why you want to know what she done?'

I looked at Ernie, who was gazing into the fire. Even without him and even though I knew he knew, I would've found it hard to talk about what Hannah does. But this time I had to. 'She said she went with men in the forest.' I spoke quickly and averted my eyes from everyone.

'She told you that?'

'Yes.' I looked up into the girl's face again. 'Well?'

'And the coppers? She told them that too?'

'Yes.'

'Well, thank you, Jesus!' I heard *drabalo* Mary say. 'My goodness, but you've certainly got a good woman there, my *rais*! She'm a proper friend to Romany people, that lady!'

'Hannah lied.' I felt a lot of tension leave me all in one go.

'Course!' Mary laughed. At that minute I didn't find it funny.

'She a Jewish lady so she know the evil that has come in Germany. Our Gentleman, Mr Stojka, he tells of Romany people being buried alive in the forests there, he talks of Jews beaten to blood and bone on the streets.' Her eyes filled with tears. 'Us, we don't matter, but the Nail, well, that is power, and Mr Hitler he shouldn't be having any more of that, now, should he?'

'By power,' Ernie began, 'what do you mean? Does it produce miracles?'

I remembered the flash of light I'd seen as Stojka had taken the Nail out of his jacket and the suddenness with which it was embedded in Mansard's eye. I shuddered.

'The Nail gives power to those who have it,' Mary said, 'power of God, power over folk. But you shouldn't use it if your heart is black. Then it will go bad and God and Jesus will be angry with you. It's why the Stojka family always took care of the Nail. They was good folk, wanted nothing.' She looked at me then. 'Like your ladyfriend Miss Jacobs.'

'Yes.' I sighed. 'But by not telling the police the truth about what happened to her that night, to protect you, I think she has become very frightened. She's gone, the coppers say, to the country. She doesn't know anyone outside London!'

'No, but we do,' Mary said. 'And when the coppers let Danny Boy and the others go, she'll get back home after a while. She didn't like the coppers' questions – or yours.'

'So, you know where Hannah is?' I said. I was open-mouthed with shock. 'Why didn't she tell me?'

'Because she didn't want you to have to lie,' Mary said. 'She'd asked you not to talk of Romany folk when you was in the hospital and she knew you didn't like that. So she just trotted off from you without a word.' She smiled. 'She's safe. She's with travelling folk. The coppers really ain't got nothing on our boys – who'll never say a word – and they'll have to let them free by and by. Then she'll be home agin 'fore you know it.'

Many flashes in the sky were followed by the vibrations from those dropped bombs humming beneath us. For a moment the sky was almost as bright as daylight. If I'd had a full and unquestioning belief in their Holy Nail, then maybe I could have had an appreciation of how my life and the lives of many others had been either taken or turned upside-down because of it. Hitler was plainly very interested but, then, a madman like him would be. For me the Nail was something, like Lily's visions, that I didn't understand. Nevertheless I had to ask what I did next because I felt I deserved to know. 'S-so where is the Nail now?'

Ernie stared eagerly at the two women.

'Oh, it's safe,' Mary said. 'Mr Hitler won't get it now.'

'But hasn't the – the chain been b-broken?' I said. 'What I mean is, aren't the Stojka family meant to look after the Nail? Without them, surely, it can't be safe.'

Mary said nothing, watching only as what I knew, but until that moment had forgotten, dawned in my mind and showed itself on my face. As one of what Mr Lee had called Martin Stojka's 'own', the Nail would let him, or presumably some other member of his family, look after it, as he'd said, 'for a while'. And who among his family had survived the carnage at Woodford Wells? Who had been in the darkness of the forest when it happened?

'You're going to look after it until you can find a member of Stojka's family, aren't you?' I said to Beauty Lee.

'The Gentleman has brothers, dead now,' the girl said, 'but as for their *chavies*, we don't know.'

'There's a sister too, Maria Stojka,' Mary added. 'Maybe when this war is over and that German devil and his generals are dead, Beauty and the girls and me, we can find that family again.'

'And what if you can't?' I asked.

'We will,' Mary replied, with complete confidence in her voice.

'What if we lose the war?'

'That won't happen,' Mary said. 'Ain't the way the world works.'

I looked into the fire. The sky was dark again now and the drone of German bombers was moving out towards the east. Although the all-clear had yet to sound to let the city know the raid was officially over, I knew that it was. The bombers had come, done what they had to, and now they were going back to Germany again – for a little while. They, or others like them, would be back.

'But we're losing,' I said. 'We're dying.'

'Frank.' I felt one of Ernie's hands on my shoulder. 'Frank, you have to believe . . .'

I gazed up into his clear blue eyes and I said, 'I can't.'

A movement across the other side of the fire caught my attention: Beauty putting one of her hands in her blouse. Normally I wouldn't have noticed, but the girl leaned across the flames towards me and showed me something that lay in the palm of her hand.

This time the Nail didn't glow. It just dripped a thick, dark liquid into the flames, which sizzled and sang as she held it there.

'My God!' I heard Ernie say. 'Is that . . .'

'The Fourth Nail, yes,' Beauty said. 'See how it bleeds?' And then she looked right at me and said, 'That is the true blood of Christ, Mr Undertaker. It bleeds for us that our suffering might one day be at an end. 'Tis a good thing, a pure thing . . .'

I contemplated the long, dark spike as the liquid oozed from its ancient, stubby head in what was, I admit, a most miraculous fashion. But even then my brain was searching for how it was done, eyes raking the girl's hand for signs of injury.

'You must have faith in the power of the good,' Beauty said.

'But only if you're a bit stupid.' It was a male voice. A little sharp like a Londoner's, but not as harsh as that. It certainly wasn't in the least bit countrified, like the Gypsies' way of speech. I didn't even have to turn to see who it was, though, because he'd already moved himself between me and the fire and taken hold of Beauty's wrist in one of his big, hard copper's hands.

Chapter Nineteen

'What are you doing here?' I asked Inspector Richards. Just beyond the fire I could see that Beauty's face was contorted with pain as the policeman twisted and pummelled the hand with the Nail in its grasp.

Ernie Sutton, ever the gentleman, jumped to his feet and said, 'Stop that! You're hurting her!'

But Richards's other hand held a gun that he pointed very quickly at the clergyman.

I swallowed hard to lubricate my throat, then said, 'You've been looking for the Nail all the time.'

But Richards wasn't listening to me. 'Give it!' he said to Beauty, as he dragged her hand into the flames below. Beauty screamed. I looked at *drabalo* Mary, my mind shouting that she wasn't doing anything to help Beauty Lee. It was only then that I realised Richards wasn't alone.

'Thank you very much, Miss Lee!' Richards held the Nail aloft so that the three men with him could see it.

Beauty, now in the arms of her little sisters, snarled and cursed at him as she nursed her injured hand with her undamaged fingers.

Sitting there watching all of this unfold in front of me, I'd never felt so useless in my life. In fact, not only was I useless I was also, I imagined, the reason why Richards was where he was now.

'You followed me,' I said, as the blood from the Nail rolled down his hand and on to his wrist.

'Your barmy cousin told me where you were,' Richards said, not taking his eyes off the Nail. '"Silly old Frank might want to go out, but we know that he shouldn't," is what I said to her. "But don't you worry your auntie or your cousins about it, love," I said. "You just come over to my car, parked round the back of good old Frank's shop, and you tell me. I'll take care of it for you."' He laughed.

Bloody stupid Stella!

'I work for Scotland Yard, you see,' he continued. 'People trust us. I knew you'd come looking for these Gyppos. Still got poor Lily's body and, of course, I'd put a lot of worries into your mind about what you had and hadn't seen the night you got shot. I knew if they were here they'd speak to you. All we had to do was follow.'

'So why do you want the Nail?' I asked, as one of Richards's men, a chap of about forty in plainclothes, pushed Ernie Sutton back towards the ground with the stock of his pistol. 'Is it money – or are you a friend of Herr Hitler, like Captain Mansard?'

Richards smiled. 'I'm a bit of both.'

'Oh, well, that's a new one on me,' I said.

'Mansard was put in charge of recovering this item and he failed,' Richards said. 'If you and the Jewess hadn't survived, we'd never have known where to start. You were a real stroke of luck.'

'Oh, good. So, are you saying there's groups of you Nazis?' I said, getting angry in spite of all my pain. 'You're all over the shop!'

Richards bent down and pushed his face into mine. 'We didn't just fuck off at the end of the thirties, Mr Hancock. And if you're wondering how we get into the jobs and places that we do, remember that our leader is a baronet.'

'Mosley's in prison!' Ernie said. 'Best place for him too.'

'Oh, shut up, Vicar, for Christ's sake!' Richards said. 'Can't you people see how wrong all your dealing with Jews and Gypsies and other filthy types is? We have a chance here, with Adolf Hitler, to clean up our countries and—'

'Grab whatever the Jews, the Gypsies and other dark types we don't much like have and take it for ourselves,' I said.

He gave me such a contemptuous look that I was forced to turn away.

'Well, you would say that, wouldn't you, you dirty little wog?' he said. 'God, I've been aching to say that to you, Hancock!' And then he smiled at one of his men. 'Mr Saville?'

'Yes, Inspector?'

'Go and tell the others they can make a start, will you?'

'Yes, sir.' He moved off in the direction of the larger part of the Gypsy camp.

'We've more blokes over there,' Richards explained. 'There's a lot of us.'

'All for one small piece of metal that bleeds,' I said, as I glanced once again at the still red and sticky thing in Richards's hand. Because I hadn't actually seen what had happened between Stojka and Captain Mansard, I still had it in my head that perhaps the Nail might attack a person who stole it in order to protect itself. But, of course, it didn't, because that was bonkers. It sat in his hand as he talked about our deaths.

'Once we've finished you lot off we'll be on our way,' he said. He looked at Ernie and frowned. 'Sorry about you, of course,

248

Vicar, but if we're to get this treasure and ourselves out to the estuary tonight . . . We've people there waiting for us.'

'To take you to Germany?' Ernie asked.

'Well, we can hardly go back to Scotland Yard, now, can we?' Richards said. 'We've only got a few hours before they realise something's gone wrong.'

'How do you know that honest coppers from Scotland Yard haven't followed you?' I asked.

'Because I'm a very senior officer,' Richards said. 'My guv'nors trust me. And those who don't trust me share my beliefs.' He laughed, then looked at the other two blokes with him and frowned. 'What's Saville doing, for God's sake?'

'Don't know, Guv.'

'Ah . . .'

'So, who are you meeting out in the estuary, then?' I said. No one, I think, wants to die without knowing as much as possible about why it's happening. 'We've had MPs and coppers who've turned out to be Nazis. Who else? A judge, couple of priests . . .'

Richards smiled. 'Mr Lovett makes his humble living fishing for cockles,' he said. 'We have people in all walks of life who want to help us – you'd be surprised – many of them high up too, especially in the police. We don't bother ourselves with recruiting silly little people from places like your local cop shop, Mr Hancock.'

I saw Beauty's eyes widen, and I thought it was with fear so I glanced around to see which of Richards's men was pointing his gun at her. I was about to ask him – I knew in vain – to let the girl and her sisters go. But as it happened Beauty's eyes looked as they did for quite another reason.

'You know, you should think twice or more about taking the

Michael out of stations like Plaistow,' Sergeant Hill said, as he walked towards Richards with one hand out in front of him. 'I'll have that weapon if—'

Richards laughed. 'I can shoot you along with this lot.' And then I saw his face drop. We were not alone, I found, as I looked around the fire, first at the Gypsies and then at Richards's men. There were other coppers too, some in uniform I recognised from Plaistow, and some in plainclothes, with guns, I did not.

'Your immediate guv'nor don't, I'm afraid, neither trust nor agree with you, Mr Richards, and if you want to know where your Mr Saville and them other blokes of yours are, they're with that other group of officers over there.' He pointed towards the larger Gypsy camp. 'Under arrest, for treason.'

I thought that Richards, if not the blokes with him, might put up a fight. But then I think that he recognised some of the faces of the men with guns who now surrounded us. They'd probably worked with him at Scotland Yard. And, if that was so, he had betrayed them as much, if not more than, the rest of us.

But although he gave the gun to Sergeant Hill, seemingly with no resistance, the Nail proved a bit more tricky. When the sergeant moved forward to take it from him, Richards stepped backwards and clutched the gory thing to his chest.

Sergeant Hill sighed. 'Look, mate,' he said to Richards, 'hanging on to what isn't yours ain't going to do you no good. Give it to me.'

'No.' Richards stepped back towards the edge of the fire.

'It's no use to you!' Sergeant Hill persisted. 'You don't know what it is or how to use it. Give it—'

'No!'

'Give it to the sergeant, please, Inspector,' one of the

plainclothes men said, as he trained his pistol on Richards. 'I'd hate to have to shoot you, sir.'

Richards looked mad. Before, had I been asked, I would've said he had to be one of the sanest men on the face of the earth. But he wasn't now. Ernie Sutton opened his mouth but before he could speak, Richards said, 'Save it, Vicar.' Then the Nail was in the fire. The inspector's body was between me and it, so I hadn't seen him drop it, but he must have done so. And then he ran. He was pursued and he was asked to stop and give himself up twice before they shot him. Having started firing, however, it was as if they couldn't stop. Once he was down, at least five shots made sure that he would never get up again. Ernie, his hands over his ears, shivered with fright as I watched Sergeant Hill look straight ahead as if nothing was happening.

I couldn't understand it. 'He was a Nazi,' I said. 'He could've told you things!'

'I think that Mr Lovett the humble cockle-fisher'll be able to fill in quite a few gaps, Mr Hancock,' Sergeant Hill replied.

'You were listening . . .'

'We were right behind the lot of you, all the way,' he said. 'Bent coppers don't deserve to live, they—' And then I saw his face crease as he pointed towards the fire and said, 'Look!'

Beauty Lee had both hands in the flames. Her face, calm and cool as a cucumber, was gazing downwards as her hands grasped the Nail. It was almost as if the fire had suddenly, to her, taken on the character of cold water. And as she pulled the Nail out of the flames she appeared to be unhurt.

'When the right person have it, Nail can't do him or her no harm,' *drabalo* Mary said, in answer to my silent question. 'Coppers best leave what ain't theirs to those who's meant to have it.'

Beauty Lee placed the bloody Nail in the pocket of her skirt, then returned to the arms of her sisters.

'This is Inspector Berger from Scotland Yard,' Sergeant Hill said, as he introduced a short, Jewish bloke in plainclothes to Ernie and myself. *Drabalo* Mary shoved a cup into the sergeant's hand. 'Ah, tea,' he said. 'Thank you, my dear.'

The old woman, who'd already given the rest of us drinks from her kettle, sat down with Ernie and me, then turned expectantly to Inspector Berger. The Scotland Yard man sat on the ground and said, 'Richards's original boss, a bloke called Brown, had been in with Mosley's lot back in the thirties. He got his cards but we didn't know for certain about Richards until he started getting involved with you, Mr Hancock.'

'Me?'

The light from *drabalo* Mary's fire threw his sharp features into deep shadow, making him black and red, devil-like – although I knew that what I was seeing was only frightening the Christian side of my brain. In India some of the devils have white faces, and features that are fat and bloated, rather than sharp. But at that moment Berger was every inch the terrifying fictional Jewish figure that Herr Hitler is so fond, it is said, of portraying.

'Some months ago the Yard got intelligence that someone was in this country carrying a religious relic what Hitler wanted. The Führer's keen on that sort of thing, so we had to look for it. But when we was told that this Martin Stojka was a Gypsy we had to think very hard about how we might find him.'

'They do look out for their own, the Romany people,' Sergeant Hill said, without thinking. Then, suddenly remembering where he was, and who he was with, he turned to Mary and said, 'That being a good thing, of course.'

Mary grunted.

'Every force in the country was looking for Martin Stojka,' Berger continued.

'The photograph I was shown of him was a bad likeness,' I said.

'Which didn't help. But then suddenly along comes this Captain Mansard of the Military Police saying as how he'd seen Stojka up in Epping Forest. He hadn't managed to catch him but he was convinced that he was being hidden there by fellow Gypsies. The MPs were already up in the forest searching for deserters so it was thought best, as I was told then, to let them carry on and find Stojka at the same time. I suppose Mansard must've seen him, although he never found him again until the night both he and Stojka died.'

'I can tell you a bit about how that might have happened in a little while,' I said, and glanced at Mary, who shrugged as if to say, 'Tell him about the Head or not, it's all the same to me.' Once he was found, was Stojka to be interned or imprisoned?'

'Neither,' Berger replied. 'For our part, the police told the public that Stojka was a German what needed to be interned. He was frightened, trusted no one. We just needed to get him in so we could ask him about Hitler, who, we'd heard, he had met. It was Mansard who called him a spy, so people'd help him find Stojka and what Stojka had. We were a bit perturbed when Sergeant Hill reported to the Yard what he'd heard Mansard was saying, but Inspector Richards, who was the contact between ourselves and the Military Police, wasn't unduly worried so we let Mansard get on with it.'

Ernie Sutton said, 'You didn't know that either Richards or

Mansard was a traitor? Was it a coincidence that they were working together?'

Berger put his hand into his coat pocket and took out a packet of fags, which he offered around before he replied. 'No, of course it wasn't,' he said. 'This business goes a lot higher than Richards.'

One of the men standing behind Inspector Berger cleared his throat very obviously.

'But I can't tell you anything about that because me and my guv'nors still have to deal with it.'

'Guv?'

A group of coppers were carrying away Richards's body.

'Take it to the car,' Berger said, to the tallest bloke. 'Then come back here. You and me'll need to have a chat about this Lovett bloke Richards was due to go and meet.'

'Chances are if he fishes cockles, he's from near Southend,' the tall man replied.

'We'll have a little chat with Saville and some of them other charmers Richards had recruited in a bit,' Berger said. The group carrying Richards's body moved back into the undergrowth.

I wondered who 'high up' at the Yard had been involved with Richards and, by extension, Mansard too. It was cold anyway and I was still quite ill that night, but the thought that one of our top coppers might be a traitor made me feel still colder. I hadn't realised that so many people had leanings towards Hitler and the Nazis. But as Richards had said, where had I thought all of the thousands who had followed Mosley in the thirties had gone?

'It all went wrong for Mansard on that night you got shot, Mr Hancock.' Quite an understatement, but I nodded. 'Richards, of course, was the obvious choice to investigate a very queer do, so that was what happened.'

'When did you realise something wasn't right?'

'It happened bit by bit. The MPs being found dead in your hearse and you turning up alive at Whipps Cross sent Richards into a frenzy. The whole thing was queer, especially when it was discovered that Martin Stojka was one of the victims. We couldn't work out how it had all gone so wrong for Mansard. We asked the Military Police for Mansard's records. It was me who recognised the name back from his Mosley days. Called himself Mr Clive Gillespie in the thirties.'

I told Berger about my Hannah and her experiences with Mansard/Gillespie.

'It was Dr Craig at Whipps Cross hospital who really made some of us up the Yard, mainly Richards's guv'nor, think about Richards in the way we did,' Berger continued. 'According to Richards, Mansard and his boys had only killed Stojka and the other Gypsies because they were defending theirselves. The Gypsies was the aggressors.'

Drabalo Mary, who had been joined again by Beauty Lee, made a low, disgusted growl in her throat.

'Dr Craig said that the way the Gypsies had been found showed that they had been executed. They were unarmed and they'd been executed,' Berger said. 'You, Mr Hancock, according to Richards, was either a traitor yourself or raving mad.'

'Which was when the Yard got back to me,' Sergeant Hill said. 'I told them you was neither a traitor nor raving.'

'Just mad?'

Sergeant Hill shuffled his feet uneasily.

'So I went down to Plaistow to see for myself,' Inspector

Berger said. 'I talked to Sergeant Hill, who, I knew, had had doubts about Mansard from the off and who also had an . . . an "interest", shall we say? Then when I come out of the station I took a little ball of chalk around your manor, Mr Hancock. Given the times we live in now, I was surprised to see so many of Richards's young officers apparently looking at your gaff for no good reason. You was wounded, as far as I knew, and couldn't be going anywhere. But Richards had to think that you was, so I had you watched meself. I told Sergeant Hill that if you did move he was to call the Yard and tell me. When the call came, I followed Sergeant Hill and his boys.'

'Who followed Richards first and then us?' I said.

'Yes, Mr Hancock.'

'Not really knowing what you were going to find.'

'No, not really. Something was wrong but I couldn't say for certain that Richards was a traitor until tonight. That's why we held back for so long – so we could understand what was going on. The Nail, as far as we could tell, was missing, and we had to follow any person who might possibly lead us to it, same as Richards, really.'

'Richards condemned himself out of his own mouth,' Ernie said.

'Yes, sir, he did.'

'So how much of our conversing did you hear then?' *drabalo* Mary, suddenly involved again, asked Berger.

'All of it. From the moment Miss Lee met Mr Hancock and the Reverend here.'

Mary looked at Beauty who said, '*Oh, dordi!*'

'Lucky for us your Bruno was well chained down tonight, wasn't it?'

But it was more than just the bear's life at stake now, if

256

Berger really had heard all of our conversation. It was Beauty Lee too, and she knew it.

'Can I give Mary here the Nail afore you take me away?' she asked.

'No,' he said. 'Give it to Sergeant Hill. Do it now.' It was plain that he would brook no argument.

Sergeant Hill extended his hand towards the girl and spoke at some length to her in pure Romany.

Chapter Twenty

For once I was just an ordinary mourner at a slightly unusual funeral. Arthur was conducting, and making a jolly good job of it. It wasn't easy, with so many Gypsies jostling for position around the grave, but Arthur handled it all very calmly and with dignity, and I was proud of him. Lily Lee's funeral had been organised in one single morning with most of the responsibility falling on to Arthur and Ernie Sutton's shoulders. But it had needed to be like that, because poor Lily's body wouldn't wait any longer. I heaved a sigh of relief when Walter and Doris's uncle Wolfie lowered her coffin on to her sister Rosie's. As soon as the ropes were pulled out from under the coffin and the bearers had moved away, the Gypsies came with their offerings of coins and banknotes, which they threw on to the lid of the coffin. Lily's sisters, Beauty included, howled to their two dead siblings below.

'Won't be long before you have to do this all over again, will it, Mr H?' Sergeant Hill whispered to me, as we watched the Gypsies take part in the final drama of Lily Lee's short life.

'No, it won't,' I said. Only the night before we'd all been in the forest with Inspector Richards and his murderous gang of traitors. Now we were burying Lily, and the next day I was back at work again for the funerals of Mr and Mrs Lee, all their boys and Rosie's husband Edward. Horatio Smith had already been buried by Albert Cox and his Canning Town firm, which left only the once mysterious Martin Stojka. But I knew nothing about how he was to be disposed of, beyond that Sergeant Hill – a man I now realised I didn't truly know at all – was to arrange it.

'Come on,' Sergeant Hill said, to the small group of coppers, from Plaistow and Scotland Yard, who stood inside the cordon that many other coppers had thrown around these proceedings. 'Take a stone each and place them round the grave. Be careful not to leave any gaps.'

The Gypsies moved aside to let a very old custom with their people take place. Stones around a grave, they believe, can restrain the dangerous *muló* or spirit of the dead, should it wish to move among the living once again. The coppers involved, young and old, did their job with reverence.

Inspector Berger was one of the Scotland Yard contingent, looking on, like me, with admiration. 'I don't know what we'd've done without Sergeant Hill,' he said. 'Only he knew the real importance of Martin Stojka and his family.'

I'm used to it being obvious what a person is. Everyone can see what I am and I've never tried to pretend otherwise – I've never had to. Sergeant Hill, with his fair skin, blue eyes and military moustache, was a normal English bloke, as far as I'd known. And his father had been just that. His mother, though, had come originally from Budapest. Word in some quarters was that she was a Jewess. But she wasn't. Still living right up to this day, Irene Hill is a Gypsy, who had taught her son all about the customs and beliefs of the European travelling people. So he knew what was expected of him at Lily Lee's funeral.

'God knows what Sergeant Hill and myself and maybe you,

too, Mr Hancock, would have to endure in Hitler's Germany,' Berger said, as he watched Ernie Sutton bless the graves of the Lee sisters once more. 'You know Hill speaks the Romany lingo, don't you? Incredible.'

I hadn't known – or, rather, the few Romany words I had heard him say I had either forgotten or dismissed. We use such a lot of words from all over the globe down in our manor – Yiddish, Hindi, Romany, Arabic. 'Well, at least old Herr Hitler won't be able to get his hands on the Nail now,' I said.

'No.' Berger's expression told me he thought all that sort of thing was so much tosh.

'Did Sergeant Hill—'

'I don't know where he's keeping the thing, only that it's safe,' Berger said, and held up a hand as if to bat away my question. 'The Lee girls can have it back when this war's over, if it ever is.' Then, seeing that Sergeant Hill and his men had completed their circle of stones, he excused himself and set off in the direction of the cordon of uniformed officers who hid what we were doing from public gaze. In spite of her death and all the doubt that had been cast on her experiences by the arrest of Gypsies in her group, not to mention the subsequent deaths of her parents and brothers, there was still a lot of interest in and some reverence for Lily Lee. Not a few people had wanted to pay their respects when they'd seen a load of Gypsies on the move up to the East London cemetery. The coppers made them all stand behind the cordon until the ceremony was over. Now, for a short time, they would be let in to pay their respects. Women and girls, mainly, placed tiny bunches of half-dead flowers beside the hole the grave-diggers were now filling in. I saw that it was getting dark.

'We're having a wake for everyone tomorrow, after Mum and everyone else's funeral,' Beauty Lee said to me. 'Will you come?'

She'd appeared at my side, suddenly dry-eyed and calm.

'Yes,' I said. We both watched the *gauje* pass with their little offerings, their crosses and their tears. 'Beauty, do you have any idea what Lily saw over by that tree?'

'No. I know what I believe about it, though,' she said.

'What's that?'

'I think it were Rosie's *muló*,' she said, 'but not come to do our Lily harm. Rosie and Lily loved each other and Rosie's Edward. Rosie just didn't want to go. Her *muló* were a good thing, I think. It were love.'

The *gauje* crossed themselves, some even bowed to the grave before they moved on. But that was all right. The Virgin Mary, even if you don't believe in her, like me, is a symbol of love and suffering. Lily and her 'virgin' Rosie had suffered in their own ways and so, to my mind, what these unknowing *gauje* were doing wasn't wrong. For a short time, Lily Lee had given them the miracle all people at war want: a sign of some sort that we are right and also that we are not alone.

I travelled home to the shop in Inspector Berger's car – Arthur took the Lees back to their camp in the hearse. I was pleased to have the opportunity to talk to the Scotland Yard man away from the funeral proceedings. I still had a lot of questions from the previous night. He had not, after all, arrested Beauty Lee for the murders of the MPs she had committed in my hearse and, I now found, he had let the other Gypsies in police custody go too.

'Beauty Lee killed men who were traitors. She's a heroine,' Berger said, as his car bounced up and down in the many potholes that scar almost every road now. 'Not that she's saying anything about it herself.'

'Yes, I understand that,' I said, 'but how is the Yard going to explain all those deaths up in the forest and in Leyton?'

He pulled the car into Bethell Avenue and brought it to a halt. 'We're not,' he said, as he turned a pair of cold eyes on me.

'But—'

'Mansard and the others were killed in the line of duty, probably by gangsters they'd disturbed during the course of their investigations in the forest. There's a lot of black-market activity in this part of town.'

'Yes,' I said, 'but that story isn't true, is it?'

Berger sighed. 'Mr Hancock,' he said, 'we live at a time when a few people have to make big decisions for many. Mr Churchill is one and I, to a lesser degree, am another. What has to be true for the many is that the MPs, our boys, were killed by nasty criminal types and that the poor Gypsies also suffered their losses. Lily Lee indeed saw the Virgin Mary, which means that God is on our side and all's right with the world.' He pointed a finger into my face. 'You say nothing, Mr Hancock. I can put you into Claybury if I feel so inclined.'

I don't like being threatened but even I am realistic enough to know when I'm well and truly beaten. I kept my trap shut.

'Censorship is a useful thing,' Berger said, as he started the engine of the car again. 'It has its place.'

I wanted to say that from what we'd heard Herr Hitler would probably agree with him on that score. But, again, I didn't even think of opening my mouth.

Then suddenly, as he turned into the Barking Road, he said, 'Oh, I've sent a car to fetch your friend Miss Jacobs.'

'Hannah!'

'With an old bloke who makes them models of people and animals you see in fairgrounds, a Gyppo. Lives in a village up round Harlow called Matching Green. Right out in the sticks, apparently.'

The Gypsies had said they'd hidden Hannah well.

'We need to know the truth from her,' Berger said.

I had to say, 'Why's that?'

He drew the car to a halt outside the shop and turned his ice cold eyes to me again. 'Because if we do survive this war, one day, a long time into the future, people will be able to get into our files and they will deserve to know the truth. We found the cockle-fishing traitor Richards told you about at Leigh-on-Sea, in Essex, and he told us some interesting things about one of my guv'nors. He'll leave the force, and for years no one will know what happened to him. Then they'll open the files. But we'll all be dead and gone by that time. Beyond any blame, you see.'

'And that makes what you're doing all right?'

'Anything that means you and yours survive is all right in a war, Mr Hancock,' Berger said, as I pulled myself slowly out of his car. 'You were in the first lot, you should know that.'

'The first lot went far beyond survival, Inspector Berger. Don't talk to me about it.'

I began to walk towards my battered, boarded-up shop, glad that Beauty Lee wasn't going to prison but aware of how different things might have been under 'normal' circumstances. Outside this war, Beauty Lee, the Gypsy, would have hanged for what she did and no 'excuses' about avenging her parents or recovering any holy relic would have saved her. Not even Berger, the Jew, would have put in a good word. But, then, there are people who are not Christian, there are foreigners and then there are Gypsies ... They are always at the bottom of everyone's pile.

'I'll tell Miss Jacobs you want to see her, shall I?' Berger called to me.

I didn't glance back at him, but I did say, 'Yes.'

'They don't call this a wake, it's a *pomana*,' Sergeant Hill said, as he tucked into a large wedge of rabbit pie. 'It's a meal they hold just after a person's death, and then at so many weeks and months until a year has passed. Only then, after that final meal, can the mourning stop.'

It was funny seeing him sitting on the ground in his copper's uniform. He didn't seem comfortable, in spite of his Gypsy blood.

'That's the very old way that is,' *drabalo* Mary said, with a big measure of admiration in her voice. But Sergeant Hill was going to be looking after the Gypsies' most prized possession for the foreseeable future so it was encouraging that Mary and Beauty liked him. Not that they'd had much choice in the matter. Berger had told Beauty to hand over the Nail to Sergeant Hill and, once he'd spoken to her and she'd been told the Romany-speaking copper was himself a *diddikai*, part-Gypsy, she had done so. Compared to the alternative of her dragging it around the countryside with her, always afraid that it might be stolen, it made sense. If and when this war ends, Sergeant Hill will give the Nail back to Beauty whose ambition is to journey to Germany and find whatever might remain of the Stojka family. As the girl says, any Gypsy can have the Nail but it only belongs to someone with the name of Stojka.

We'd had to borrow three vehicles from other local firms to get all of the dead Lee family members to the cemetery. I'd been in charge for the first time since I'd been shot, and although I'd felt tired, I'd managed, with the help of my lads, Albert Cox and his boys from Canning Town and a couple of men from a firm in Bow, to get the Gypsies where they needed to be. Now, sitting on the ground beside my mother and Doris Rosen, both of whom had come to pay their respects to the Lees, I smoked in silence as others filled their faces from the Gypsies' meagre larder. Still weak, I hardly noticed when Beauty Lee came to sit next to me.

'We're leaving tomorrow,' she said. 'Once we've dealt with Bruno.'

I looked at her questioningly.

'Mary give him summat to send him off gently this morning,' Beauty said. 'Old Eli was with him when he went.'

I wondered if I'd heard her right. 'You killed Bruno?'

She pointed to where her little sisters were smashing plates against a tree. 'We have to get rid of all the dead people's things,' she said matter-of-factly. 'Bruno was my dad's bear.'

'Yes, but when you told me that Bruno had,' I lowered my voice to a whisper, 'killed that sergeant, you were frightened I'd tell the coppers and get the bear destroyed.'

'Couldn't have the coppers kill him, no,' Beauty said. 'That's wrong. They wouldn't bury him right. Creatures have *mulós* too, you know. We'll do him proper tonight with money and stones and a few old spells from *drabalo* Mary. Then we'm be off.'

'Where to?'

'Travelling. Go up by old 'Zekiel's first.'

'Is that the—'

'Now, Mr Hancock,' the girl said, smiling now in spite of her sorrow, 'if there was one thing you wanted what would that be?'

'Why?'

Beauty shrugged again. 'Just askin'.'

The Duchess, who had been listening to the last part of our conversation, said, 'Well, for me it would have to be an end to this war.'

I took one of her hands in mine. 'Well, that's about the best thing anyone can hope for. So I suppose . . .'

'Yes, but what else is there?' Beauty asked. 'There must be something.'

I heard some noises behind my back, but I didn't take any more notice of them than I did of the chatter and clatter around the Gypsies' food and drink. Sergeant Hill was still chewing rabbit pie (probably not alone in wondering where the poor beast had come from), Doris was listening quietly to one of the Gypsy girls telling her about her life, and people were pouring beer, smoking and talking of anything other than the dead, as is the Gypsy way.

'I'd like to see my friend Hannah – Miss Jacobs,' I said, after a while, 'but I expect she's still answering questions from the police. I'll see her in a bit, I'm sure.'

I had asked Berger to tell Hannah to come and see me and I was sure that at some point she would. In the meantime there was nothing more I could do.

'I'm sure you will too,' Beauty replied. Then she looked behind me and said, ''Zekiel?'

Following her gaze I found myself staring into the face of a tiny, wrinkled old man. He wore a red tailcoat and top hat like a circus ringmaster and he was standing in front of a booth like the one I'd seen in Lily's tent, with the Head, Martin Stojka. For a moment I gazed at Beauty, horrified. But strangely, to me, the girl smiled.

'Mr Ezekiel Gaskin of Matching Green, in Essex, is a magician and a maker of illusions,' she said. 'But this, Mr Hancock, is real.'

The little man stood in front of the booth and waved his arms. When he moved away I saw Hannah's head floating on the table. I heard my mother say, 'Oh, my goodness, how very clever!' But I was speechless.

Hannah saw me, smiled and said, 'You know, H, that Mr Gaskin can walk in front of this table just like that Arab bloke Davy Green once saw.'

And to prove that this was so, Ezekiel Gaskin walked in front of the table. Try as I might I couldn't see a reflection of anything underneath Hannah's floating head.

'Bloody . . .'

'So, do you think we should tell David Green about this or not?' Hannah said.

Epilogue

Sergeant Hill doesn't talk about the Fourth Nail to anyone except me, and then not often.

'I do take it out and look at it occasionally,' he said, a little while ago. But he didn't say whether he did it at the station or at his home. And I didn't ask. I have Hannah back; my mother, sisters and even Stella are managing. Doris copes. Ernie Sutton has now learned his lesson and has become genuinely fond of my Jewish girl. I don't need to know much more.

The sergeant, I've known for years, lives with his mother on Tredegar Road, Bow. I'm not often up that way, but last night, after the bombing, I found myself there, among tall old houses all blacked out and silent. I couldn't've told which one was Sergeant Hill's had my life depended on it. I wasn't even thinking of him as I began to recover from my latest terrified run. I was going home until something caught my attention. It was a light and it was in a ground-floor window of one of the houses. I looked around for a warden, as you do. But then I saw what the light was and I just watched it until the blackout curtain was pulled to shut me out, and presumably the rest of the world.

Sergeant Hill and his mother, Irene, were sitting in a

darkened room. On the table between them lay something light and bright that I had last seen in the hands of Martin Stojka. Once more, the Fourth Nail was glowing brightly.

Author's Notes

Romanies (Gypsies)

A bout a thousand years ago, those people commonly known as *Gypsies* began their long wandering journey from their place of origin in northern India to the Middle East, Europe and beyond. Their proper name of Romany was unknown in the lands through which they travelled and, due to the different way they looked and behaved, people in Europe called them *Egyptians* or *Gypsies*. They were not always welcomed or understood and many of the legends that surrounded them were sinister in character. Gypsies, it was said, had forged the nails that had been used to crucify Jesus. Over the centuries they were classed as sorcerers, witches, criminals and agents of the Ottoman Empire. They were frequently persecuted and sometimes put to death. However it wasn't until Adolf Hitler became Chancellor of Germany in 1933 that a nation took systematic action against the Romany travellers.

Romanies do not call what happened to their people in places like Dachau a holocaust, it is called the *Porrajmos* – the devouring. Designated *asocials* by Hitler, the Romanies were worked to death, experimented upon by Josef Mengele, beaten, shot, gassed and, in some cases, even buried alive. Because of the shifting nature of their existence, no one really knows how many Romanies died in Hitler's death camps. Estimates range from between a quarter of a million people to one and a half million souls. The memory of the *Porrajmos* haunts the Romany people still and in this book I have turned an old legend about them around in order to explore their courage and resilience as well as the suffering they endured during the Second World War.

The language used by Romanies across the world is an Indo-Aryan tongue that has its roots in Punjabi and Hindi. There are many spoken dialects, three of which are to be found in Europe: *Dom*, spoken by the Domari in central and eastern Europe; *Lom*, by the Lomarvren of central Europe; and *Rom* spoken by the Romani of Western Europe. However these dialects do share many similarities and so my Romany characters, who come from western and eastern Europe, understand each other's dialects and customs. This may not always be so, but I have used this device in order to facilitate the reader's understanding and, I hope, enjoyment of the book.

East End Anti-Fascism and The Battle of Cable Street

Sunday 4 October 1934

I n the 1930s a British politician and aristocrat called Baronet Oswald Mosley (1896–1980) rose to prominence as the leader of a party called the British Union of Fascists. Otherwise known as the Blackshirts, these people modelled themselves on Hitler's followers and were violent anti-Semites who took great delight in terrorising the poor Jewish population of the East End. And although when caught the perpetrators of these acts were punished, when Mosley wanted to march his Blackshirts through the East End in what he assured the authorities would be a peaceful way, he was given permission to do so. Local Jewish and Communist organisations had other ideas and when the marchers reached the mainly Jewish road called Cable Street in Stepney, they fought to keep the Fascists out. So violent was the struggle that the Commissioner of Police was eventually forced to curtail Mosley's march and that night a great victory over Fascism was celebrated in pubs all over the East End. But many, many people did march with Mosley on that day and I have often wondered where they went after the defeat of

Cable Street. This book, though fictional, addresses that question.

The Disembodied Head Illusion

What is referred to in the novel as the 'Head' or 'Egyptian Head' illusion is based upon a trick that was first performed by the English magician Colonel Stodare in London in 1865. This trick, which was called the 'Sphinx', involved the apparently sentient disembodied head of an ancient Egyptian man appearing on the top of a table. It could move its eyes and speak and at the end of the act, when Stodare covered it up with a box, the Sphinx disappeared leaving behind it only a small pile of ashes. How was it done?

First take one four-legged, round-topped table and remove one leg. Position the table so that one of the remaining legs points straight out towards the audience, with the other legs at equal distances to either side. Then fix two mirrors from the front leg to those at either side at 90-degree angles. The mirrors must be clean and must be constructed to cover the whole distance between the bottom of the table and the floor. Behind the mirrors, cut a hole in the table top through which the head may appear and then surround the table on three sides with a booth and/or curtains which are reflected into the mirrors. Then place the performer under the table until the audience is distracted from the set by a puff of smoke or other mis-directional device, whereupon his or her head pushes through the hole in the top of the table. The mirrors reflecting the curtains at the side of the set create the illusion that the audience is looking underneath the table and the head to the curtains at the rear. However the magician performing this trick must be careful where he or she stands in relation to the set lest his legs or other body parts reflect in the mirrors and give the trick away. Simple!

On the other hand, how this trick may be done where the magician, and sometimes the audience too, walks around the head, I do not know. My mother saw such an illusion back in the 1950s and is still baffled by it to this day. But then maybe that particular trick was not an illusion at all. Maybe that really was magic.

Barbara Nadel

Glossary

Ackers	slang for money, from the Egyptian *akka* (money)
'Atchin 'tan	Romani – stopping-place
Av	Romani – come
Ball of chalk	rhyming slang for *walk*
Bonkers	slang – mad, crazy
Butchers	rhyming slang, 'butchers hook' – look
Chavies	Romani – children
Crackers	slang – mad, crazy
Diddikai	Romani – someone with half Romany, half *gaujo* blood
Dinilo	Romani – stupid, foolish
Dordi	Romani – dear (*Oh, dordi!* = Oh dear!)
Drabalo	Romani – doctor
Drom	Romani – road
Friar's balsam	an aromatic inhalation to relieve respiratory diseases and infections
Gaff	slang – home
Gas mantle	replaceable element of a gas lamp
Gaujo	Romani – a non-Romany (plural *gauje*)
Ha'porth	slang – silly person; also meaning a 'halfpenny's worth'
Jock	slang – Scotsman
Kate	rhyming slang, Kate Karney – army. Kate

	Karney was a nineteenth-century music-hall star from Canning Town
Lelled	Romani – arrested
Lingo	slang – language
Marimè	Romani – contamination by the dead
Meshuggeneh	Yiddish – a crazy person
Muló	Romani – spirit of the dead
Mullo	Romani – death
Muskero	Romani – police
Mutt and Jeff	Rhyming slang – deaf
Pinny	apron (*pinafore*)
Pomana	Romani – meal to mark the passing of the dead
Rais	Romani – gentleman
Romanipe	Romani – the Romany way (of life)
Schtum	Yiddish – quiet
Sit shiva	Yiddish – Orthodox Jewish seven-day mourning period
Tan	Romani – tent
Tom	slang – prostitute
Tosh	slang – rubbish
Two and eight	rhyming slang – state
Va	Romani – yes